CHRISTMAS WISHES AT THE STATION BOOKSHOP

MARGARET AMATT

LEANNAN PRESS
INDEPENDENT PUBLISHER

LEANNAN PRESS

First Published by Leannan Press 2025

Book Cover designed by Margaret Amatt

eBook ISBN: 978-1-914575-26-6

Paperback ISBN: 978-1-914575-22-8

Chapter One

Scarlett

Being single, jobless, and glaring at puddles from a railway footbridge like she was auditioning for a discount version of *The Girl on the Train* wasn't how Scarlett Finch had expected to spend her twenty-fifth birthday. Shouldn't something more exciting happen when you turned a quarter of a century? Her friends moaned about turning twenty-five. Scarlett felt like she'd earned double.

She inhaled the metallic smell of Glenbriar Station, staring at the tracks below. What was she doing here on a damp November morning? If she started thinking about it, it would open a bigger question – what was she doing here at all? How had she gone from being the life and soul of friend groups and parties to little more than a cardboard cutout? From being loud and gregarious to wanting to curl up in a ball and hibernate... not just for the winter.

She wrapped her scarf tighter, picking at the frayed bit that looked increasingly like a noose. The wind cut across her face and made her eyes water – just the weather, not the fact that she'd royally screwed up her life.

Beneath her, the main platform hunched under the drizzle, its old-fashioned metal and glass cover already strung with Christmas lights. Two men in hi-vis jackets were putting up what looked like a light-up decoration on one of the lampposts. It was kind of cute. Even through her bleak mood, she gave a little smile. The scene reminded her of TV shows she'd enjoyed as a kid. Postman Pat and his friends would fit right in here, stringing lights, organising Christmas shows, wishing for snow, and making everything magical.

And completely unrealistic. Which was, of course, why people loved it – escapism at its finest.

Well, she couldn't stay here all day and watch – or she could, because it wasn't like she had any other pressing engagements, but she really should walk on. This was what she did. Just walked around Glenbriar. It was slightly better than sitting in her mum's house, hoping she'd find a dream job online.

If she knew what that dream job even was.

It wasn't being a relief cleaner for an agency, which was all she could get at the moment.

As she turned to walk back, her eyes landed on the Station Bookshop. It was a cute little place built into the old Victorian ticket office. Scarlett had never even been in it. She wasn't much of a reader or a book lover – not that she had anything against books – it just wasn't her thing.

A shape caught her eye – something moving in the dead zone between the ticket machines and a row of benches. Not something. Someone. A bundle of clashing prints and wool, swaying side-to-side like a malfunctioning Roomba, herding a dog that looked like a potato on legs. The woman was maybe late sixties, with hair like an untamed snowball and a headband that looked like a nineteen-eighties tennis player's. She wore a cardigan that could have been knitted by a hallucinating magpie, a skirt patterned with reindeer and fingerless gloves... very Bob Cratchit.

The dog – was it a pug? – wore a Santa vest. It was trying to chase a pigeon twice its size and failing so hard it looped back into success, because the pigeon seemed to take pity on it and simply walked away.

Scarlett couldn't stop herself; she grinned. This was even more like an episode of Postman Pat, but what a bizarre way to be living out her childhood fantasies. Still, it had got her smiling. And the sensation felt strange, like stretching a muscle that had atrophied since August.

Her heart iced over.

She mustn't think about that.

The woman below was trying to coax the pug back with something from her pocket. She called out, but Scarlett couldn't catch the words. A train was due in two minutes; a few more people arrived on the platform. The woman caught the dog and tucked it under one arm. She seemed to be scolding it, albeit very gently.

Scarlett's cheeks ached from holding the smile. She wiped it off, scowled for balance, and reached into her jacket for her phone. No new messages. Not that she was expecting any. Most people were busy. It was a Thursday afternoon. People had work and jobs to go to. She'd already had all the birthday cards and good wishes that morning. There was nothing left for people to give. She'd already said she didn't want a fuss or a party, and they were respecting that.

She wasn't sure what she'd expected. Or what she really wanted.

What would she wish for if she truly believed it could come true?

Below, the train thundered in, rattling the bridge. Scarlett stared down at its roof. The doors hissed open, and some people got off.

Scarlett walked to the end of the bridge and made her way down the steps as the passengers boarded the train. She didn't want to look like she was getting on and hold the driver up waiting, so she ambled across the platform and up to the window of the bookshop. The display was an array of romance books with topless men on the covers. A very quirky, handwritten sign read:

Glenbriar Station Lost Property:

These poor lads have lost their shirts.

(If you find them, don't return them – we prefer them like this!)

She raised an eyebrow, in little doubt that this had been put here by the woman with the dog. Her gaze drifted to the door, which had two more handwritten signs pinned to the glass. One read: *Help Required – Apply Within* and another in green glitter gel pen: *NEW! WISHING CHRISTMAS TREE inside! Cast Your Wishes Here!*

The thought she'd had just moments ago fluttered into her mind again. What *would* she wish for?

But really, it wasn't like there was any point. Still... She sucked her lip for a moment. Why not? It wasn't like she had anything to lose. She turned the handle and pushed.

The bell above the door didn't tinkle; it exploded in a jangling burst, and Scarlett cringed. No one else seemed to be in here, which didn't help. Every surface was rammed with books, so tightly packed they formed a labyrinthine grid. Maybe she should just go straight back out, but the woman behind the counter was smiling at her. The pug was on a bed near a low shelf, snoring. A parrot in a battered cage squawked from a perch above the till.

'I saw you looking at the sign,' the woman said, eyes bright behind her large glasses. 'And I'm very glad you're here.'

Scarlett hesitated. Why was the woman glad? Did it look so obvious that Scarlett was due at least one good turn from the universe round about now? 'I—?' What the hell should she say? *I just nipped in to make a quick wish.* Even in her head, it sounded silly.

The woman clapped her hands, then beckoned Scarlett closer with a movement like shuffling a deck of invisible cards. 'Don't be shy. You've got the look for it.'

'The look for what?' Was she a medium or something? She certainly had an aura of mystic about her. Did she perhaps grant wishes? Scarlett frowned. Ok, this was getting weird.

'What's your name?'

Why did she need to know that? Maybe it helped her with clairvoyant vibes or something. 'Um... Scarlett.'

The woman made a pleased noise. 'Of course. I'm Eunice. This is Clarence.' She gestured at the pug, then upward. 'And that's Captain Beaky. Ignore him if he insults you. He's been stuck with me too long.'

Beaky shrieked, 'ARSE! ARSE!' and laughed like a lunatic.

Eunice didn't blink. 'He's from a broken home.'

Scarlett stayed within running distance of the door. 'So, um—'

'You're timing is perfect.'

'It is?'

'Oh yes. I was wondering how on earth I was going to get to my appointment today. It's not like I can be in two places at once. That's why I put the sign up. So, if you wouldn't mind looking after the place until I get back, that would be wonderful.'

'Hang on... What?'

'You were looking at the sign, weren't you?'

'Well, yes, but...' That wasn't the sign she'd focused on, but she couldn't deny she needed a job. Maybe if she did well here, Eunice would consider hiring her for a more permanent job. 'Do I get paid?'

'Oh, yes. I'll get you something.' She waved an airy hand.

'And it's only for today?'

'Just a couple of hours, yes... Though heaven knows, you can have the job. I can't be bothered with it all. But anyway, let me show you how the till works.' She frowned at it. 'Though that's a contradiction in terms if ever there was one. Never trust a machine, dear.' She opened and closed the drawer at high speed. 'If you get stuck, just hit it.'

Scarlett's insides were knotting. What the hell was she getting herself in for? But then again, the shop wasn't exactly over-flowing with customers even when a train had just come in. So hopefully she'd survive. It was better than her other options.

Eunice rattled off some shop rules like she was making them up on the spot. 'No loud voices. No charity – they pay for the books. If someone asks for a book in the window, only give it to them if it's not in the middle and doesn't ruin the display.'

Captain Beaky provided a soundtrack of garbled football chants and rude noises. At one point, he yelled, 'DO ONE!' and tried to peck Scarlett's hand as she wiped biscuit crumbs from the till.

Scarlett tried not to look overwhelmed. She'd survived worse – a lot worse. This was nothing compared to what she'd gone through in the summer – being pushed around by her now ex-boyfriend on a coach full of people, only for him to be thrown off, making it her most spectacular breakup to date. Then she'd become a spectacle for the rest of the trip... and made a de-cision that could be considered the stupidest thing she'd ever done. She'd jumped into bed with another passenger. It had been meant to be a distraction, nothing more, but since that fling, her mind, heart and soul had been elsewhere. Those few days had rerouted her thoughts on love and attraction. Her whole relationship history was full of short-term stints with guys who were rough and treated her like shit... But the guy on that fling, Lloyd – she could barely even bring herself to think his name – had been so kind. So gentle. So caring.

Perhaps that was only because it had been a fling. Her mind was probably skewed by the fact that it had only been a few days in a different place without the stresses of real life. And now she had to accept that she wouldn't see him again and probably wouldn't meet someone like him again either.

'What if someone actually wants to buy something?' she asked.

'Just scan the barcode or write it down if the scanner plays up.'

Scarlett nodded. She'd worked in shops before, so this shouldn't be much different.

'Right, now I need to get to the dentist. Clarence will protect you. And Beaky. Don't let him out, though, or he'll start a turf war with the crows.'

'The pets are staying too?' A panicky ripple ran up her spine. What if Clarence did a runner again?

'They'll be fine. I'll be back by three, or earlier if the anaesthetic wears off. I'm allergic to painkillers, but don't tell them that, or they refuse to treat you.' Eunice shrugged into a raincoat with padded shoulders and grabbed her tartan bag. 'Thank you very much, dear. I can't tell you how much I appreciate this.' She patted Scarlett's hand. 'And feel free to make a wish on the new Christmas Wishing Tree. It's got an almost one-hundred per cent success rate.'

'Does it?'

'Yes. I put it out this morning, made a wish that someone would help me out with this appointment and voila! Two love-birds just put another one on, but we haven't had enough time for theirs to come true yet, so, try it... You never know.'

Scarlett barely managed to open her mouth before Eunice was halfway out the door. The bell went berserk, then the shop was weirdly silent, just the faint rumble of Clarence's snores and the distant football score update from Beaky.

Left alone, Scarlett was acutely aware that she had just become the sole human employee of the Station Bookshop. She tried the till drawer, which opened and closed with all the subtlety of a car crash.

'Well...' She let out a slow breath. This was beyond weird.

Beaky fluffed his feathers and belched out, 'TWAT!'

'Delightful.' She ambled over to the wishing tree. It was cute, but she could think of nicer ways to display it. Would Eunice be annoyed if she changed it? Maybe she could just add a few book stacks. Everything looked like it could do with a good dusting. She could do that if nothing else.

After finding some ancient cleaning supplies in the cupboard under the till, she dusted around, passing the time in a weird kind of blur, and resisting the urge to call her mum or her half-brother, Aidan, to come and rescue her. She could do this... And it would be a talking point if nothing else.

She served a single customer, a guy in a thick coat who wanted 'something with a plot and no politics.' As she had no idea what to advise him on, she suggested he look in the crime section.

A couple of commuters wandered through on their way to the platform, mostly ignoring Scarlett, and left without buying anything.

Hopefully Eunice would be back any minute. Scarlett went back to the wishing tree and lifted one of the bauble-shaped bits of paper and a glitter pen. On the tree were two wishes looking rather lonely.

The first read: *I wish someone would come along and help me.*

Scarlett smiled at it, then turned the second one over.

The second read: *We'd like a real-life happy ending!* And it was decorated with little hearts.

'Wouldn't we all?' Scarlett muttered. That was someone aiming big. She knew what she wanted to wish for, but it seemed silly. Almost shameful. She didn't want to wish for something as airy fairy as happy endings and true love – though if they came along, she wouldn't turn them away. But no... she wanted something much more specific.

To see Lloyd again.

How could she write that? If she did, Eunice might see it and guess who'd written it. That could lead to questions. Questions Scarlett didn't want to answer.

She uncapped the pen. It was her birthday. So why not make a birthday wish?

Please let my birthday wish come true.

With a deep breath, she hung it on the tree, capped the pen and stepped back. There. She didn't need to spell it out. The universe or the Christmas spirits or whoever was granting these wishes knew what she wanted.

Of course it was stupid, of course it wouldn't happen, but still. Stranger things had happened… some of them in the last hour.

She glanced at the shelves of books, and the half-hearted start Eunice appeared to have made on Christmas decorations. Really, if wishes were to come true, this was exactly the kind of magical place for it.

CHAPTER TWO

Lloyd

The house was even smaller than Lloyd remembered, which was an impressive feat considering he'd spent the last two days mentally shrinking his mother's place to the size of an advent calendar. Boxes colonised every surface. The hallway was completely covered and not helped by the fact that Lewis had constructed a fort out of the clutter and was attempting to make himself some kind of armour out of bubble wrap. Oh, to be ten again.

At thirteen, Harry obviously saw himself above all that and had retreated to the darkest corner of the living room with his Nintendo, where he was poking repeatedly at the screen, every third tap punctuated by a new variation on, 'Dad, when can I get the Wi-Fi password?'

Lloyd let out a sigh. 'Two minutes and I'll see if I can find it. Or ask Gran.'

'She doesn't know where it is.'

That seemed unlikely. She probably just didn't want him disappearing into a game for the rest of the day. But really, that was the least of Lloyd's worries right now. Moving house a month before Christmas was crazy enough, but when the sale of his previous place had gone through before the new one was ready, it left a gap. So now he was basically moving twice. First to camp in his mother's cottage in Sweetwater Lane – a very quaint little street near the start of the climb up Ben Vrack. And sure, the cottage was cute too, but it wasn't really big enough for Lloyd and three kids. Just a few days to get through before the house was ready. And those few days in the grand scheme of things were nothing. Not after what Lloyd, Lewis, Harry and Eve had been through in the last few years.

Eve had disappeared the instant they'd unloaded the car, trailing up the stairs with her rucksack, headphones, and the hunched posture of a girl who wanted to hide from the world until spring... possibly longer. Of all of them, she was the one who'd suffered the most from losing her mum. Now she was stuck in a house full of boys without her mum to confide in, when really, she just wanted to be a normal fifteen-year-old.

Lloyd took a breath. He needed to talk to her. Again. But she didn't want to talk or listen. Sometimes she got so angry, he wasn't sure it was worth stirring the pot, but he didn't want her to think he'd given up or wasn't available. God, it was so difficult.

His mum swept into the hall and shook her head. 'I thought you'd put all this stuff into storage?'

'Some of it. But this is the necessities.'

'Dad, do I have to start the new school tomorrow?' Lewis popped up from behind a box.

'No. On Monday.'

'Yaas.' He punched the air. 'Another day off.'

That would be Monday's fight. Lewis was still at primary school and seemed to be ok about changing schools, but Eve and Harry were not amused at being ripped from their friends and their social circles. And nothing Lloyd said could change that.

Eve already seemed to think it base treachery that Lloyd was moving them away from the home they'd been a family in. And he got it. Of course he did. But he also got the practicalities of life as a single parent better than she did. In Edinburgh, the flat they'd lived in was nice, but too small. They'd meant to move into a family home in a place like Glenbriar some years ago, but when Amy got sick, staying near the hospital became more important. With the two older kids in secondary school and Lewis still in Primary, it was a logistical nightmare. The catchment schools had terrible reputations, so Lloyd and Amy had opted for schools further afield, but that meant so many school runs, breakfast clubs, after-school clubs, or taxis to ferry them places if two of them had something on at the same time. He'd also had to factor in time off when they were sick – and that happened frequently, because all of them were in a tough place. His kids needed him present, not fobbing them off to a club and then not seeing them again for ten hours.

He'd taken steps to change that, got a new job with more work-from-home days, but he couldn't do it alone. And they'd outgrown the flat. They needed space to breathe – a garden. It took a village, and the village he needed was Glenbriar. His mum had lived here for the past fifteen years. And the kids' other grandparents lived in Perth, which wasn't far away. Both were happy to help with after-school care if needed. And with both schools within walking distance, it would be so much easier – for him.

His insides knotted. Was he the world's worst parent? Though he knew the world in general was not kind to families or single parents. This was part of his accepting he couldn't do everything alone.

After Christmas, his mum was giving up the Station Bookshop that she'd owned for as long as she'd lived here. Lloyd was taking that on too—which was perhaps rash. His mum had already signed it over to him but was still running it from day to day. Just as well, because on top of everything else, he hadn't got around to figuring out how to staff the place.

'Lloyd!' His mum bent to pick up a bundle of clothes from the stairs. 'Is this meant to be art, or shall I put them in the wash?'

'I-I don't even know.' He took off his glasses and pinched the bridge of his nose.

Rita's eyes narrowed as she looked him up and down. 'You look like you haven't eaten since breakfast.'

He couldn't recall even eating breakfast but nodded anyway.

She called into the lounge, 'Anyone want a hot chocolate?'

From the depths, Lewis shouted, 'Will it have cream?'

'I'm sure that can be arranged,' Rita said. 'Harry?'

'Yeah, ok.'

'Please,' Lloyd added.

'Please,' Harry muttered.

'Go and ask Eve if she wants some.' Rita chivvied Lewis towards the tiny stairs as he approached making ka-pow noises and doing karate chops in mid-air.

'Why me?'

'Because you're the one with ninja powers,' Lloyd said.

Lewis vanished up the stairs, yelling, 'Eve! Do you want hot chocolate with cream?'

Rita headed for the kitchen, but not before patting Lloyd on the arm, steering him in after her. 'Come on. You need tea.'

'I think I'd prefer hot chocolate too.'

'Nice and easy then.'

Rita put the kettle on and gestured to the only available chair at the little table. The other one was already taken by the cat. 'Sit. You look like you need to.'

'Eve says no,' Lewis shouted in the door, then returned to the living room.

Rita studied Lloyd for a moment, her mouth doing a thing that could have been either a smile or a warning. 'It's not forever, you know. The house. You'll get your keys soon enough.'

'I know. I'm sorry for all the chaos.'

She gave a sympathetic nod, reached for a biscuit tin, and slid it across the table. 'Don't worry. It was never going to be easy.'

Wasn't that the truth? No one could have prepared him for any of this. Amy was gone, so was the mess of her illness and treatments. But it left such a gap. Things hadn't been 'normal' for so long, and this new reality was punishing.

His mum leaned in, lowering her voice. 'And are you alright?'

It was a question he dreaded. 'Yes,' he said, because that was always the answer.

She watched him, waiting to see if he'd expand. When he didn't, she clicked her tongue. 'Oh, Lloyd. My poor, poor boy.'

Except he wasn't a boy anymore. She could help with the kids, which he appreciated immensely, but she couldn't get rid of the pain in his heart. In fact, sometimes she made things worse when she tried to protect him. His mind fleetingly whipped back to the summer. It was only a few months ago, but he wanted to bury the memory of it so far below the ground that it would never be seen again.

He'd behaved like a fool. Rita's idea to take him on a coach tour with her hadn't exactly been his first choice of trip, but with Amy's parents looking to spend time with the kids, he'd agreed. It had turned out to be exactly the hell he'd imagined – stuck in close quarters with some very dodgy passengers, including a guy who'd verbally and physically abused his girlfriend, then shoved the tour guide onto Lloyd's knee, and eventually got himself thrown off. The gossips on the bus – including his mother – had a field day. Only Lloyd hadn't stopped there with the crazy.

The woman who'd been getting all the abuse – Scarlett – started talking to him randomly – in corridors, outside in the hotel garden when they'd both been seeking peace. Things had developed. And Lloyd had done something he'd never done before. Had a fling.

The thought made him feel sick. The gossips had found out. His mum had assumed Scarlett had 'seduced' him – whatever the hell that meant – and had berated the poor woman. The whole thing was like a horror movie.

Well, most of it. And the bits that weren't horrible made him prickle with guilt. Because he'd liked Scarlett... when really, he shouldn't. Because he was only recently widowed. He'd betrayed Amy and her memory barely a year after she'd died.

'So...' Rita handed him a mug, bringing him back to the present. 'I've got news.'

Lloyd blinked. 'What?'

'I'm not actually taking a day off today to help you.'

'I don't follow.'

'I haven't worked in the shop for the past few weeks. The whole thing has got too much for my back.' She gave a sad shrug. Lloyd knew she didn't like admitting it bothered her. She'd had ankylosing spondylitis for years but tried not to let it get the better of her. He could often tell when she was having a flare up, however, as her moods were all over the place. 'I've delegated to my friend Eunice,' she continued.

He took a second to process. 'Eunice?'

'You know her. She was doing part-time hours before, usually weekends, but she's agreed to take it on for the time being. Mad as a box of frogs, but she loves putting up displays and that kind of thing.'

Lloyd's insides curled up and died. 'She's running the shop?'

'For now.' Rita's eyes were twinkling. 'I mean, you can employ someone else if you like.'

'Doesn't she have a contract?'

'She had one, I'm sure, for the weekend hours she did before... though I'm not entirely sure where it is.'

'Have you been down there to check since she took over?'

'Um... once.'

'Oh god.' Lloyd let out a low groan.

'It'll be fine. You'll see.'

He looked up, trying to summon a smile. If only he could believe her, but very little felt fine right now.

'Let me deliver the hot chocolates to this lot. I made one for Eve anyway. She might come down. Maybe we could get them all settled with a film.'

She bustled off, and Lloyd dropped his head into his hands, not sure whether to laugh or cry.

His mother didn't return, so he got up and went to the doorway of the living room. He leaned on the frame, feeling almost like a ghost in his own family. For a moment, it almost looked normal. Like something they might have done before. His mum skimmed through the film library while the kids moaned at every choice. Even Eve had come down, though she still had one ear-bud in.

The ache in Lloyd's chest throbbed. He took out his phone, flicking through old photos. There were dozens – hundreds – of Amy: with the kids at the beach, at birthdays, in the garden. Her smile was so real even when she was in the darkest days of her treatment.

What would she make of all this? The new house, the new life. Had he made the right choice? He'd promised her he'd try, that he'd keep them together and safe. But he'd never promised her he wouldn't fail.

Maybe he already had.

When they finally agreed on a film, Rita joined Lloyd at the door.

'Would you mind watching them for an hour? I need some air. And I feel like I should check the shop and see how Eunice is getting on.'

Rita grinned. 'I can't believe you're so worried about it. But of course I'll watch them. You go and get some air. But leave the shop for now. That's one stress you don't need.'

Maybe that was true, but he didn't find that shop stressful. He never had. In fact, he loved it, which was why he couldn't bear for it to shut down – which was what his mum had wanted to do with it. There was something peaceful about being there with the books, even though he knew it made very little money. It needed something to liven it up and bring it back to life – much like him. Maybe Eunice was the person to do that. For the shop... not him. But he had his doubts.

The walk to Glenbriar Station took him through the High Street, which was a busy place even at this time of year. Two men in hi-vis jackets had a mini cherry picker and were attaching Christmas lights to lampposts.

Lloyd reached the station platform and approached the door of the bookshop, pausing to take in the hand-written signs.

Help Required – Apply Within and another in green glitter gel pen: *NEW! WISHING CHRISTMAS TREE inside! Cast Your Wishes Here!*

Seriously?

He shook his head, not sure what was worse – a Christmas tree for wishes or the fact that she was advertising for her own job.

He opened the door, and a very noisy bell jangled. A dog in a Santa outfit was sleeping by a shelf, and on the counter, a parrot in a battered cage muttered something that sounded very much like 'wanker.'

No one was behind the counter, but as he opened his mouth to call hello, someone came out from behind the shelf carrying a small duster, a young woman with vivid red hair. She stopped dead when she saw him, eyes going wide.

Lloyd's brain jammed.

What the hell? Just what?

He couldn't begin to figure out what was going on. No way on earth had his mother hired her – not after the coach tour fiasco.

So how…? Why?

This made zero sense.

And Lloyd was trapped.

CHAPTER THREE

Scarlett

Scarlett was frozen. Her brain refused to load the scene in front of her, like the universe had jammed the buffering wheel on her actual, physical existence. Lloyd Miller, the man from the coach trip – the one she'd wished she could see again – was here, standing in the middle of the Station Bookshop, looking right at her. Not just at her – through her, over her, around the back and through her again, like a bullet she wasn't even remotely prepared for.

He looked exactly the same as the last time she'd seen him. Hair a little mussed, blue eyes doing that quiet, appraising stare that made her tremble. He was wearing a dark wool coat, open over a shirt, so normal it made her own getup feel zany and cheap, despite how much she'd dumbed herself down in the past few months. The contrast should have made her snort. It didn't. She couldn't move a single muscle.

He didn't speak. Didn't raise his hand or nod or anything. For a full ten seconds – felt like an hour – he just stood, mouth slightly open, eyebrows halfway up his forehead. He didn't look confused or even shocked. It was more like he was bracing himself for something.

Scarlett's stomach did a perfect gymnastic somersault, landing in her shoes and then trying to climb up her spine to escape through the top of her skull. She forced herself to breathe, but it was like her lungs had suddenly switched to manual control and she'd missed the training video.

A million memories detonated behind her eyes, one after the other, all starring Lloyd in various states of undress or emotional vulnerability, none of which she wanted to see right now. There was the way he'd held her on that last night in the hotel on Skye. The way he'd looked at her in the half-dark, like she was a real person and not just a warm body, a mess to fix or a temporary patch job. These memories lived rent-free in her head, though none more so than the one she pictured as a photograph, her naked in his arms, their bodies joined so intimately, and him watching her with an intensity that made her want to crawl out of her own skin and hide, but she hadn't. She'd stayed and listened to his words... she could still hear them as if he were saying them to her right now.

'Why are you looking at me like that?' she'd asked.

'Because I want to,' he'd said. 'Is there something wrong with that?'

She'd shrugged, because admitting that she wasn't used to being looked at – really looked at – wasn't something she was ever going to say out loud. 'Guess not.'

He'd drawn a line with his finger across her bare shoulder, tracing something invisible, and then gently kissed her neck. 'What do you see?' she'd asked, and he'd given her a soft smile, the kind that made her stomach pull tight.

'I see someone bright. Spirited, with a lot to give. Someone who's a little lost, a little broken. Kind of sad. Someone who has so much more going on inside than people usually get to see.'

Back in the present, the words felt like a splinter under her fingernail, something she couldn't get out. Did he actually mean any of that? Or was it just something people said when they were naked and high on endorphins? She wouldn't know. He was the only man who'd ever treated her so gently, and she'd stupidly mistaken that for love. When really, it only showed how little she'd expected from previous partners – because kindness should have been the bare minimum.

And now he was here. In Glenbriar. In her orbit again. How the hell had this happened?

She tried to break eye contact, but it was like his gaze had some kind of tractor beam, yanking her back every time she even glanced away. She tried to say something, anything, but her voice-box had gone on strike.

He finally moved, just a twitch of his hand as if to say, 'Well, here we are then.' Still nothing out loud. She wanted to laugh at the absolute cosmic joke of it. Of course he was here. Why wouldn't he be? Her wish had been granted in the most literal, least convenient way possible.

And then, just as she was about to force herself to say something – maybe a witty 'Long time no see' or a much less witty 'Please tell me you're not a ghost' – she caught sight of her reflection in the shop window behind him.

She looked small. Older than she felt. A twenty-five-year-old who alternated between feeling sixteen and sixty.

She blinked hard and tried to reset.

Somewhere behind the counter, Captain Beaky yelled, 'ARSE!'

Scarlett almost smiled.

What would happen if neither of them moved? Would they turn to statues? Fossils? Did anyone ever die of mutual embarrassment?

She forced her mouth open. Something had to give, or she'd combust. But just then, Lloyd opened his own mouth, as if the idea had struck him at the same instant.

They both closed them again, in perfect awkward sync.

Her entire life had been leading up to this moment, apparently: the universe presenting her with the man she'd never managed to get out of her system, in a second-hand bookshop that she had somehow agreed to work in for the afternoon, while a parrot screamed expletives in the background and a pug slept in the corner.

'Well... hm, hi,' Scarlett said, the words so feeble they evaporated as soon as they left her mouth.

'Scarlett,' Lloyd said, but it sounded like a question. He cleared his throat.

Oh god, when he said her name, it was enough to give her a minor existential crisis. He had a low voice that scrambled her insides. Perhaps it had been that as much as anything which had drawn her to him in the first place.

She grappled for something clever to say. Maybe an icebreaker. Maybe just a normal-person conversation. But her mind delivered nothing but static, and in the same instant, Lloyd opened his mouth to speak, too.

'So—' he started.

'Are you—' she blurted, which made him shut his mouth again, lips pressed tight.

It was like being in a sitcom, except neither of them knew their lines, and the laugh track had gone on strike.

She had a split-second urge to just blurt out: I thought you were a hallucination! Or: I swear I haven't stalked you; I didn't even know you lived in this hemisphere! But nothing came out.

'I, um—' Lloyd said, but whatever followed was steamrolled by the shop bell detonating above their heads, loud enough to set off a car alarm in the next postcode.

Eunice was back, trailing a strong scent of peppermint, her cheeks pink from the cold. She swept in with the energy of a marching band and immediately started chattering to Scarlett, not even noticing the tension in the air.

'Was it busy? I saw the train come in. Sometimes you get odd-balls, but most people are very nice. Ooh, you dusted the shelves, that's marvellous. Oh, Clarence, look at you, you silly thing, you've got a new friend, have you? And Beaky hasn't pecked your fingers off? Yet.'

Scarlett gave her a weak smile, but her focus was still on Lloyd, whose entire posture said, "I wish I could disappear into the floorboards."

Eunice fished a bag of dog biscuits from her pocket and threw a chunk to the pug, who caught it mid-air and swallowed without chewing. 'Now then, what did I miss?'

She finally turned and spotted Lloyd. She gave him a cheery nod.

'Hullo there, can I help you with anything?'

There was something almost blissful about it – she'd just erased every ounce of tension with her bulldozer in a cardigan personality.

Lloyd smiled. 'Hello, Eunice. I'm – uh. Lloyd Miller. Rita's son?'

Eunice's face underwent a slow-motion transformation as the penny dropped, rattling through several emotions before settling on delight. 'Oh. Goodness, well I never. You've changed... or maybe I have. I didn't recognise you.'

'I'm just here to check how things are going.' His eyes darted from Eunice to Scarlett, then down at the counter, then back at Eunice.

Scarlett could tell he was wondering why the hell she was in the shop and where Eunice had been.

'Everything's going fine,' Eunice said. 'I had a dental appointment, so I put a note on the door asking for help. I also asked the wishing tree, and my wish came true.'

Lloyd raised an eyebrow, not unkindly, but more like he was wondering if perhaps he'd stepped into an alternate reality rather than the shop.

Scarlett had lost the ability to think or speak. Of all the things she'd imagined could go wrong today, seeing Lloyd Miller was so far down the list it was basically a footnote. Because in her mind, seeing him again had been a fantasy. One where she curled up in his arms and everything was fine, but the reality was not like that. She kind of wished it could have stayed a fantasy because his existence here would make her brain short circuit. With the fantasy Lloyd, she could make him whatever she wanted, imagine him as she pleased... But real-life Lloyd had his own reality. And it didn't match hers *or* her fantasy.

And he owned this shop. On the coach trip, they'd chatted about so many things; he'd told her he lived in Edinburgh – worked in finance, had three kids, was a widower, but he hadn't realised he had any connection to Glenbriar. Maybe she hadn't asked. Or maybe she didn't remember properly. Or maybe he'd lied, as so many of her past boyfriends had. It was hard to know what was real when every conversation had filtered through a haze of break-up misery and post-coital dopamine.

She needed out. She needed to get as far away as possible. Why had she made that crazy wish? Not that it was even real. Sometimes her head needed clearing out, and right now, she couldn't think straight.

Eunice was deep in conversation with Lloyd, but his eyes kept returning to her. Scarlett couldn't stand it anymore. She lifted her coat.

'I should go.'

Eunice caught her arm before she could slip out. 'Oh, you can't go yet. I need to pay you—'

'No, really,' Scarlett said. 'It's fine. Just take it as an early Christmas present.'

Eunice blinked at her. 'I insist.' She pulled a tattered purse from her pocket, so stuffed with receipts it barely shut.

'Honestly. It was no bother.'

'Here's your money. I hope ten pounds is enough.'

'More than. Thank you.'

'No, thank you, my dear. You saved my teeth.'

'You're welcome.' Scarlett pocketed the money and almost ran to the door. The bell shrieked in her ears, and she blinked in the cold November light.

She stood for a second on the platform, trying to work out where to go, whether she was supposed to run or just evaporate. Lloyd was just visible through the window, talking to Eunice, but half looking at Scarlett like he might come out after her. She wasn't sure if she wanted him to or not. He seemed so unflappable compared to her, and so perfectly out of her league.

Their eyes met again, and for a moment, the world froze.

She wasn't sure what was written on his face – regret, maybe, or confusion, or just polite curiosity. There was nothing cruel in it. Nothing smug or angry or disappointed. If anything, he looked... sad. Or maybe just tired.

She hated that it made her want him more. Because she needed to stop thinking like that.

She turned away, boots crunching on the frosty paving, and set off towards the exit. The air stung her cheeks, clearing her head just enough to let her feel the full blast of embarrassment.

By the time she reached the main road, she'd convinced herself it was fine. Nothing had happened. She'd just survived an ambush by the universe, that was all. Inside her pocket, she felt the edge of the money Eunice had given her, and she clenched her fingers around it. She'd go home and chat to her mum – not about this, but other casual stuff. She'd laugh about this. Eventually.

Wouldn't she?

But she knew, deep down, that she wouldn't. Not ever. Not when every step she took away from the station felt like moving further from something she'd never get back.

She didn't stop walking until she was nearly at her mum's house, and by then, the shock had curdled into a single, solid thought:

You can never go back.

Not to the bookshop. Not to the way things were. Not to who you were before this summer.

Scarlett wiped her nose on her sleeve, pushed her hair out of her face, and kept going. She wasn't cut out for real love or a real job... maybe even real life. Her fantasy was so much more joyful.

But she'd survived another day – her birthday – and that was the best she could do. Keep putting one foot forward.

Chapter Four

Lloyd

Lloyd's pulse was still hammering. He couldn't stop staring at the shop door, half expecting Scarlett to ghost back through it, but to what end? He wanted to call after her, but he hadn't even managed a proper hello. Had he just made things worse? Was he always going to be this useless at life?

'She seemed lovely, that one.' Eunice dropped her bag behind the counter and removed her scarf. She gave Lloyd a look over the top of her enormous glasses. 'I've a sixth sense about these things.'

'What was she doing here?' Lloyd said, not quite looking at Eunice.

'She was working.'

'Does she normally work here?' Lloyd's confusion grew.

'No, no. She just walked in at the perfect moment, like the answer to my wish.'

'Sorry, I don't follow.'

'I had a dental emergency. Got to save as much of the originals as you can when you're my age.'

Eunice's energy was somewhere between a street busker and a malfunctioning wind-up toy. She began re-arranging a display of books in what looked almost like a Christmas tree, which Lloyd assumed was the goal. He took a deep breath, steadying himself.

'So you just... left her in charge?' he said, a little sharper than intended.

Eunice looked at him, mildly affronted. 'Well, yes. She had the right look for it. And she knew how to work the till. More or less. Though she was nervous about the parrot.'

'She's not the only one,' Lloyd muttered.

Captain Beaky squawked, 'ARSE!'

'Exactly,' Eunice said, with a triumphant little snap of her fingers. 'See? Beaky always knows.'

Lloyd massaged his forehead. A headache was forming behind his right eyebrow, a direct result of the last half-hour, if not his entire existence.

'It's just...' He let the sentence trail, not wanting to become the kind of person who shouted at sweet, mad old ladies. 'It's not really safe. What if something had happened?'

'Oh, but nothing did. And besides, you never know who's a diamond and who's a dud until you give them a chance.'

He wanted to argue, but it was no use. Eunice had the 'wisdom' that his mother would consider completely accurate. Facts were optional, anecdotes were gospel, and the rules were whatever you decided they were on any given day.

'I don't think my mother—'

'Rita knows I'd never leave the shop unless I was desperate. And she knows I wouldn't trust just anyone. Besides, I used the wishing tree, too. Have you seen it?' She gestured to the artificial pine in the corner, decorated with tinsel, some very suspect fairy lights and two paper baubles.

He frowned at it, then crossed the room and read the messages. 'Is it your birthday?'

'No, let's see that.' She bustled over and took the bauble from him. 'Someone else must have been in and written that. I wish I'd seen who it was. But no, this is my wish.' She pointed at another bauble. 'See?'

In looping script, it read: *I wish someone would come along and help me.*

'And they did.' Lloyd raised an eyebrow.

'Exactly! The universe always provides.' She grinned. 'You should try it. Make a wish.'

He stared at the tree and the wish written in shaky block capitals. The green glitter pen had bled slightly:

Please let my birthday wish come true.

'I'll not bother. I'm sure there are people who need the wishes more than me.'

'If you say so,' Eunice said. 'I'm told you're taking over in January. Is that right?'

'I've already taken it over. It's all in my name now, but I didn't realise my mother had employed someone to run it. I thought she was still doing it.'

'No, she practically begged me to do it. I'm an ex-librarian, you know. But I've bitten off more than I can chew. It's too much for me. Weekends were fine, and some of it I enjoy. The displays and whatnot, but it's a long week doing it every day.'

He nodded. 'I haven't looked into staff yet.' It hadn't been a priority.

'You should hire that young woman – Crimson, I think her name was.'

'Scarlett,' he said automatically, forgetting he hadn't told Eunice that he already knew her, but she didn't appear to notice.

'Ah, that's right. She had a good energy. And she's spruced this place up nicely in the hour or so she was here.'

Lloyd couldn't bring himself to speak. It wasn't like he could tell Eunice that employing Scarlett here was something he really couldn't do. For his own emotional wellbeing more than anything else.

Eunice beamed at him. 'I could make a cuppa, if you're staying?'

Lloyd tried to smile. It landed halfway and died. 'Thanks, but I can't stay long. I left the kids with Mum, and I don't want to be away from them for too long.'

'Do you miss them?'

'Yes, and they... well, they need me.' They needed him to be sensible and reliable. And he had to remember that. What would they think of him if they knew how he'd carried on that summer? The thought made him cringe.

Eunice returned to the counter, straightening her skirt and giving Lloyd a look that was both sharp and concerned. 'Are you alright?'

'Fine, thank you. It's been a long week, that's all.' He took off his glasses and sighed. 'Listen… a couple of things.' He crossed to the counter, lowering his voice. 'And please don't take them the wrong way, but you can't leave the shop with a stranger again. We shouldn't really have pets here either. If you need help, you should have called my mother. I'm sure she'd have done something to help, or we could have closed for the afternoon.'

'Oh no, I didn't want to do that. What if we'd had a pre-Christmas rush?'

Chance would be a fine thing. Lloyd glanced around the small, cluttered space. This place was almost beyond saving, and yet he'd promised he'd try. But he struggled to see why. It was the kind of place people raved about and called it a quirky local asset, but hardly anyone actually came in and bought anything.

'And Clarence is practically staff,' Eunice was still speaking. 'You'd be amazed how many people come in just to see him. He's good for business.'

If only that were true. 'There are health regulations,' he said, and immediately felt ninety years old.

She laughed, a chesty, brassy laugh that could have been either joy or contempt. 'There are regulations for everything, dear, but that doesn't mean anyone follows them. You should see the state of the chemist's back room. And don't get me started on the bakery.'

He pinched the bridge of his nose, which was fast becoming his default pose. 'Look, I'm just saying. The next time you have an appointment, just close the shop for half an hour or call my mum. Please.'

Eunice gave him a soft, forgiving look. 'If you insist. I only took the extra days as a favour to Rita. I told her, "I'm not a details person. I'm more of a creative whirlwind". She said that's exactly the kind of management she needed. And now look. We're in the Christmas spirit. People are making wishes. We've got some wonderful displays.' She swept a hand towards the window.

Lloyd couldn't see it properly from inside, but from the reflection he saw dark covers and what looked like topless men... He wasn't sure he needed to see the rest of it. 'You've done a good job, thank you. If you don't want to remain here full time, that's fine.' Probably good. 'But I'll need time to advertise the post.'

Eunice's eyebrows bounced. 'Why not her? The red-haired girl. She seemed exactly right. She reminded me of how I used to be. Before I got old.'

'She...' He searched for the words. 'We don't even know who she is. I mean, do you know how to contact her?'

'Hmm... No, I don't. But let's not be too worried. We can solve that easily.'

'How?' Though knowing the Glenbriar gossip network, he didn't think it would be too difficult.

'We'll make another wish.'

Lloyd almost groaned as Eunice stood and shuffled over to the tree. 'Please let us see Scarlett again,' she said aloud as she wrote, then hung the bauble on the tree.

'Well...' Lloyd almost gave up, but he had to be sensible – just in case. 'If this wish comes true, just remember, you can't go offering her a job without speaking to me first. She needs interviews, CVs, that kind of thing.' His insides twisted at the thought until he reminded himself of the unlikelihood of the wish coming true anyway.

'DO ONE!' the parrot screamed.

'Hush, Mr Beaky.' Eunice flapped at him. 'Yes, yes. If she comes back, I'll do it all by the book – get my pun?' She winked at him.

He nearly laughed. If he didn't, he might weep. With a gentle smile, he thanked her again and headed for the door. His eyes lingered for a moment on the Christmas tree with the wishes. He'd mocked the idea, but part of him wanted to believe and leave a wish there too. Only he didn't know what to wish for. Or maybe he did deep down, and it scared him to death.

He left without writing anything.

Out on the platform, the air felt fresher. His breath huffed in front of him in little clouds. Fairy lights had been strung across the lampposts, and some larger decorations had been put up but presumably wouldn't light up until the 'switch on', whenever that was. Lloyd didn't really care. Christmas didn't feel special anymore. It was just another period to get through without Amy. This would be their second one without her and was unlikely to be much better than last year – not when the kids were already upset with him for dragging them across the country.

In his mind, this was a better place for them in the long run – they would all have their own bedroom, plus more space downstairs, a garden, and the proximity of their grandparents. But was that a selfish way to look at it?

He couldn't start this argument with himself again. Not when he'd already been over it so often. But in the back of his mind, guilt mites were already nibbling away, suggesting this whole move was based more on his own needs than those of his kids.

He walked fast, trying to clear the static in his head. It didn't work.

Every time he blinked, Scarlett appeared in his mind's eye. She'd probably wanted to forget all about him. He doubted he'd been the highlight of her year. Why would he be? She'd told him at the time she needed a distraction. And he was it. He got it. She'd been pushed about and dumped very publicly by a disgrace of a human. All she wanted was some tenderness. She deserved it and more. She had a right to shine the light Lloyd knew was inside her and not have it dimmed by ugly users. He'd convinced himself a fling would be fun for him too. At the time, it had been. He'd definitely been distracted, but he wasn't quite so good at the forgetting part.

Had she told him she was from Glenbriar? Maybe she had, and he'd not registered. Maybe he'd just assumed everyone on that coach tour was a tourist from elsewhere. He remembered her saying she'd won the tickets, which was why she was there in the first place. Maybe she was only passing through now.

He didn't believe in fate. He believed in luck, and mostly in the lack of it. If fate was real, Amy would still be alive, and he'd be home with her in their new house, cooking and helping the kids with their homework while she folded laundry and listened to Eighties power ballads. The ache of that parallel life made him want to punch something.

Instead, he balled his fists and walked faster. When first he'd kissed Scarlett, it had almost been a mutual dare rather than anything else, both of them punch-drunk on sadness and dysphoria, clinging to each other like they were the last two people on earth. It should have been a disaster. It should have meant nothing.

Except it hadn't. Almost every night – and day – on that tour, they'd sought each other out. The sex had been wild, but it wasn't just about that – not that he could explain it to anyone, least of all himself. There was a kind of honesty to it, a desperation to feel alive, that he hadn't known he was missing until it happened. They'd talked about everything and anything and been happy just existing together as two people who understood each other, and their need to do something crazy and step away from normal life for a few days.

On the way home, the guilt had crashed down so hard he'd almost thrown up. Not because of what he'd done, but because of how much he wanted it to happen again. Because for the first time since Amy's diagnosis, he'd stopped counting days and started wanting to make more of them.

That was the worst part. Wanting.

Scarlett was a fling. Someone he never expected to see again. He'd never prepared for that possibility. It seemed too insane to be real.

What would Amy say if she could see him now? He wasn't sure he even knew. She'd said she was ok with the idea of him seeing other people after she was gone, but Lloyd had never been able to think about it. The curse of denial.

He followed the main road up to Sweetwater Lane, passing the golf club and the new houses on The Fairways Estate. He was nearly back now, and he had to make sure he didn't betray himself. No way could he let his mother know he'd seen Scarlett again. Rita had the worst opinion of her – most of it built on a series of misunderstandings and gossip on the trip. Scarlett's breakup had caused such a furore, and everyone was out to criticise her. She'd done a crazy thing to get people off her back and told Lloyd's mum she'd heard him sleeping with the tour guide. He shook his head, almost laughing. She'd apologised so hard to him – which had been the prelude to their first kiss – but Rita wasn't as forgiving. And when rumours started kicking about that were closer to the truth, scratch that, *were* the truth, she was fizzing with Scarlett for 'seducing' her son. It was ridiculous. Neither of them had seduced anyone. What they'd done had all been consensual. But while Lloyd had fobbed his mother off and claimed it was nothing more than a drunken kiss, she didn't know the half of it.

Because it had been a lot more than that. A whole lot more.

Did Scarlett hate him for it now?

Did it even matter?

Even if he saw her again, nothing could happen there. What had happened with her was a blip – just a temporary moment of happiness, not something for the long term.

He stepped through the gate into the quaint little garden of his mother's cottage. Even in its winter dead state, it had a charm about it. It was almost fully dark now. The nights were drawing in. Above the front door, his mum's security light flickered weakly. As he placed his hand on the doorknob, he took a final cleansing breath, to hopefully rid Scarlett from his mind once and for all. The light pulsed almost in time with his heart. He stared at it a moment longer than necessary, a whisper of a thought brushing his mind:*Amy always hated when lights did that. Said they were a migraine waiting to happen.*

The light went out entirely.

He shook his head. Just a loose wire, not the ghost of Jacob Marley... or anyone else, no matter how Scrooge-like he felt about everything remotely related to Christmas – and most of his life in general.

Right now, he had to focus on his kids and make their happiness his number one priority. Because happiness was fragile. He had to maintain the fragments he had – cling to them like the fraying ends of a rope – and not reach for anything new. Because if he lost it again…

He didn't think his heart would survive.

CHAPTER FIVE

Scarlett

The walk home had done nothing to calm the riot in Scarlett's chest – if anything, it had made it worse. Every step away from the station felt like she was abandoning something important, which was mental because what exactly had she abandoned? A man who probably saw her as a regrettable blip? A bookshop run by a woman who dressed her pug like Santa?

She pushed open the door, ready to slink upstairs and bury herself under her duvet until the universe apologised for its sick joke, but instead she was assaulted by singing.

'Happy birthday to you, happy birthday to you...'

Three voices, wildly out of sync. Her mum stood in the hallway holding a chocolate cake, while Aidan lounged against the wall looking pleased with himself, and Lilah – sweet Lilah – was actually harmonising.

'Oh my god,' Scarlett said.

'Surprise!' Patricia beamed, though it was less surprise and more ambush. 'We thought you'd be back earlier but never mind. Come on, coat off, cake time.'

Scarlett let herself be herded into the kitchen. 'You didn't have to do this.'

'Course we did.' Aidan reached over and ruffled her hair, which she'd normally murder him for, but right now, she was too shell-shocked to care. 'Twenty-five's a big one. Quarter of a century. Practically ancient.'

'Cheers, thanks for that.' She shrugged off her jacket and realised she was still clutching the grubby tenner Eunice had given her. As she unravelled it, her jaw dropped. It wasn't a tenner, it was a fifty-pound note. Christ. She'd never even seen one of these in real life, never mind had one. The colour was much like a tenner. Eunice obviously hadn't meant to give her this. Shit. She'd have to go back and return it to her. No way could she keep it. That felt so wrong.

Patricia set the cake on the table – chocolate with wonky icing that said 'Happy Birthday Scarlett' in what looked like a child's handwriting, though more likely Patricia's after a glass of wine.

'Where've you been all day, anyway?' Patricia lifted a tray of mini sandwiches and sausage rolls onto the table. 'I texted, but you didn't reply.'

'Oh, I forgot to check it.' Scarlett dropped the money into her pocket. 'A weird thing happened this afternoon.'

'What kind of thing?' Aidan's eyebrows did their concerned-brother thing. She could only imagine what he was thinking – that she'd got entangled with another toxic boyfriend, perhaps?

'I was at that little bookshop on the platform at the station, and this batty woman who worked there asked me to watch her bookshop while she went to the dentist.'

Lilah leaned forward. 'What?'

'I know. Mental, right? She'd put a sign in the window saying help required, and it literally meant required for that afternoon. She just assumed I'd do it because I looked at the sign. She was crazy, though sweet. And she had a pug in a Santa outfit and a parrot that kept calling me an arse.'

Patricia laughed so hard she nearly dropped her wineglass. 'You're joking.'

'I'm not! She was called Eunice, and she literally just left me with the shop and her pets.'

'Did you actually serve anyone?' Aidan asked.

'One bloke – that was it. It wasn't exactly crawling with customers.'

'Shame. It's such a sweet little place.' Patricia gazed into the near distance. 'But fancy leaving you in charge like that when you could have been anyone. I've never heard such nonsense.'

They were all laughing now, and something loosened in Scarlett's chest. This was good. This was normal. Her slightly dysfunctional family had got so much closer in the past few years – mostly thanks to Lilah. That thought made Scarlett feel a little guilty too. Scarlett had been awful to Lilah at school, but now she was one of her only friends.

And Scarlett was very glad to have people here now, making her feel less alone on a day when she'd been prepared to wallow.

'You should go back,' Lilah said. 'Sounds like the perfect job for you.'

'No way.' The word came out a little too fast. 'I can't do that. I know zero about books.' If she went back, it would literally be to hand back Eunice's cash as quickly as she could then run.

'I love books,' Lilah said. 'If I wasn't doing the Crafty Bee Barn, it would be a good job for me.'

Scarlett smiled. Lilah and Patricia were both into crafts, and Aidan kept bees. Together, they sold their produce in a yellow shed next to Aidan's house called the Crafty Bee Barn. For a while, Scarlett had worked there too, but it wasn't really her thing. Nothing was, it seemed.

'You should add it to your CV,' Patricia said.

'I don't think one afternoon in a practically empty bookshop really counts as work experience.'

'I don't know. It's better than another temporary cleaning job.'

Scarlett almost groaned, but she didn't want to lower the mood again, which also meant keeping schtum about Lloyd. Her family knew what had happened in the summer. Scarlett had confessed when she'd been overwhelmed by it all. The whole thing had been so messy, and weirdly it had been Aidan's ex-girl-friend, Elise Reid, who'd helped Scarlett find clarity. Elise had been their tour guide – awkward! – but she was someone Scarlett had always liked and looked up to. She'd suggested Scarlett went for counselling, and Scarlett had.

She picked at the sausage roll crumbs. In counselling, she'd learned about patterns. Like how she kept choosing guys who treated her badly. And how the fling that summer wasn't actually what made her feel shit. It was just the last straw. Losing something good had made her realise how much bad stuff she'd accepted before.

'Maybe temporary cleaning jobs are what I deserve.' She finished off a sandwich.

Patricia reached over and squeezed her hand. 'No, you deserve good things, love.'

Scarlett's throat went tight. Did she? Because good things required being a functional human who could handle normal relationships.

'Right then,' Patricia said. 'Let me light the candles and you can make a wish.'

Scarlett stared at the candles as, one by one, her mum lit them. She'd already made one wish today, and look how that had turned out. The universe clearly had a sadistic sense of humour.

'I don't know what to wish for.'

'World peace,' Aidan suggested.

'A job you actually like,' Patricia offered.

But Scarlett's brain had already betrayed her, sliding back to Lloyd, to the way he'd looked standing in that bookshop – tired, melancholy, but still unfairly magnetic

What would she wish for? To see him again? To never see him again? To go back to summer and make different choices? To be someone else entirely, someone who could cope with complicated feelings?

'Come on,' Patricia prompted. 'Candles are melting.'

Scarlett leaned forward, closed her eyes, and tried to think of nothing. But her subconscious, the treacherous cow, whispered: *I wish I could be with him.*

She blew out the candles in one go.

'What did you wish for?' Lilah asked.

'Can't tell you or it won't come true.'

Though given her track record today, maybe she should've specified that she wanted it not to come true. The universe seemed determined to grant her wishes in the most painful way possible.

'Good girl,' Patricia said, already cutting generous slices. 'I still can't get over that bookshop. It's the weirdest thing ever.'

Maybe... But she didn't know the half of it.

The smell hit Scarlett first – that unmistakable cocktail of floor polish, teenage desperation, and whatever crimes against nutrition they were committing in the canteen. Glenbriar High School hadn't changed its signature scent in the eight years since she'd escaped, which was either comforting or deeply depressing.

She was leaning towards the latter, given that she was back here with a mop bucket and a tabard that looked like it had been designed by someone who actively hated human dignity.

The agency had given her roughly three minutes of training, which boiled down to 'clean things that look dirty' and 'try not to break anything expensive.' Revolutionary stuff. The regular cleaning staff seemed too busy to elaborate on that – so she was basically winging it.

She started in the main corridor, pushing a trolley past the noticeboards that looked so familiar. The floors were that special kind of shiny that showed every footprint, which seemed like a design flaw, but what did she know? She was just the woman in the dignity-destroying tabard for a few hours – and right now she needed anything that would make her some money, otherwise no one would be getting any Christmas presents. And while she couldn't get herself buzzed up about Christmas, she hated being stingy.

'Scarlett?'

She froze, hand halfway to the mop, then slowly turned to find Eddie Caldwell, her old history teacher, looking exactly the same except for a few more distinguished greys at his temples. He'd aged like a fine wine and looked proper handsome despite easily being old enough to be her dad.

'Mr Caldwell.' Her voice came out approximately two octaves higher than normal.

'Nice to see you.' He was smiling, but there was something in his eyes – not pity exactly, but close enough to make her want to dissolve into the floor she was supposedly cleaning. 'How are you? I usually forget students' names as soon as they're out of the building, but your hair is a good reminder.'

'Yeah.'

'And how are you?'

What was she supposed to say? That she was living her dream of returning to her old school as a skivvy? That she'd peaked at seventeen and it had been downhill ever since?

'Living my best life.'

He laughed. 'Aren't we all? Well, lovely to see you. I'd better dash – meeting about to start. Take care.'

'Thanks.'

He strode off down the corridor in his neat chinos and pressed shirt, probably heading to do something meaningful with his life while she contemplated whether drinking the cleaning fluid would be less painful than this entire situation.

She attacked the floors with unnecessary vigour, working her way down towards the meeting rooms. The school was that weird after-hours quiet – not empty but holding its breath. Teachers still hunched over desks, marking papers or planning lessons or whatever it was that kept them here.

Scarlett was wrestling with a particularly stubborn stain when she heard voices from a room just off the corridor. The door was slightly ajar, probably for air, and she could see slivers of the scene inside – a bright room with motivational posters that reminded her of her counsellor's office.

'I really appreciate you taking the time,' a man's voice said, and Scarlett's whole body went cold.

Lloyd. Of course it was Lloyd. Because the universe wasn't done with her yet.

She should move. Should grab her supplies and clean literally anywhere else. Instead, she found herself frozen.

'Not at all,' a woman's voice replied – warm, genuinely caring. The kind of voice that probably never told kids they were disappointments. 'Starting a new school is tough for anyone, but especially after everything Eve's been through.'

Through the gap, Scarlett could see the woman – youngish, pretty in that wholesome way that made her immediately seem trustworthy. She was leaning forward, hands clasped, radiating empathy, and Scarlett had a weird desire to be her friend.

Lloyd was in profile, and Christ, he looked tired. Good tired, still annoyingly attractive tired, but tired nonetheless. He was wearing a smart white shirt that showed a tantalising glimpse of his forearms, and his hair looked accidentally perfect. Scarlett's insides flipped. This was how it had started on the coach – with her eyeing up his forearms, his neck, his hair, even his glasses, and then the rest of him.

'She's just so angry,' he said. 'At me, mostly. She had friends in Edinburgh, a whole life, and I've ripped her away from all of it.'

'Fifteen is such a difficult age anyway,' the teacher said. 'Everything feels like the end of the world, and for Eve, some things actually have been.'

'I know. I just...' He rubbed his face. 'I want to make this work. The boys are younger, they're adapting, but Eve – she won't even talk to me half the time. Just locks herself in her room with her music.'

Scarlett's chest ached. She remembered being fifteen, feeling like nobody understood her, like the whole world was against her. Except she'd had friends, a whole familiar world. Eve had lost her mum, and now her dad had dragged her to a small town where she knew nobody.

'Give her time,' the teacher said. 'And maybe... is there anything she's interested in? Clubs or activities where she might meet people naturally?'

'She used to love drama. But she's not interested anymore.'

'Well, Mrs McArthur will be back from her maternity leave after Christmas, and she's a truly wonderful drama teacher who is amazing with the students. We also have a really great stand-in teacher who's doing *A Christmas Carol* with the students this year. The rehearsals have already started, but I know a couple of pupils have dropped out, so there are auditions for one or two smaller parts. And if Eve didn't feel like acting yet – it might be too exposed right now – then she might think of joining backstage. I could work with her to help integrate her into the group.'

'Thank you, I'd appreciate that.'

They kept talking; Lloyd's voice was heavy with the weight of trying to do right by his kids, and Scarlett felt like an intruder. Which she was technically, but it cut deeper than that. She was eavesdropping on pain that wasn't hers to witness, on a life that was so far removed from her own that it might as well be happening on another planet.

Here was Lloyd, killing himself to be a good dad, worried about his daughter's emotional wellbeing and school transitions. And here was Scarlett, twenty-five years old, living with her mum, cleaning her old school because she couldn't hold down a proper job. She couldn't even take care of herself, let alone three grieving kids.

This was why they only worked as a fling. Anything else was laughable. She grabbed her supplies and moved to the next corridor, but the voices followed her out.

'...I really appreciate this,' Lloyd was saying. 'I know Christmas is probably the worst time to be starting somewhere new.'

'Yes,' the teacher replied, 'but at least there are lots of things happening. Maybe some of them might help to take your mind off things.'

'I haven't even thought about Christmas properly. Last year was... well. This year I wanted to make it special, but instead I've dragged them here.'

They were in the corridor now, still talking, and Scarlett ducked into an empty room that was actually just a walk-in cupboard, heart hammering. Through the open door, she could hear the teacher's voice.

'You're doing your best. That's all any of us can do.'

'Is it enough though?'

'It has to be.'

'Well, thank you, Miss Morgan, that's been really helpful.'

'Anytime. And I'll make sure I catch Eve before classes start tomorrow, and we can work things out.'

His footsteps faded down the corridor, and Scarlett slumped against the wall. Her eyes burned with tears she refused to let fall. She wanted to help him so badly it felt like a physical ache. Wanted to make Christmas magical for his kids, wanted to take some of the weight off his shoulders, wanted to be the kind of person who could actually contribute something useful.

But she wasn't. She was just Scarlett Finch, disaster in human form, whose greatest achievement this week was getting three hours' work cleaning floors and toilets.

She wiped her face with her sleeve.

'Oh, hello.' The cupboard door opened, and the friendly teacher, who'd been talking to Lloyd, smiled at Scarlett. 'Are you ok, my love?' she said.

'What? Um... Yeah. Just the bleach making my eyes water.'

She gave Scarlett a quizzical look. 'Are you new here?'

'Just covering... Though I'm not sure I'm doing it right. I appear to have found a cupboard that I thought was an office.'

The teacher smiled. 'My office is empty now. It's next door. You could do that, and both the deputy head and the principal are in the meeting room, so their offices are empty too. That's them just over there.'

'Thank you.' Scarlett wheeled her cart back into the corridor. 'That's helpful.'

'No problem, my love. You take care. And thank you for the good work. We often take the cleaning staff for granted, but we couldn't work without you, so everything you do is appreciated.'

Scarlett nodded, wishing even more she could be friends with someone as lovely as her. Well, if Lloyd had her to fight the corner for his daughter, then he was a lucky man. And Scarlett should be satisfied with that.

Because realistically what could she do to help him? Other than stay away. It was abundantly clear he didn't need a distraction or further complications in his life right now.

But as Scarlett emptied the bin in the principal's office, she found herself making another wish. Not out loud, not on a tree or candles or stars. Just a quiet, desperate thought:

Please let them be ok. Let his kids find happiness here. Let him find peace.

It wasn't for her. Maybe if the universe was listening and feeling generous, it could do something nice for someone who actually deserved it.

Chapter Six

Lloyd

After the performance of the first day of school, Lloyd's hopes of day two being any better were quickly dashed. His plan to get all three kids and himself dressed, fed, and out of his mum's cottage by 8:20 had spectacularly failed. By 8:19, they'd had a minor nosebleed – Harry, not him – a coffee stain on his shirt, and a mental note that his mum's cat absolutely could not be allowed in the bathroom with Lewis, even for one minute.

Utter chaos.

Eventually he got the older two out, then walked Lewis along Sweetwater Lane past the tennis courts and along a little path that joined up with the larger road leading to the primary school.

A clutch of other parents and kids were heading that way too. Lewis was doing ninja moves at Lloyd's side instead of walking, his little backpack bouncing. Lloyd glanced at him, struck by the difference between this and how Eve had skulked out, barely speaking, glowering at the world with headphones jammed so tight she might as well have been in another galaxy. Harry had sloped after her in sullen silence, not so much angry as resigned.

'You don't need to walk me to the gate,' Lewis said. 'I remember the way myself.'

'Yeah, but you're not familiar with these roads yet.'

Lewis pulled a face. 'Can you wait on the street and not come into the playground then?'

'Ok.' God forbid he embarrassed a ten-year-old. Kissing him goodbye was also a no-no. Lloyd hovered near the scrum of small kids, buggies at the perimeter, and ruffled Lewis's hair. He twitched his head away and marched up to the gate without a backward glance. A little bubble of pride swelled in Lloyd at how well his youngest was dealing with everything, though he also felt a twinge of sadness at not getting a kiss goodbye. They were all getting too grown up to do such things – especially in public.

'Good morning.'

Lloyd tensed, turning to see a woman with sleek, highlighted hair, immaculate makeup, and a coat that probably cost more than his laptop.

'Are you Lewis's dad?'

Lloyd nodded.

The woman stuck out her hand. 'I'm Amanda Reid.'

'Lloyd.'

'I'm the chair of the parent council. Delighted to meet you. My eldest is in Lewis's class. She was telling me about him yesterday.'

'Oh really? Hopefully nothing too incriminating.'

Amanda laughed. 'Not in the least. She just said he was new. Where have you moved from?'

'Edinburgh. But my mum lives in Glenbriar and has done for some time.'

'Lovely. And where are you staying?'

'At the moment with my mum. She has a cottage on Sweetwater Lane, but we've bought a house on Golf Course Road – it's not ready for us to move into yet.' The words 'we' and 'us' still rolled off his tongue and while they applied to him and his kids, it felt more like he was discussing himself as still being part of a partnership – even though he knew that wasn't the case anymore.

'Wonderful.' Amanda clapped her hands. 'We'll be neighbours. I live on Golf Course Road too.'

'That's good to know.' Lloyd gave her a little smile.

'And is your wife around, or...'

'She's not.' He tried to say it as gently as possible. 'She passed away last year.'

Amanda's face froze for a split second, then rebooted with a smile so warm it was almost too much. 'Oh, I'm so sorry; that's dreadful. You must let us know if there's anything we can do. Anything at all.'

'Thanks,' Lloyd said, heat blooming in his neck. 'I think we'll be fine.'

'Well, I won't keep you. But if you're ever stuck for a coffee, just give me a shout.'

He nodded as she flounced back to the other parents. The bell rang and Lloyd craned his neck to look over the fence and the hedge. Hopefully Lewis was in the line. Lloyd eventually spotted him. He seemed to be chatting to another child. Well, that was something.

Lloyd made his way back to the house. His phone buzzed, and he dug it out. One missed call, number withheld. One voicemail.

The speaker was so immediately frantic, he nearly walked into a wheelie bin.

'Lloyd! Oh, it's Eunice, dear. I'm so sorry to bother you, but I've done something extremely stupid – well, Clarence has, but technically I'm the one with the opposable thumbs so the blame is shared – and now I'm at A&E and it looks like I've broken my shoulder or possibly dislocated it – can you possibly open the shop today? I'm at the hospital, and they say I'll be here a while. They've given me lots of pain relief. It was quite agonising. I tripped over a branch when Clarence decided to go after a deer ten times his size and then proceeded to yank my arm in a direction in isn't meant to go in, especially at my age... oh, hang on, nurse is coming. Must dash. Sorry again.'

Lloyd groaned and headed back to the house.

Rita was in the kitchen, feeding the cat.

'Mum, I just got a voicemail from Eunice.'

'Yes, she called me too. She sounds in a state.'

'She wants someone to open the shop today. Can you?'

'Sorry, I can't. I promised Eunice I'd look after Clarence and the parrot. The poor dog will be traumatised. And Beaky hates being left alone. You'll have to do it, or I suppose you could close it, though that always feels like such a waste. Or why not take your laptop and do your other work there too?'

That might work today, but the rest of the week he had online meetings. His head buzzed, and for a moment he couldn't see straight. It seemed like people were pulling him in all directions, and he wanted to give them all the time and care they deserved, but he just didn't have the energy.

His mother gave him a look. 'I know it's not ideal, but it can't be helped. I'll try to make it up to you in other ways. If I'm honest, I find all the lifting and bending in the shop too much.'

He nodded, knowing it was this issue that had made her want to give it up in the first place. And she definitely seemed a lot better. She'd been in a good mood ever since they'd arrived, with none of the short tempers or the loss of patience that often accompanied her flare-ups.

'Ok. I'll do what I can.' He slung his laptop into his bag and headed out. Sweetwater Lane was quite a way from the centre of Glenbriar and the station. It was a pleasant enough walk down-hill through the chilly streets. With December just around the corner, all the shops had already fully embraced the Christmas spirit and windows glowed with Christmas trees and fairy lights. Lloyd felt like a veritable Scrooge as he looked at them all with complete indifference. Or maybe it wasn't Scrooge-like at all.

Because he didn't feel animosity towards the displays – he didn't feel anything. And sadly, that wasn't just related to Christmas. His whole body was numb. So were his insides.

When he reached the station, he unlocked the door to the bookshop and stepped inside.

He dropped his bag behind the counter and took a moment to look around. This place was a higgledy-piggledy mess, but there was something quaint about it. If he could channel the quirky side of it but somehow modernise it and make it look more cottage-core and whimsical rather than dusty jumble sale, then maybe more people would enter in. But he wasn't sure he had the skills. And sweet as Eunice could be, he wasn't sure she did either. His brow furrowed as his focus landed on a large sign pinned to a shelf: *BOOKS TO MAKE YOU HAPPY*. It had at least three crime novels on it.

He let out a breath and pulled his laptop from the bag. She was something else.

The bookshop had two rooms: the main retail space and a little overflow nook where the stock migrated. It was a mess – boxes half-unpacked, a sale table blocking the fire exit, and three Christmas trees, each decorated in a different but equally questionable style. At least they hadn't been turned into wishing trees. One of them was quite enough. Lloyd eyed it with a raised brow and rubbed the back of his neck. Maybe he should make a Eunice-style wish that someone would come along and help him.

Or maybe just that someone would appear and tell him what the hell to do with his life.

He left his laptop on the counter and held his palm to his forehead. Where to even start?

Flipping the sign to OPEN, he straightened a few books, turning the best covers face out.

At the back of the shop, next to the cookbooks, there was a narrow stairway. Lloyd hadn't been up there in years. He climbed up, careful on the creaking steps, and found the old staffroom exactly as he remembered – except now, it was two-thirds storage, one-third desk, and the rest a shrine to Eunice's taste in instant soup. There was an ancient kettle in the kitchen area, a couple of mugs, and a faded tartan sofa. A tiny bathroom was squeezed in at the top of the stairs. This had possibly once been home to the station master – not a grand abode by any stretch. It was basically a bedsit.

He boiled water, made a cup of coffee, and carried it down to the counter. His laptop pinged as he set it up, new work emails appearing like mushrooms after rain. He clicked through them half-heartedly, eyes glazing over the spreadsheets, the endless loop of audit reminders, deadline extensions, and "gentle nudges" from his boss. He'd asked for this – more flexible hours, less time in the office – but it came with its own challenges.

He stared at the screen for ten minutes, answering the easier messages first. Then he started a to-do list.

There was something about the stillness of the shop, broken only by the rumbling of trains every half hour or so, that made him want to stay here forever. No one needed anything from him. He could just be.

The lack of customers was a little disturbing. He kept glancing at the clock, waiting, though not sure what for. A shiver ran through him. Why did it feel like something was going to happen? An odd sense of foreboding spread through him.

The bell over the door jangled, and Lloyd almost jumped out of his skin. Over the door, the clock was at precisely midday.

A woman in a green coat came in. She had dark hair, cut straight and long, and a quick, birdlike way of scanning the shelves. She didn't look at him as she moved through the shop, but something about her profile made the bottom drop out of his stomach.

It was the hair, maybe, the way it fell almost covering one eye. He watched her, frozen. She was so like Amy. Or if not Amy, then the closest approximation he'd ever seen. Even her sister didn't look that much like her. She turned a book over in her hands, pursing her lips exactly the way Amy would have when she didn't want to pay full price.

The woman circled the shop once, then came over to the till without a word. She slid a book across the counter. *Take a Chance*, the cover said. It was a romance novel. Amy had loved these, especially the ones with cartoon people kissing.

Lloyd took the book, scanned it, and tried not to stare. 'Would you like a bag?'

She looked at him then, and the illusion wavered. Her eyes were a different colour, and her face shape was wrong.

God, his mind was on a bender these days.

'No, thank you.'

He passed her the card reader. She tapped her card, took the book and left. Lloyd watched her go, feeling like he'd been struck in the chest.

An unsettled sensation had plagued him since he'd arrived this morning, and he couldn't shake it. What the hell was wrong with him?

Grief, no doubt.

Or maybe he needed more coffee. He retreated upstairs and boiled the kettle, looking out of the little window at the train that had just arrived and watching the passengers alight.

Sitting for a moment on the tartan sofa, he let the mug warm his hands. The adrenaline from earlier had faded, replaced with a slow-motion fatigue.

The bell on the shop door clattered, loud enough to wake the dead. Getting to his feet, he headed for the stairs. From the top, he heard a voice.

'Hello? Anyone in? Eunice?'

His whole body went cold.

It couldn't be. Could it?

He forced himself to go down the stairs slowly so he had time to recalibrate his face into something neutral. Not happy, not desperate, just... normal.

Scarlett stood in the middle of the shop in a long black coat. She looked up as he came down, and for a moment they just stared at each other. Again.

Christ. Why did he lose the power of speech every time he saw her? This time he needed to say something.

'Hi.' He swallowed as he reached the bottom of the stairs, clutching the banister.

'Hi,' she said, voice small and tight. 'I... um...'

He walked behind the till, desperate for something to do with his hands.

Scarlett stayed on the customer side, twisting a strap of her bag between her fingers. She had the look of someone who regretted every decision that had led her to this exact spot, at this exact time.

'Is Eunice here?'

He shook his head. 'Sorry, no. Just me.'

She reached into her pocket and pulled out a fifty-pound note. 'Eunice gave me this the day I helped her out. I was supposed to get ten quid, but she paid me fifty by mistake.'

'Wow, she's something else. Who carries fifty-pound notes around?' His lip tugged into a smile, but when he met Scarlett's eyes, he stopped. She didn't look at all happy about being here.

'Will she be back here? Or can you give it to her? I can't keep it. She's a pensioner, and—' Scarlett shrugged. 'I don't want her to think I was scamming her. Especially not at Christmas.'

She slid the note across the counter.

'I'm sure she wouldn't,' he said. 'I'll give it to her as soon as I can. She's... Well, she had a fall this morning, and she's at the hospital. She thinks she's maybe broken her shoulder.'

Scarlett's face slipped. 'Oh shit, that's horrible.'

'Yeah. My mum's going to look after her animals.'

Scarlett's eyes flashed, and Lloyd knew why. His mum and Scarlett's history was not pleasant. 'So... do you live here now?' she asked.

He nodded, fiddling with the fifty-pound note. 'I've just moved. My mum's lived here for years, running this place.'

'Oh... I didn't realise.'

'Same.' He met her gaze again. 'I mean, I assume you live here too. We didn't really discuss it.'

Her cheeks looked a little pinker than before, and his felt equally warm. They'd talked a lot, but for some reason, Glenbriar had never come up – possibly because their mouths had been busy with other activities.

'Yeah, I've always lived here.'

'I see.'

Another silence followed. She didn't move. Neither did he. They just looked.

It was like the universe was daring them to say what they actually meant. Lloyd wanted to tell her how much he'd missed her, how the idea of her had got him through the last five months. But he couldn't.

Because his life was way too full of baggage, and that was assuming she even wanted anything from him, which was a pretty big assumption considering the flimsy foundation their fling had been built on in the first place.

A mutual distraction did not equal relationship potential.

Scarlett shifted her bag, looking at the floor. 'Well. I'll get out of your way.'

'You're not in my way.'

Her teeth grazed her lower lip, and for a second, it was like being back on the coach trip, both of them lonely and weary but alive. So alive.

The bell exploded again, shattering the moment.

A man in his late fifties stomped in. 'Have you got any Lee Child books?' he asked without preamble.

Lloyd had no idea. He hadn't even had a proper look at the inventory.

'There's a whole shelf of them around here.' Scarlett walked to the end of a row and pointed. 'In the middle, there.'

The man grunted, then nodded, and even managed what could be mistaken for a smile. 'Thank you.' He made his way down the row and peered at the shelf.

'Thanks,' Lloyd whispered.

She shrugged. 'It's fine. I noticed them when I was dusting the other day.'

'I don't suppose you actually want a job here?'

Scarlett blinked. 'You're not serious.'

He rubbed the back of his neck. 'I kind of am. I've got work meetings, kids, a new house to move into, and Eunice is out for at least a week. I suspect longer.'

'Even though...'

The man appeared holding two Lee Child books. Lloyd scanned them through, while Scarlett hung about fiddling with her long scarf and thumbing aimlessly through a book on Christmas crafting.

When the man left, and the howling bell calmed down, Lloyd turned back to Scarlett. 'If you want the job and you don't have anything else on, I'm sure we could work something out. You did better than I did in that one afternoon.'

'You think? I mean, I might burn the place down by accident or offend someone and get banned from the station for life.'

'I'll take the risk.'

Scarlett looked at him, and he pushed down all the rising fire in his gut.

'Can I think about it?' she said. 'I mean, I'll let you know by the end of today.'

'Of course. Do you want my number?'

'Um... Yeah.'

He pulled a bit of paper from a deskpad and wrote it. 'There you go.'

She took the paper from him like she was holding her breath. Maybe he should say more. Tell her this was all professional, and he expected nothing. Tell her not to worry on that front. He understood what they'd done in the summer was nothing and they could move on.

If he could start by telling his heart that it might be best.

'I'll let you know.' She backed to the door, then left with the bell clanging wildly.

Lloyd closed his eyes and breathed slowly. If she didn't bin his number and disappear from his radar, he'd be very much surprised. His insides contracted, and he groaned. Why the hell was his life such a horrible mess?

Chapter Seven

Scarlett

Scarlett almost tripped as she left the bookshop, which was exactly the kind of flourish the universe liked to give her. That silly ledge at the door was not only a hazard to people like her but made it inaccessible for people in wheelchairs. She pressed the door shut behind her and waited for the insane bell to stop its war cry. Still clutching the scrap of paper with Lloyd's number on it, her fingers locked so tightly it was almost painful.

The platform was almost empty except for a bunch of pigeons, a couple at the far end, and a woman on her phone. Scarlett walked to the bench under the shelter and collapsed onto it. The air was weirdly still, almost like it might snow.

She stared down at Lloyd's writing, neat and square, totally at odds with her own messy scrawl.

Did she actually want this job? Or did she just want to orbit the possibility of Lloyd? And either way, she'd have to deal with Rita, who hated her on a molecular level after the summer fling cock up.

Scarlett leaned back and exhaled. She should be happy. This was the closest thing to a real opportunity she'd had since… pretty much ever. But was this just an opportunity to rerun old mistakes on a brand new stage?

A few more people appeared on the platform, and Scarlett checked the electronic board. A train was due any minute. She should probably go. She was cleaning the school again later, but not for the rest of the week, so if she wanted to accept the job, it wouldn't clash, unless the agency called early the next day. That was a possibility, but she could say no to the cleaning… especially if she had something else lined up.

At the far end of the platform, the train rattled in, sending a cold blast down the shelter and making Scarlett tuck her hands into her armpits. Two passengers got off – a woman with a very large suitcase, and a man with long dark hair and a biker jacket. Scarlett recognised him as a singer in a local band. She'd been to a couple of their gigs last month with Elise, who'd been kindly trying to help her get out of her funk since the coach trip. It still felt strange to be friends with her brother's ex. When Elise was dating Aidan, Scarlett had almost hero worshipped her. Maybe she should call her now. Elise was five years older and had the benefit of experience. She could help Scarlett decide. But she also knew about Lloyd and would probably try to talk Scarlett out of it.

Did she want to be talked out of it?

A clamour of loud voices made Scarlett look up. A gang of young men barged onto the platform. Six or seven of them, already tanked on cheap lager, bottles clutched in gloveless hands.

Scarlett did a double take.

No. Please no.

Leon Fletcher, her ex-boyfriend, was at the head of the pack, his eyes giddy with the energy he only ever mustered for a midweek session. Scarlett's throat tightened, and she curled into herself. When they'd been together, she'd dreaded days like this, knowing how he'd come back loudmouthed and violent.

'Hurry up, get the fuck moving. It's another hour if we miss this.'

Next to him was Zeb Buchanan, another of her exes. He was laughing at something, then he paused to scratch his stomach and spotted her.

The recognition hit like a backhand.

He jabbed an elbow at Leon, pointed straight at Scarlett, and cackled.

The bottom dropped from her stomach. Leon's face twisted into an ugly grin.

She stood as fast as she could and made a beeline for the bookshop, keeping her head down.

The bell above the door sounded less aggressive than before, almost welcoming.

She shut it tight behind her and breathed out a long sigh.

Lloyd was behind the counter, hunched over his laptop. He looked up, and it was like watching someone take a breath after being held under for too long. He straightened, took off his glasses, and set them carefully on the worktop. 'Are you ok?'

She shook her head, then caught herself. 'Yeah. Actually, no. I just—'

He waited, his eyes soft and kind, though perhaps a little concerned.

She peered at her shoes, chewing her lip until the words fell out. 'Leon's on the platform... along with another of my exes. They're drunk and are probably going on a bender. I just... didn't want them to see me. Or talk to me.'

'Leon?' Lloyd's hands curled on the counter like he was gripping very tightly. 'That piece of work.'

Of course he would remember what had happened on the coach tour. It was likely the stuff of legends these days. The memory made her cringe.

'Yeah,' Scarlett said. 'The same.'

Lloyd moved around the counter and walked to the door. As he passed her, she caught the scent of his sandalwood cologne, and it transported her straight back to the summer. How she'd felt so perfectly safe in his arms. He looked through the window in the door. 'I'll lock this until they're gone.' He leaned forward and turned the key. 'Though I don't see them, so I think they must be on the train already.'

'They'd never come in here anyway. Unless the pub ran out of beer and they had to eat the furniture. I don't think Leon can read much more than his own name and the football scores.'

Lloyd let out a low chuckle. For a second, Scarlett forgot all about the platform and the ghosts of boyfriends-past that had given her such a jumpscare.

The sound of the train's engine rumbled, and it slowly pulled away from the platform. Lloyd waited a beat, then unlocked the door. 'They're gone.'

Scarlett exhaled. 'Thanks.' Even now, the sense of reassurance she felt when she was close to him was almost overwhelming.

He went back to the counter. She didn't move, just stared at the spines of the romance novels. If she was bone-deep honest with herself, the only place she wanted to be was near him and there seemed only one way to do that without being sneaky or crazy – which her past self would probably have done without question, however she was twenty-five now, plus she'd had coun-selling which had taught her a thing or two.

This may still be the stupidest decision of her life, but after seeing two examples of past mistakes, she was ready to take a chance on something better.

'I'd like to take the job,' she said.

Lloyd blinked, as if he hadn't expected her to say yes. 'You would? Don't you want to think about it?'

She nodded, twisting the fabric of her sleeve. 'I have. And I want to. I have to do a cleaning shift at the school later, but after that, I'm free. If that's still ok.'

A smile started to edge its way onto his face. It wasn't smug, just surprised, and maybe a bit relieved. 'Of course it's ok. I can show you how the computer system works and everything. Properly, not the Eunice version.'

'Probably sensible.' Scarlett grinned.

'I'll sort out a contract. Terms and conditions. We'll make sure everything's done by the book.'

'One of your puns?' She couldn't help saying it. He'd been full of them those few days they'd been together, but drawing attention to those memories seemed reckless.

'I can't take the credit this time; Eunice got there first.' He gave her a weak smile, and the tension in her shoulders unravelled just a bit.

'Thank you,' she said.

He nodded, and she saw the faintest blush on his cheeks. 'If you can come in tomorrow morning, I'll show you around properly.'

Scarlett gave him a thumbs up. 'I'll be here.'

They lapsed into another silence, and Scarlett found herself staring at the little wishing tree in the corner, now with a few more baubles in varying shades of glitter pen.

'I, um... will see you tomorrow then.'

'See you then... Oh... and can you get some kind of ramp at the door? That ledge is a trip hazard, and the shop really should be accessible.'

He gave her a soft smile. 'I'll order something straight away.'

'Thanks.' Scarlett left, the bell giving its usual show of melodrama as she stepped carefully over the ledge.

She walked up the road towards the school, her hands in her pockets, her brain crowded with every feeling she'd ever tried to bury. She still wasn't sure she was doing the right thing. But she'd given herself a small window to try.

And for once, she wasn't going to slam it shut.

She'd see Lloyd again. She'd face the past, even if it meant risking her heart all over again. The world was full of past mistakes, but maybe she didn't have to let them win.

CHAPTER EIGHT

Lloyd

Lewis launched himself out of the school doors and bar-relled straight into Lloyd's arms, backpack thudding like a brick.

'We have to collect jars,' Lewis announced, 'to make Christmas candle things for the fayre.'

Lloyd smiled, pulling the bobble hat lower over his son's head. 'Maybe Gran's got some. We haven't really got anything except what's in the boxes.'

'Can we eat pasta sauce and get some?' Lewis was walking backwards, coat flying open to the point of almost falling off. 'I want to make a Samurai one with Ninja cats.'

'Is that Christmassy?' Lloyd raised an eyebrow.

'Sure. I'll put a tree beside them.'

Lloyd steered them out of the gate and onto the pavement. 'I assume you had a good day by the sound of things.'

'It was ok. And can we go to the Christmas light switch-on? It's at the weekend,' Lewis said. 'Everyone's going. The whole of Glenbriar is going to be there. Can we?'

'Yeah, I'm sure we can.' Lloyd ruffled his son's hair, then tried to hold his hand. Lewis resisted but let it happen when a car went by a little too close. Moments like this were precious. Lewis was already ten. The years went by so fast. It seemed like yesterday he was a baby. That was in the good old days, before Amy was diagnosed. Who would have thought that in the ten years since Lewis was born things could have changed so dramatically?

Sweetwater Lane looked especially narrow with the cars parked on one side and bins out for collection. A light mist drifted over the hedges in the impending darkness, and with coils of smoke coming from the chimneys in the row of cottages, it really looked very atmospheric.

As they went inside, Rita's voice echoed from the kitchen.

'Lewis, take your shoes off before you trample mud across the carpet.'

'We didn't go anywhere muddy,' Lewis called back. 'Just the normal way.'

'It's muddy everywhere this time of year.' Rita appeared in the doorway, glasses perched at the end of her nose. 'How was school?'

'Dad said we can go to the light switch-on. My new friend Robbie is going. His dad is in a band, and he's going to sing there.'

'That's good that you've made a friend,' Lloyd said.

'Can you go into a band, Dad?'

Rita smirked and returned to the kitchen. 'I've got soup on. And cheese scones.'

'No, I can't sing,' Lloyd said. 'But I could get into a waistband if Christmas dinner doesn't stretch it too far.'

'That's not even funny.' Lewis unzipped his coat and dropped it on the stairs.

'Pick that up.' Lloyd gave him a look.

Lewis snatched it up, flung it at the hook, then headed into the kitchen after Rita. 'Can we get a tree? Like a real one? Or will we have a fake one at the new house?'

'We'll have both if you want. The new house is big enough.' Lloyd shrugged, already regretting the two-tree future he was creating, but really he should attempt to do something festive – or at least go through the motions to appease Lewis. 'We could have one in the dining room and one in the living room.'

Lewis scrunched up his face. 'Can one of them be black?'

'Why do you want a black tree?' Rita passed him a mug of hot chocolate loaded with marshmallows.

'So it can be a ninja tree.'

She snort-laughed behind his back. 'I heard from Eunice, by the way,' she said to Lloyd. 'She's still at the hospital. They're waiting to see if they need to operate.'

'She's still in?'

'Yes. A friend has taken Clarence and Mr Beaky for the time being, which is just as well. I didn't want to bring them here. They'd petrify Cali.' She ruffled the cat's neck.

'Poor Eunice,' Lloyd said.

Rita nodded. 'She was quite chipper, considering, but it does leave a problem about the shop.'

'Don't worry about that, I've... I've got it covered.' But a gaping hole had opened up in his plan. He couldn't let his mum discover who he'd hired. How would it look? *Lloyd moves to a new town, happens to be the place his summer fling lives, and he suddenly hires her to work in his shop?* Rita would flip her lid and assume he'd lost his mind – which was a possibility, of course. His sense had already been called into question on the coach trip. He'd thought he'd been discreet enough, but he hadn't banked on a whole cohort of gossips, most of whom had it in for Scarlett because of her alternative dress sense, and who made her business their business, especially if it was something they could get self-righteously angry about. Someone had clearly seen or heard something, and Rita had found out, which had led to a highly unpleasant spectacle where Rita had shouted at Scarlett.

It hadn't helped that Rita had been going through a big flare-up in her ankylosing spondylitis – and hadn't told him. She'd taken out her pain on Scarlett, and nothing Lloyd had said at the time could change her mind. Scarlett was not a suitable person to get involved with as far as she was concerned. Now the trip didn't feature in any conversations. Rita had boxed it away, and Lloyd certainly didn't want to bring it up.

'How exactly?' Rita frowned slightly.

'I... um... I'll be there.' He could clean up the upper floor and use it as an office. It would actually be a better space for him than being here with Rita. The new house had plenty of room to work from home, but in Rita's house, he was always in her way.

From the hall, sounds of Harry and Eve arriving home from school filtered through.

'Hey, you two.' Lloyd went to the kitchen door.

Lewis jumped up. 'Guess what, we're going to the Christmas light switch-on at the weekend. And there's a Fayre at my school next week.'

Eve shook her head. 'I'm not going.'

'But it's fun,' Lewis said.

Eve didn't look at any of them. 'I don't want to go.'

'It might help to get out a bit, Eve,' Rita said.

'I'm not a little kid.' Eve's voice cracked at the end.

'You don't have to do anything you don't want,' Lloyd said. 'But Gran's right, it might do you good.'

'It won't.' She stalked up the stairs, feet thudding like gunshots. A door slammed overhead.

The silence she left behind was raw. Harry picked at his sleeves, not meeting anyone's eyes. Rita cleared her throat and busied herself with getting cheese scones out of the oven.

Lewis looked to Lloyd for guidance, but there was nothing in the manual for this. Lloyd just reached over and squeezed his youngest son's shoulder, then turned to Harry. 'How was your day?'

Harry shrugged, his face mostly hidden by his fringe. 'Boring.'

Lloyd nodded. What else did he expect?

With a sigh, he went upstairs and tapped on the boxroom door. This room was barely big enough for a bed, but it gave Eve a bit of privacy. Lloyd, Harry and Lewis were sharing another room, and Rita had her room to herself.

'Go away,' came the voice through the wood.

He considered turning back but then tried the handle. It was blocked.

'Eve, I just want to talk.'

'Well, I don't.'

He let his forehead touch the door.

'You can be as upset and angry as you want,' he said gently. 'You don't have to pretend. But you don't have to hide either. We're still a family, even if we're not doing a great job right now.'

No answer. Music started up.

'I love you,' he said, then left her alone and went downstairs.

For a moment, Lloyd just stood in the hallway, not sure what to do with his hands, or his heart. He was so tired of being strong, of pretending he had answers. The truth was, he was winging it. He didn't know how to fix any of this. And there was no light at the end of the tunnel.

The next morning, the sky looked so cold and white it might shatter. He dropped Lewis at school, then headed to the station again.

Letting himself into the shop, he flicked on the lights, and for a minute just breathed. In his backpack, he had some cleaning products he'd bought at the store and a roll of black bin bags. Part of today's work would be to start cleaning the upstairs room.

He'd just started the computer when he saw Scarlett through the window. She paused on the platform, then squared her shoulders and came inside, the bell above the door still going berserk.

'Morning.' She met Lloyd's eyes as soon as she came in. She'd dressed down – black jeans, a slouchy red jumper, hair in a side ponytail.

'Hi,' he said. 'How are you today?'

She smiled, and it lit up her whole face. 'I didn't sleep very well, but I'm fine. You?'

What had kept her awake? An old story, or a new one? He shook off the thought. 'There's coffee upstairs if you want. Have you seen the upstairs room?'

'Not yet.'

He glanced around, then took off his glasses and sighed. 'Listen, there's been a slight change of plan.'

'Oh? Do I not have the job anymore?'

'You do. It's just that I'll be here too for a week or so. I need to use the room upstairs as an office.'

She gave a little shrug. 'Ok. That's fine.'

'I just don't want you to think I'm spying on you, or monitoring your work or anything. It's not like that. It's... Well, because of my mother.' He replaced his glasses. 'I didn't want to say who I'd hired. You know... she might—'

'I get it.'

'So, it's easier if she thinks I'm here. I won't get in your way though. I've got so many meetings to get through, I'll be stuck up there for hours.'

'It's fine.'

'Good.' He pulled in a breath, then let it out slowly. 'If you want to come around, I can show you the contract on my laptop. If you agree to it all, I'll print off a copy.'

She dropped her backpack behind the counter and moved in beside him. He stepped back to look at the screen. Lloyd couldn't stop looking at her hands: her red nails with snowflake designs on them, and pale delicate fingers. He'd never cared much about hands before, but this hit different. Maybe because he'd spent so many pleasant hours that summer with those hands on his body.

'What does this mean?' She pointed at a line on the screen.

He leaned in beside her and read: *This agreement does not constitute a contract of employment under the Employment Rights Act 1996.*

The space behind the counter was barely two feet wide, so they had no choice but to be close. Her orange blossom and jasmine scent was so sweet it made him dizzy, and he remembered kissing her neck, sliding his palms over her naked back, and holding her so close.

'Does that mean it's not a real job?' She turned to him, and little fires started in his gut.

'It is. That just means it's casual; you're only filling in for Eunice short term. No holiday pay, sorry. But I'll treat you right.'

'I know you will.' Her voice was soft and a little hoarse. Lloyd glanced at her, then blinked. Was she still talking about the contract?

'So... what can I actually do here? Do I just have to sit at the till, or can I change things about? No offence, but it's a bit stuffy in here.'

Lloyd huffed. That was more like her. 'Knock yourself out... just not literally.'

'Too much paperwork?'

'Way too much. Oh, and leave the wishing tree. I don't think Eunice would survive if you took it down.'

'I'll leave it... though it might have to move. Can I change the window display? I'm kind of a Scrooge, but really, it should be Christmassy.'

'I wouldn't have thought you were a Scrooge. You seem too...' She raised an eyebrow.

'Bright.'

'Bright?' She grinned. 'As in, I have red hair, so that means I should act like an all-singing, all-dancing elf?'

'It might get the customers in.'

'Too bad you didn't put it in the contract then.' She smirked at him, and he smiled back. A raging urge to hug her assaulted his brain for a moment, but he didn't.

'Yeah... Well, thanks for all this. I should go upstairs and set up for my meetings. If you need to come in for coffee or a break or whatever, it's fine; just be aware that I'll probably be on a live call.'

'So no swearing or anything? Is that what you're trying to say?'

Clicking his fingers, he pointed at her. 'One hundred per cent that.'

He was about to head up when she caught his sleeve, gentle but deliberate. He froze. Her face was serious, maybe even a little scared.

'I need to tell you something.'

He braced himself for a conversation he'd been dreading since their first run-in here. Maybe she wanted to clear the air or tell him she was in love with someone else and needed closure or assurance from him that what they'd had was nothing. He had a thousand guesses in a few short seconds.

'Of course,' he said.

'So, this is going to sound mental,' she said, 'but I sort of... overheard something, and I feel like I have to say.'

He raised an eyebrow. 'Overheard what?'

'The other day,' she said, 'I was doing relief cleaning at the high school for an agency. And I... kind of overheard you and a teacher talking about your daughter.'

Lloyd exhaled, almost laughing. He'd been ready for pretty much anything, but not that.

'I see,' he said.

She grimaced. 'I wasn't trying to be creepy or anything. I just... Well, I didn't know what I was supposed to be doing. They didn't really tell me, just that I was on the ground floor. I was just mopping floors and dusting desks, and then I heard you.'

He shook his head, opening his mouth, but not sure what to say.

'I'm sorry,' Scarlett said. 'I'm always doing stuff like this, aren't I? This is a bad habit of mine, making things weird for everyone.'

Lloyd shook his head. 'You haven't made anything weird.'

She didn't look convinced. 'I thought I'd confess. I made a real mess... well, on the trip, when I said some stupid stuff to your mum.'

'It's ok.' He reached out and gently touched her hand. 'You were in one of the worst places in the world on that trip. The stuff you said then was armour. You were trying to protect yourself.'

'By getting other people into shit, yeah.'

'Don't beat yourself up about it. Nobody's perfect. And when you've been through a rough time, keeping it together is hard... almost impossible.'

'But you've been through a lot worse than me, and you didn't do anything stupid.'

'Didn't I?' He met her eyes directly. 'We're all different. We all react to situations in different ways. And what I've been through isn't the same as what you've been through. It's not a competition or a comparison.'

'I just—' She ran a hand through her hair, breaking eye contact. 'I just want you to know I think you're a really good dad. Because you try, and you show up.'

How would she know really? But he appreciated her saying it. He'd heard plenty of sympathy, but very little praise or acknowledgement.

'Thanks,' he said.

'My dad doesn't exist in my life and never has. Seeing you so involved... I dunno. It's just nice to see.'

'Thing is, it doesn't feel good. It's like pushing a truck up a hill, and every time you think you're getting somewhere, it rolls back and crushes you. My kids are not happy – except maybe Lewis – and I have no idea what I'm doing.'

Scarlett was quiet for a moment. 'I can't imagine what it's like for Eve. I mean, I was a mess at her age, and my mum was still around.'

'She won't let me in,' Lloyd said. 'I can't even get her to eat dinner with us. She used to talk to me. Now it's just... silence.'

'Maybe she just needs time,' Scarlett said. 'Or maybe she needs to scream at you first.'

He laughed, not because it was funny but because it was probably true.

'Was it really that bad, being a teenage girl?' he asked.

'Yep. I was never good at being a person, let alone a girl. Too loud, too much, too weird. My mum never knew what to do with me. Still doesn't.'

He cocked his head. Maybe she didn't see what he saw. Maybe others didn't either, especially ones who'd known her for a long time. Perhaps she was someone who was better to meet now. She'd grown up and learned a lot if what she said about herself was true.

'I moved us here thinking it would help,' he said. 'That maybe being closer to family would fill the hole. But now I wonder if it was just for me, to make my life easier.'

Scarlett considered this. 'Why did you move?'

'Amy's parents live in Perth. My mum's here. I thought... if I could work from home, maybe I'd actually see my kids. Instead of farming them out to after-school clubs and childminders. In Edinburgh, everything was rushed. Here, I thought it would be different. More of a chance for us all to bond again. I feel like they're slipping away from me and the family's fallen apart.'

Scarlett reached over and laid her hand on his wrist. Her palm was cool, but the touch sent a hundred electric sparks up his arm.

'You're doing the best you can,' she said. 'It's not your fault it didn't turn out perfect straight away.'

He swallowed. It was the kind of thing Amy would have said – except coming from Scarlett, it wasn't reassurance, it was defiance. Like she was daring him to argue.

'Thanks,' he said. 'Since when did you get so wise?'

She laughed and squeezed his wrist, just for a second. 'It's this place. There's something spooky about it. Good spooky, you know?'

'Maybe I should start believing in stuff like that.'

'Or at least make a wish.' She winked at the wishing tree.

'That thing scares me a bit.'

'Why?'

How could he tell her he'd wished for her, and she'd appeared, without sounding insane?

'It just does.' He checked the time on the clock above the door. 'I should get ready for my meeting. I don't want to miss the start.'

'Ok.'

He gathered his things and turned towards the stairs, glancing back just once. Scarlett was still watching him. The part of him that knew better braced for the slow torture of being near her without reaching out. But deeper still – beneath the logic, beneath the guilt – his heart surged with quiet relief. She was here. She was safe. And if he needed to speak to her again, he could. That thought alone lit something in him he hadn't felt in months, and he climbed the stairs with a smile he couldn't suppress even if he wanted to.

Chapter Nine

Scarlett

The first order of business was to do something about the featured table display. At the moment, it was a bloodbath of genres – pop-up fairytale books wedged between a dark biography of Rasputin and three separate "Sexy Santa" paperbacks, all with suspicious creased covers.

Scarlett eyed the display with the air of a bomb disposal expert, then pulled out every book featuring tinsel, snow, or an animal in a scarf. In twenty minutes, she'd assembled a half-decent "Festive Reading Nook," complete with pinecone garland and a tiny set of battery fairy lights she'd found in a box behind the counter. Clearly Eunice had left it there, meaning to add more festive decorations. Some of them were usable, but others were so worn and tatty that they belonged in the bin. She pulled out a paper chain that looked like it had been made before she was born.

Was it just her lack of Christmas spirit? Should she try to salvage this stuff? Or was it ok to let it go and start afresh?

Lloyd was speaking upstairs, presumably to his online clients or colleagues, though she couldn't hear what he was saying. His voice, however, was soothing, and just knowing he was there gave her a deep sense of safety.

The crazy bell rang, and the first customer blundered in. He was the sort of man who probably said "ho ho ho" unironically: broad, round, with a beard that glistened in the morning damp, and a very loud scarf and jumper combo. He looked around, then beamed at Scarlett.

'Morning!' he boomed. 'Isn't it a cracker of a day!'

'Um... yeah.' Scarlett smiled. 'Morning.'

'I love this cold weather. Puts the roses in your cheeks, doesn't it? Gives you a real boost and makes you appreciate the warmth when you go inside.' The man bustled around the display, breathing so heavily she thought he might fog up the books. 'I'm after a gift for the wife,' he said. 'She's into crime. Got any good murders?'

Scarlett led him to the shelf, where Eunice's "BOOKS TO MAKE YOU HAPPY" sign still lorded over several volumes about serial killers.

'We have these,' Scarlett said. 'Or, if you want something lighter, there's a new one about a "kilted detective" in—' She flipped the cover '—Culloden Moor.'

The man grinned. 'Ooh, that'll do. She loves the Highlands, and Culloden has such an interesting history. Ever been?'

Scarlett shook her head. 'I'm not well travelled.'

'Oh, you should try. So much to see, and you don't have to go far to see it.'

'Maybe one day,' Scarlett said.

'Oh, a wishing tree.' The man clapped his hands. 'This is excellent. I will definitely make one... or two. Is there a donation box?'

'No, it's free. It's not like we can guarantee they'll come true. Best not to charge in case anyone sues us.'

He barked a laugh. 'Good point.' He thumped the kilted detective book onto the counter, then went to the wishing tree and scribbled something on a bauble, then hung it on the tree. With a grin, he did another. 'Are you all ready for Christmas?' he asked, capping the pen.

'Almost,' Scarlett lied. 'Just got to do the panic-shopping bit.'

'Ah, it's best to do it that way. Shopping too early takes all the fun out of it.'

'Yeah.' Scarlett scanned the barcode. 'That'll be six ninety-nine.'

He tapped his card and looked at her over the top of his glasses. 'And will you have family around for the big day?'

'Oh... no. Just quiet, you know.'

'Can't say I do. I enjoy Christmas and being together with loved ones is probably the best part for me, so we always have a full house, though I don't deny it comes with its own drama at times. Still, it's worth it. Christmas can be joyful for people of all ages, if we choose to honour it in our way. It doesn't have to be about expensive presents and fancy decorations. It's more about sharing the love in your heart to enrich other people's lives as well as your own.'

Scarlett smiled. 'That's a really lovely message.'

'Well, I hope you have a good one. I better dash in case I miss the train.' He gave her a double thumbs-up and lumbered out, nearly colliding with the postie at the door. The bell went mental. Scarlett watched him go.

'A couple of letters.' The postie handed them to her. 'Are you new here?'

'Yeah... just covering. Eunice hurt her shoulder, so she's out of action.'

'Ah, shame. She's a funny and sweet old dear. Are you her daughter?'

Scarlett shook her head. 'Na, just... well, I'm just working here. No relation to anyone here. I was just in the right place at the right time.'

'Nice.' He looked around. 'You've brightened it up a bit. Looks good.'

'Thanks.'

He left with a little wave and the crazy bell went off again. Was there a way to dismantle it? It was really annoying.

The train pulled away from the platform, and Scarlett caught a glimpse of the jolly man in the second carriage. He seemed to have found some other people to chat with.

She returned to her tidying, trying to make more room be-tween displays so that it didn't feel so cramped. As she passed the wishing tree, she couldn't resist a peek. "I wish for a white Christmas" and "I wish you love and joy this Christmas".

Scarlett smiled despite herself. What a sweet guy.

A creak on the stairs caught her attention, and she looked around to see Lloyd on his way down. He had a mug of coffee in each hand, a small miracle of dexterity considering the stairs were steep enough to trip a mountain goat.

'Here you go.' He handed her a mug. 'It's that time of day.'

Scarlett accepted it with a nod. 'Thanks. You read my mind.' Her eyes met his, and a current of electricity ran along it. No, what he was doing wasn't mind-reading. He just instinctively knew what she needed. It had been the same during their fling. He'd been there when she felt lost – offering comfort when she wobbled, listening when she needed to spill her thoughts, making her laugh when the mood threatened to sink. He never rushed her, always seemed to know when to give her space and when to draw her closer, and somehow he made her believe she was stronger than she thought. One day they'd gone canoeing, and Scarlett had been sure she'd have to go alone, even though she wasn't confident, but Lloyd had offered to go with her. They'd had some laughs, even stolen some kisses when they were out of sight of the others. Later, they'd made love, and even then, he'd done things to her no one else had. He knew how to make it good. How to be gentle. How to make her feel safe.

She took a sip of coffee and blinked – he even knew how to make the coffee the way she liked it. One sugar, and a splash of milk. He remembered.

'This is good.'

He gave her an almost shy smile, cradling his mug. He'd rolled up his shirt sleeves, and Scarlett tried not to stare or fixate. From the outside, he might look like an average guy in smart clothes and glasses, but there was so much hidden. He was fit... and annoyingly hot. She burned her mouth taking another sip, trying to force her mind to go elsewhere.

He leaned against the counter and nodded at the window. 'Who was the jolly man who came in earlier?'

'No idea. He was waiting for a train.'

'He sounded like Father Christmas.'

'He looked like him too.' Scarlett laughed. 'Well, he had grey hair and a white beard anyway.'

'Oh well,' Lloyd said. 'That seals it then. He was the real deal. Maybe if I grew a beard, it'd help me get in the Christmas spirit... and I don't mean breaking into the spiced rum.'

Scarlett shook her head. 'If only it was that easy... though I'd settle for the rum as I can't exactly grow a beard.'

'Maybe I should buy some shots to try to channel Christmas spirit.'

'Not fair, is it? Some people get all the serotonin and none of the trauma.'

He snorted into his coffee, and for a second, it was like all the awkwardness had faded away.

'I always thought Christmas would be different when I had kids,' he said, in the soft way people have when they're talking more to themselves. 'But it's never worked out like that. Well, maybe the first few. But recently, at best, it's controlled chaos. At worst, it's just a long reminder of how you can't fix the stuff that's broken.'

Scarlett said nothing, just watched the steam curl from her mug. She discerned the real wish underneath: he wanted to be enough for his family and doubted he was.

'I think Lewis still believes in Santa,' Lloyd said, voice rougher now. 'Or at least he wants to. Maybe he's just clinging to anything that ever brought him joy. Who knows? He's desperate to go to the light switch-on this weekend. Which is fine. I'll take him, but the other two think it's babyish. I don't want their indifference – or mine – to rub off on him.'

'Sometimes it's hard to enjoy things when life is a mess,' Scarlett said. She wasn't sure if she meant Lloyd's kids or herself. 'Or to give yourself permission to enjoy things when you feel like you should be upset or mourning.'

He held her gaze and nodded.

That was exactly how she'd felt on the coach trip – guilty for finding joy with Lloyd so soon after breaking up with Leon. It still lingered, even though her counsellor had told her it was ok –

necessary, even – to find moments of light during dark times, no matter what others expected.

People had judged her for sleeping with Lloyd just days after the breakup, but she'd needed that connection. The comfort she found with him would've been impossible to find elsewhere. The real problem was how good it had been – she missed what she'd shared with Lloyd for a few days more than anything she'd had with Leon... or anyone else.

'You should make a wish.' She pointed at the tree.

He gave her a look. 'I already did.'

Her heart stopped, but she breathed through it. No way did he mean that he'd wished to see her. That would be crazy. 'Make another one then. One for your kids.'

'Ok, if you insist. I'm not sure I'll ever be able to say no to you.'

'Really?'

'Yeah.' He uncapped the pen.

'Can I have a pay rise then?'

He snorted, his hand hovering over the bauble. 'No.'

'There you go. Job done.'

He was still smiling and shaking his head as he wrote in blocky letters, then hung it low on the tree.

Scarlett waited until he stepped back before reading it.

I wish my kids could be happy this Christmas.

'Aw,' she said, and her throat tightened. She silently wished she could help somehow to make it come true.

'Well, I suppose I should get back to work.'

'Do you have another meeting?'

'Not until after lunch.'

She hesitated, sucking her lip. 'So, you know the Light Switch-On you mentioned?'

'Yes,' he said.

'What if we did something here? Something that made people actually want to come inside?'

He blinked. 'Like a sale?'

Scarlett pulled a face. 'Does anyone care about book sales? I meant more like something festive to get people in. They might buy a book while they're here if we're lucky.'

Lloyd's lips parted and Scarlett tried really hard not to think about how good they'd felt on hers, but a butterfly storm took off in her stomach.

'Yeah. I'm happy with that. But it's just a couple of days away, so there's not much time to prepare, and how will you let people know it's happening?'

'Social media. It's the quickest way.'

'So what kind of event?'

'I'm not sure, but maybe something your kids will enjoy too.' She shrugged.

Lloyd stared at the floor for a moment. 'I'm not sure Eve or Harry will go for it.'

'Probably not,' Scarlett said. 'I wouldn't have either at that age, but ask them anyway because then they know you haven't given up on them. My mum was always desperate for me to do stuff with her, but I didn't. I wish I had now, but I'll never forget the effort she made, time and time again.'

Lloyd nodded. 'Ok. I guess that's the key. Just to keep going.'

Scarlett took a deep breath. 'OK, so here are some ideas...We could do mince pies and mulled wine? But the alcohol might be a problem. Kids and all.'

'Hot chocolate?' Lloyd suggested. 'With marshmallows. Could do it in takeaway cups.'

'Yes! That's festive. And easy. People love free stuff.'

He raised an eyebrow.

'Well...' She gave him a crooked smile. 'What do you think?'

'Yeah, that's easy enough to get, and I'll buy a new kettle. We can use it for the hot chocolates, then afterwards it can replace that dreadful thing upstairs.'

'Perfect. And how about some kind of lucky dip?'

'A tombola? Won't that mean buying a whole lot of plastic tat?'

'No, I was thinking more for books. What if we wrapped books and just wrote a vague clue about what's inside?'

Lloyd's eyes lit up. 'Blind date with a book?'

'Exactly. I saw it once at the library. They'd written little phrases on the wrapping to tease the reader into taking a chance. It was really cute.'

He scratched his jaw, thoughtful. 'That could work if you're up for wrapping lots of books.'

'Sure.' Scarlett shrugged. 'That's what you're paying me for.'

'Ok. I'll grab some wrapping paper on my way home and bring it in tomorrow.'

'And some tape.'

'Ok. I'll get the full works, plus a kettle, some paper cups and some tubs of drinking chocolate.' He grabbed a paper bauble from the wishing tree and wrote the items on it.

They both lapsed into silence, staring at the bauble, and then each other.

'Thank you,' Lloyd said finally.

'What for?'

'Bringing the sparkle.'

Scarlett shrugged, suddenly shy. 'I'm not sure that's what I'm doing.'

Their eyes met, and for a beat, it wasn't about the bookshop anymore.

He broke the spell first. 'Well, I appreciate it anyway.'

'We haven't survived the hordes of Glenbriar locals yet.'

He laughed, and it lit up his whole face. 'Well, at least we're trying.'

She felt stupidly happy then, for no reason at all. Was this what Christmas was supposed to feel like? If she had more nerve, she'd hug him, but for once, sense outweighed her urge.

'I'm glad you came back. I thought it might be weird, but... well, it's ok, isn't it?'

She returned his smile with a nod. 'Yeah, it's ok.'

Maybe even a little better than ok.

Chapter Ten

Lloyd

Around noon on Friday, Scarlett called up to Lloyd, asking him to come down when he had a moment. The interruption was a welcome one as he'd had enough spreadsheets for the week. Downstairs, it sounded like there were more customers than usual. The violent shriek of the bell had been a constant interruption, but he liked hearing it. It meant that the bookshop was alive. That was good but weirdly unsettling for a place that had always been a crypt. Still, he wasn't complaining.

He closed his laptop, then headed down to see what Scarlett wanted.

'There's a delivery on the platform,' she said. 'I think it's the ramp for the door.'

'Great.' He glanced around. The shop was unrecognisable.

Scarlett had replaced every trace of dust and daylight-starved darkness with something twinkly and festive. The window was frosted with fake snow, fairy lights drooped from the shelves, and she'd wrapped the counter in dripping icicle garlands. The display table was glittering and laden with books that looked happy and inviting.

Lloyd went outside to open the package, and Scarlett followed him.

'Are you any good at DIY?' she asked.

'Not too bad.' He ripped open the packaging to reveal a sturdy metal ramp. 'I'll give it a go. There are some tools in a cupboard upstairs.'

'Do you need help? I'm hopeless at this kind of thing, but I don't mind trying.'

'If I need a hand, I'll give you a shout.' He returned upstairs, grabbed some tools, then went back to the platform. Placing the ramp was fairly straightforward, but it took a bit of jiggling and manoeuvring to line it up with the ledge and ensure it was a smooth surface. When he'd finally got it perfect, he glanced up to see Scarlett watching him. She instantly glanced away, busying herself, but Lloyd felt the heat in his neck.

Two women appeared at the door as he stepped back to check his handiwork.

'Is the shop open?' one woman asked.

'Yeah, sure. In you go. You can test the ramp.'

They walked over it, nodding. 'Very good. It'll be much easier for buggies and wheelchairs now.'

'Yeah.' He tidied away the tools. When he went back inside, Scarlett was mid-conversation with the two women, who were now both clutching Christmas romance novels. She caught his eye and winked. When Lloyd had first seen her again, she'd been in almost subdued outfits, but today she was in a white off-shoulder sweater, a short red tartan mini-skirt, and black combat boots. The sleepy butterflies in Lloyd's gut burst to life again.

'I haven't read them.' Scarlett scanned the books. 'In fact, I have a lot of catching up to do with books.'

'Well, you're in the right place for it.' The women laughed, and one added two more books to their stack. Scarlett scanned them too.

Lloyd didn't want to interrupt, so he went upstairs and put the tools away. When he came back down, Scarlett and the women were still chatting, so Lloyd meandered into the other room. What had been little more than a junkyard just a few days ago was now a reading nook by the little window. In fact, it was a full-on hygge sanctuary: two beanbags, a tartan blanket, plush cushions, and a floor lamp.

He drifted over and sat on the edge of the beanbag. Beneath the tree – a convincing synthetic – there were at least two dozen books wrapped in Christmas paper with handwritten clues on the covers.

The manic bell rang, sounding the departure of the two women. Scarlett appeared in the doorway.

'The ramp looks great. Well done.'

'Thanks. It was a really good idea.' He looked up. 'And this room is... amazing. I love it.'

Her eyes met his, and she swallowed hard.

'I haven't finished wrapping the books for the lucky dip.' She dropped down next to him, closer than necessary, but he didn't mind at all. 'It reminds me of Secret Santas at work.'

He groaned. 'Yeah. Thankfully, I'll bypass that this year.'

'I've only done it once. Last year when I was cleaning for the agency in an office and they included me.' She adjusted her red bra strap so it stayed close to the edge of her sweater, leaving her shoulders bare. The skin there looked so soft and inviting.

'That was, um, nice of them.'

'Yeah…' She pulled a face. 'The thought was nice, but I got a set of edible underwear.'

Lloyd slapped his hand across his mouth. 'What?'

'You heard.'

'I'm not sure I want to know the answer to this but… well, did you try it?'

She laughed. 'I don't think the point of it was to eat it myself.' She snuck a shy grin at him. 'So, no, I didn't.'

He didn't dare ask if anyone else had done it. If she'd been wearing it in the summer on Skye, he would have. And that thought both ignited a fire in his gut and made him cringe.

'No,' she said, and he glanced at her.

'What do you mean? I didn't say anything.'

'You didn't have to. I can hear your thoughts. No, no one else ate them either.'

He huffed out a laugh. 'Why not? Wrong flavour?'

She nudged him and giggled. 'Apparently. More like... well, no one I was with would have wanted to.'

He side-eyed her. 'You sure?'

'Well, no. But I didn't exactly think to pack them on my holiday. Not when I thought I was going with Leon the prat. And he definitely wasn't into that kind of thing.'

'Yeah.' Lloyd stared at the Christmas tree. Scarlett had already told him during their fling that Leon was a wham-bam-thank-you-ma'am kind of guy who didn't give a shit about his partner. Lloyd hated that her experiences had all been so crap – though hopefully not the ones she'd had with him.

A lull settled. They thumbed through some unwrapped books in silence, listening to a train rumbling away.

'Do you want help with anything?' he asked. 'I'm done working for the day. I thought I might do a bit more tidying upstairs, but if you want me to do anything here, just tell me.'

She flicked her red hair over her bare shoulder. 'Yeah, I could do with some help to wrap and think up clues... That's actually really difficult. I also want to do some kids' ones, but I'll need to label them for the right age.'

'Ok, let's do it.' He met her eyes and smiled at her. The electricity crackled between them. If he was a single man with no responsibilities and ten years younger, he would have used this moment properly, leaned in and kissed her. And if he were that man, Scarlett would probably want that too. Maybe she even wanted it now. And if that was the case, then he had to be even more sensible. He didn't want to give her false hope.

She pulled over rolls of wrapping paper, a tape dispenser and labels. As she sat back down, the bell rang. 'Back to the till I go.' She jumped to her feet again, and as she did, Lloyd caught a glimpse of the lacy edge of her hold-ups. He turned his gaze straight back to the wrapping paper, suppressing every ache in his body, all the bolts of lust that were firing around him.

Contemplating the heap of books, he wrote a label, then wrapped the first one. He'd done three more when Scarlett returned. She plopped down beside him and lifted a book.

'Do you think people will like this?' she asked.

'I'm sure they will. Even if the books aren't all sold tomorrow, we can keep it going right up until Christmas.'

'Yeah, of course. I'll make a sign for the door. I hope you don't mind, but I made a page for the shop on social media, and I've joined some local groups with it, so I can do some shouting about what we're doing.'

'Great idea. And you can add that we're now accessible, thanks to you.'

'And you.' She beamed at him. 'You fixed it up.'

'Teamwork makes the dream work.' He gave her a little wink.

For the next hour, they wrapped books side by side. It was companionable, and every time their hands brushed, or their knees knocked, an electrical storm erupted inside him, sending sparks straight to his groin. They talked about nonsense, and

Scarlett hummed along to Michael Bublé playing faintly from her phone.

Between books, Lloyd watched her. He loved how animated she was when she let go, how every emotion flashed through her face in fast-forward. Sometimes she bit her tongue in concentration, eyes narrowed. Other times, she laughed at her own terrible tape jobs and then started folding off-cuts of paper into eights and chopping them into snowflakes.

'They actually look really good.' He squinted at the small pile of paper snowflakes. 'Though I'm not sure about the mess.' Tiny clippings covered the carpet.

'I'll hoover it. Don't worry.' She wiped some wayward clippings from her thighs, then surveyed their handiwork. 'I think that's looking good.' Her gaze lingered on him for a moment, and despite only having a couple of shirt buttons open, he felt way too exposed.

'Yeah... all good.' His cheeks heated up.

'Let me just arrange them.' Scarlett crawled over to the tree on her hands and knees and started stacking books.

Lloyd had to look away. Having her positioned like that messed with his brain, reminding him of hot moments in the summer, but also teasing him with what he couldn't have.

When the shop bell went, Scarlett got up and went to the till, and Lloyd used the moment to tidy up and go back upstairs. This area really let the place down now that the shop was looking so good. He filled some binbags and pulled all the soft furnishings off the old sofa. Maybe he should just replace them. They all looked worse for wear. And the sofa needed a good scrub. He made a note on his phone to buy some upholstery shampoo and, as he did, he noticed the time. Shit. It was almost time to get Lewis.

'I need to go,' he told Scarlett as he reached the bottom of the stairs with his laptop bag. 'But I'll be here tomorrow. With at least one child in tow.'

She gave him a smile over her shoulder as she tidied a forgotten shelf behind the counter. 'Great, see you then.'

There was a beat of silence, something hesitant and a bit raw. Neither made a move to end it.

'Thanks for today,' he said, voice catching a little. 'I... honestly, I don't know what I'd do without you here.'

She made a face, but her eyes were soft, and she came out from behind the counter with a pile of books that she sat on a low end table. 'Just fulfilling my job description.'

He nodded, then found himself standing awkwardly near the door, hands stuffed in his coat pockets. He wanted to say more, but it was too risky.

Scarlett sucked her lip, then came closer. Very quickly, she reached up, put her arms around his neck, and pulled him into a hug. It surprised him a little, but he didn't back away. He freed one hand from his pocket and gently returned the hug.

It was just a quick press of her arms around him and her cheek against his, but he felt it everywhere. The shock of heat, the surge of longing. He squeezed her for a single beat before letting go.

She pulled away first, blinking up at him with a weak smile. 'Sorry. I—'

'It's fine,' he said. 'But I really need to go.'

'Yeah, see you in the morning.'

He stepped into the cold, his heart hammering so loud it drowned out the train at the platform.

Dinner at Rita's house was always a tightrope. Lloyd had learned to appreciate the stability – a hot meal at a set time, everyone at the table, even if the atmosphere ranged from mildly awkward to catastrophic. Tonight, it was somewhere in the middle.

Lewis was already at the table, narrating the day's school adventures to a disinterested cat. Harry hovered in the hallway, earbuds in, and Eve was still upstairs.

Rita ladled soup into bowls. 'Wash your hands, Lewis,' she barked, though he'd already done it.

'Eve, dinner's ready,' Lloyd called up the stairs.

Lewis dunked his bread in the soup, then sucked it in with a slurp. 'Can I go to Robbie's house after school one day? He has an Xbox.'

'And we have a Playstation,' Harry muttered. 'And they're better.'

'But I want to try the Xbox.'

'Well, if I speak to Robbie's mum or dad. I'm sure we can arrange something,' Lloyd said.

'Robbie lives with his dad – you know, the one I told you about who's in a band. His mum doesn't live with them. So, we kind of get each other.'

'You do?' Lloyd raised an eyebrow.

'Yeah, we both live with grumpy dads.' Lewis laughed.

'I'm not grumpy.' Lloyd put his hands on his hips.

Harry sat down and immediately started scrolling his phone under the table.

'Eve!' Lloyd called again.

A full thirty seconds passed. Then Eve thumped down the stairs, hoodie up, face pale and set. She slid into her seat, stabbed a piece of bread, and glared at her soup.

They ate in relative silence, broken only by the occasional sniping between the siblings or Lewis's chatter about his new friend. Lloyd was very pleased to know he'd found someone.

'So, tomorrow's the big day. The light switch-on in the town,' Lloyd said. 'The shop is running a special event, and it would mean a lot if you guys helped out. It'll be fun. There's free hot chocolate, and I could do with some help to serve it—'

'I will,' Lewis interrupted. 'Is there like marshmallows and stuff?'

'I bought some, yes.'

Harry shrugged. 'Maybe. If I don't have to talk to anyone.'

'I don't want to,' Eve said, not looking up.

Lloyd ignored the pang in his chest and focused on the win. 'Great. Lewis, you're on marshmallow duty. Harry, you can help me with making the drinks where you won't have to talk to any-one. And Eve, if you change your mind, you're always welcome.'

Eve kept her eyes on her food. 'I won't.'

'Ok.' Lloyd took a mouthful of soup, sure his insides could easily shut down and stop working at any second. Was the life-force in him strong enough to keep going? To get up every day and face this?

Rita leaned over and patted his arm, but nothing brought him comfort.

He went to bed that night in the small double in the spare room. Lewis was snuffling on the other side, and Harry was zonked out on the camp bed next to the window. Lloyd kissed them both goodnight before lying awake for hours wishing he knew what to do for best. A weird sense of displacement swarmed in his head. Almost like he was two different people. One of them was dad to Eve, Harry and Lewis, with all the trou-bles and worries that brought with it. The other was just a man. A man whose heart yearned for companionship. But bringing those two lives together would be like trying to mix oil and water.

The next morning, Lloyd woke to see drops of sleety snow falling on the Velux window. The kids were already up. He rolled out of bed, stretched, went to the loo, then padded downstairs to the kitchen; his mum was already there.

'Atmospheric weather for the switch-on.' He pulled back the curtain to look out.

'I hope it doesn't lie,' Rita muttered. 'It's a nightmare walking back up the road if it does.'

Lewis was fully dressed already as he raided the cereal cupboard, and Lloyd was halfway through a mouthful of toast when Harry wandered in.

'When are we leaving to do that thing today?' he asked.

Lloyd put his arm around his back. 'In about an hour. The lights aren't getting switched on until five when it's dark, but the shop even is on all afternoon.'

They all got ready. The wind picked up quite dramatically outside, rumbling down the chimney, rattling the letterbox, and making the windchimes in the garden ring like crazy. Sleet was still falling in on-off showers.

After putting on his coat, Lloyd rubbed his hands together. 'Good weather to lure people in for hot chocolate.'

There was a thud overhead. Eve's footsteps were unmistakable. She came down the stairs, black hoodie over her head, not looking at anyone as she went into the kitchen. Lloyd followed her.

'Hope you're ok to stay with gran. We're just leaving.'

'I'm coming with you.' She grabbed a cereal bar from the cupboard.

Lloyd caught Rita's eye, and they both stared at each other. 'To the shop?'

Eve nodded. 'Well, it's not like there's anything else to do in this town.'

He grinned, the corners of his mouth stretching further than they had in months. 'Aw. Thanks, snookleberry.'

'Don't call me that,' she muttered. 'It's silly.'

Outside, the sleet had stopped, though the wind still bit hard. Christmas lights blinked in windows, and a few plastic reindeer stood sentry on front lawns. Lewis did ninja kicks all the way down Sweetwater Lane. Harry mostly kept pace with Lloyd, hands stuffed in pockets, while Eve walked a few paces behind, earbuds jammed in, head lowered.

When they reached the High Street, shop windows glowed with decorations, each one trying to outdo the other. For a moment, Lloyd felt like he was in a Hallmark card, and he quite liked it.

He slowed down to let Eve catch up. 'You know, I'm glad you're coming today,' he said.

She didn't answer but gave him the smallest of smiles.

Maybe, just maybe... could this be the start of one of his Christmas wishes coming true? Perhaps he could manage at least one happy day with his family.

Chapter Eleven

Scarlett

Scarlett checked her reflection in the window for the sixth time in ten minutes. The glass warped her face, so her nose looked like a pig snout, and her eyeliner was slightly wonky. She pressed her lips together, then fluffed her hair. It was getting long. For a while, she'd liked it in a pixie cut, but she'd grown it past her shoulders now and she preferred it around her face. It softened her look. She yanked her skirt an inch further down her thighs. Was this too short to be appropriate? She'd never managed 'appropriate' very well. Her black jumper with a sequinned skull that said "Bah Humbug" pretty much confirmed that. But it was as Christmassy as she got.

Maybe she should have stuck with something duller, but this felt so much more her. And this last week she'd had so much fun here, she felt like she was getting something of her old self back. Seeing Lloyd again was a factor because, no matter how much she tried to deny it, she still liked him, but it wasn't just that. She liked the shop and having some responsibility. Something to work towards and a reason to get out of bed, leave the house and get out from under her mum's feet. Lloyd's presence added to that. Having him nearby was comforting, and when he came down to talk to her, she liked him in a different way than she had in the summer. She liked the chat, the company, his faith in her to do the job. Because although he was here every day, he didn't pry, hover, or hang about expecting her to fail or have a meltdown. He just let her get on and trusted her to do it.

He'd been sweet and kind on the trip too, but lust had played a big part in it then. Now, she liked his company in other ways – though she couldn't deny that thoughts of physical pleasure with him had crossed her mind. For all he was mild-mannered and sensible, he knew what to do between the sheets – better than anyone else she'd ever been with.

Why was she thinking about this stuff now? Her stressed-out brain was going every which way. And why? It wasn't like she was meeting Lloyd's family for a special occasion... or because she meant anything particular to him.

She'd already decided, no matter how much she liked him, that his lifestyle wasn't for her – how could she even contemplate being anything to his three kids when she couldn't even take care of herself? And that was leaping fifty stages ahead. It wasn't like she was going to come out on top of Lloyd's list.

Sure, they had something. But as her therapist had taught her, something wasn't always enough. The excitement of new beginnings wasn't enough to carry a relationship.

Her hands shook as she stacked the "blind date with a book" pile into a perfect pyramid.

The wishing tree glared at her from the corner, now dense with paper baubles and a worrying number of wishes about "new iPhones".

From outside came the muffled rumble of a train. Scarlett peered through the frosty glass and spotted a cluster of people moving towards the shop. They stopped to look in the window at the display, and she retreated behind the counter in case she scared them away.

The door shrieked its welcome as a blast of December air cannoned into the shop. Half expecting some of the people from the train, Scarlett didn't look up until she heard Lloyd's voice. He ruffled his hair, his cheeks slightly pink. His youngest child bounded in right behind, shaking wet slush off his boots with dramatic ninja kicks.

'Lewis. Use the doormat.' Lloyd shook his head. 'You'll get the books all messy.'

'Oops.'

The other boy slouched in wearing a hoodie and the classic teenage expression of "please let me die".

Lloyd's daughter appeared last, her face a thundercloud, hands jammed so far into her coat pockets it looked like she was about to punch her way out. She reminded Scarlett so much of herself at that age. The transition period of not being a child but not being an adult either. She wore make-up and looked a little older than fifteen, but the way she carried herself screamed teenager.

Scarlett's heart did something weird, like a dropped ice cube hitting the floor. She found her smile, gripped it tight.

'Hey,' she said, louder than she'd meant.

Lewis grinned. 'Whoa, it's like a Christmas cave in here!' He darted into the other room, to the lucky dip books, and started shaking them like presents. 'Are these real?'

'Lewis, put them down.' Lloyd followed him to the door. 'They're for sale.'

'You can open them,' Scarlett added. 'If you buy one.'

'Dad, do I have any money?'

'You do but maybe come and say hi first. This is Scarlett, who's working in the shop until Eunice recovers.'

'Who's Eunice?' Lewis frowned. 'And hi.' He waved to Scarlett.

'This is Lewis,' Lloyd said. 'You might have gathered. And Harry.'

Harry hovered near the door. 'Hi,' he said, polite but flat.

'Hi, Harry.' Scarlett gave him a wave, then immediately felt like an idiot. What were you supposed to say to a teenage boy?

'And this is Eve,' Lloyd finished.

Eve didn't even look at her. She peeled off her hood, eyes flicking to the wishing tree, and she screwed up her nose.

'This is amazing.' Lloyd gave Scarlett a smile that made her knees wobble. 'You've outdone yourself.'

'Thanks,' Scarlett replied, ignoring the heat crawling up her neck.

'Is this where the hot chocolate is happening?' Lewis bounced on his toes, eager.

'Yeah, but you have to help make it,' Lloyd said. 'You'll be helping me make them behind the counter. Harry and Eve are going to go up and down to get water.'

Eve let out a huff.

Lewis practically sprinted to the counter. 'Can I do the marsh-mallows?'

'Yeah.' Scarlett lifted the bag. 'There's a scoop. So, it's like one scoop in each cup.'

'Except my own.' Lewis smirked up at her. 'I can have as many as I like, right?'

'Wrong.' Lloyd ruffled his hair. 'Behave.'

Eve folded her arms.

'Let me show you upstairs.' Lloyd eyed Eve and Harry. They followed him, neither speaking.

Scarlett's stomach churned a little when she realised she was alone with Lewis.

'Are you a singer?' Lewis asked.

Scarlett shook her head. 'Definitely not. I absolutely can't sing.'

'You look like a singer. And your hair is cool. My friend's dad is a singer. He has a band, and they're singing in town today.'

'Is that Tavrach?'

'Yeah, that's it. I can't say that name. It's weird.'

Scarlett chuckled. 'It is a bit. I love Tavrach. They're a really good band. I'm going to see them play tonight at the Stagger Inn.'

'What's that?'

'A pub in the town. I'm meeting some friends there.'

Lloyd came back down the stairs, his expression a little grim. Scarlett had a weird out-of-body moment where she imagined herself at The Stagger Inn with Lloyd, sitting hand in hand, listening to Tavrach singing some of their own music as well as some traditional Christmas songs. But that couldn't happen. Lloyd wasn't free to go to gigs and do stuff like that. He was in a different place in his life from her. That's why meeting a few old school friends who were back for the switch on was a better option... or so she kept telling herself.

'Are you two ok?' Lloyd looked between the two of them.

'Yes,' they both said at the same time.

'Are Harry and Eve ok upstairs?' Scarlett asked.

Lloyd gave a little shrug. 'I think so. They're not the most communicative people on the planet though, so it's hard to tell.'

'Can I go out and watch the trains?' Lewis asked. 'Someone said a steam train is coming through. And I can tell people to come in and get books and drinks.'

'Yes, but stay just outside the door. Don't wander off and don't go anywhere near the edge of the platform.'

'Well, duh, as if I would.' He made an attempt at sarcasm, then laughed and opened the door. The bell screeched.

Lloyd looked at Scarlett. 'Sorry. This seemed like a better idea in my head. As many things do. I'm not sure why I haven't yet learned to make my expectations more realistic.'

'You're an optimist.' Scarlett raised an eyebrow.

'I'm not sure I am in general, but when it comes to my family, the rose-tinted glasses often go on... And frequently I end up disappointed. Still...' He let out a sigh. 'At least they all came. I thought Lewis might be the only one.'

'They might be grumpy, but they still want to be near you.' She blinked as she tried not to look at him. She knew how they felt. If she met his eyes now, she'd want to hug him again like she'd done yesterday when he left. It had felt so damn good.

'Did you do some more tidying upstairs after I left yesterday? It looks great.'

Scarlett nodded. What else did she have to do? She'd come back after closing time with some cleaning products, including upholstery shampoo, and cleaned up.

With the old radiator on, it'd dried quickly and left the place smelling great too.

'Thank you,' Lloyd said. 'You didn't have to do that, but I appreciate it. My mum has some cushions and throws she's getting rid of. I've got them in the car. It'll make it a much nicer office and staffroom.'

'Sounds like a good idea.'

The door shrieked again. This time it was a woman in a puffer coat, trailed by two girls in matching jackets, and a large baby buggy.

'Oh, this looks much better than it used to,' she said. 'Last time I was here, I couldn't get the buggy in, and there was barely room to move.'

Lloyd beamed at Scarlett, and she felt her ears getting hot. 'Scarlett had the wonderful idea of putting in a ramp,' he said.

'Such a sensible idea. My grandma – that's great grandma,' she added to her kids '– needs a wheelchair to get out and about. She'd love this place, but she probably hasn't realised it's suitable.'

'Well, I hope she'll enjoy it now,' Scarlett said.

'I'll be bringing her for sure. The boy outside said there's a wishing tree. The girls would like to use it.'

'It's here.' Scarlett pointed it out and passed over a tag and pen. The woman smiled. 'Write your wish and hang it up. You never know...'

Scarlett returned to the desk, and Lloyd leaned in. 'We should have charged for that.'

'Don't be a Scrooge.' She poked him in the chest. 'It's fun.'

He huffed out a laugh and gave her the briefest, gentlest touch on the back. The bell screeched, and Lewis yelled, 'Come see this. It's an actual steam train.'

Lloyd, Scarlett, and some of the other customers went to the door as a huge green engine huffed and hissed as it puffed through the station, pulling some old-fashioned and rather posh looking coaches.

'Doesn't it stop here?' Lewis asked.

'I don't think so,' Lloyd said.

Some of the people in the carriages waved. Lewis waved back, and Lloyd walked along the platform with him as the train moved out of sight in a cloud of smoke.

Scarlett ducked back inside, heard a creak on the stairs and looked up to see Eve at the bottom, arms crossed, watching her. Scarlett blanched, nausea rising in her gut.

'Where's my dad?'

'Out on the platform with Lewis. They're watching a steam train go through.'

'The Wi-Fi isn't working,' Eve went on.

'Um...' Scarlett checked the router behind the counter. 'It should be. All the lights are on.'

'Well, it isn't, and I need it.'

The doorbell sounded off again, and Lloyd came back in.

'Dad, can you fix the Wi-Fi?' Eve said.

'Again?' he muttered.

'All the lights are on,' Scarlett said, 'so it should be working.'

Eve gave a shrug. 'Well, it isn't.'

The woman who was in with her kids came up to the counter to buy some lucky dip books and hot chocolates, while Lloyd went upstairs to look at the Wi-Fi booster. Scarlett heard him talking to Eve and Harry like he was trying to get them to help rather than just sitting around.

As more people came in, Scarlett found herself on autopilot. She took money, made drinks, and chatted. Lloyd helped her and Harry traipsed up and down the stairs with water jugs, occasionally helped by Eve. All the while, the awkward current between Scarlett and the kids buzzed louder and louder. Lewis was fine. Harry was Switzerland – neutral, unbothered. But Eve had great thick walls, and every time Scarlett caught her looking, it felt like the defences increased.

Maybe I'm just being dramatic. Maybe it would pass. But what if she ruined this, like she'd ruined everything else? Maybe she just wasn't cut out for a real job... or real love. That would explain why she'd never managed to make a relationship last longer than six months.

Lloyd glanced around from the kettle and caught her eye. She gave him a tiny smile, hoping it looked more convincing than it felt.

The day trudged on, a conveyor belt of hot chocolate and forced cheer. The shop was full of sound – kids squealing about the wishing tree, parents discussing which books to buy, customers trying to figure out which books in the lucky dip they fancied just from the clues, and the bell periodically shrieking at maximum volume.

Scarlett caught sight of Eve slouched at the bottom of the stairs, phone in hand, occasionally glancing up and biting her lip. Now and then, her eyes would flick to Scarlett like she was looking for a weak spot.

Scarlett could guess how she felt. She'd been a tricky teen herself not so long ago. In high school, she'd disliked everyone and everything, even her friends, and especially Lilah, who'd been her mortal enemy after she'd knocked Scarlett's front tooth out during a P.E. hockey game. It had taken many years and for Lilah to become her sister-in-law before Scarlett forgave her enough to be friends.

Circling the shop, Scarlett picked up stray books, pretending to neaten displays, but mostly orbiting Eve.

'So, do you go to Glenbriar High?' she asked.

Eve didn't look up from her phone. 'Obviously.'

'Do you like it?'

Eve gave a shrug so minimal Scarlett almost missed it.

'What year are you in?'

'Fourth.'

'Are you doing exams this year?'

'Yep.'

Scarlett resisted the urge to smack her head against the shelf. She'd expected resistance, so she shouldn't be surprised.

'You know,' she tried, 'when I was your age, I was a total nightmare. Teachers hated me.'

Eve's gaze snapped up. 'Congrats.'

Scarlett bit her tongue, forced a smile. 'I mean, I get it. It sucks having to start over in a new place.'

Eve blinked, then stared back at her phone. Scarlett caught her own reflection in the glass. She looked like someone who was trying too hard.

She tried another tack. 'What are you listening to?'

Eve pulled one earbud out. 'What?'

'Your music. Who is it?'

'It's a playlist.'

'Oh, cool. What kind?'

'You wouldn't know it.'

Scarlett fought the urge to laugh. 'I probably wouldn't. I'm twenty-five, practically an old woman now.'

Eve's mouth twitched, but she killed what might have been a smile before it could escape.

Scarlett walked away, heart pounding. She'd been so sure she could break through, but the wall was higher and thicker than she'd imagined. Remembering what she'd been like as a teenager herself, she knew the best thing to do would be to leave her alone – but that also felt like a copout as an adult... It was so hard to find the right balance. Impossible maybe.

She busied herself behind the counter, hands shaking as she counted coins and straightened receipts. Lloyd was watching her from across the room, his brow furrowed.

A lull in the crowd let her breathe. Lewis had come inside and was "helping" with the marshmallows, mostly by eating them. Harry was reading a manga in the nook, hood up, happy as a clam. Eve had gone back upstairs.

Scarlett sank onto a low stool, head in hands. For a second, she thought she might cry, but the shop was too public.

This is what you get, she thought. For thinking you could just step into someone's life. At least now, she knew she was right to think she couldn't handle it.

The bell at the door went off, two notes apart, like the warning signal on a sinking ship. She looked up and felt her entire ribcage seize.

Lilah and Aidan.

Scarlett's eyes darted to the stairs. Lloyd, with his infinite timing, had just appeared on the steps, already halfway down. Scarlett moved before thinking, crossing to the steps in three fast strides.

'Stay up there,' she hissed, not even bothering to whisper. 'Please. Just for a minute.'

Lloyd blinked, surprised, but nodded and retreated, eyebrows raised. Scarlett spun, plastered on her biggest, most artificial smile, and stepped behind the counter.

'Hey, you two,' she called, as if her pulse wasn't hammering in her ears. 'What brings you to my lair?'

Aidan glanced around. 'So you really do work here.'

'Did you think I'd made it up?' Scarlett replied.

'We thought it best to check.'

'Do you want a hot chocolate?' Lewis asked from behind the counter.

'Um... ok. Thanks.' Aidan frowned, and when Lewis turned away, he whispered, 'Who's that?'

'The owner's son,' Scarlett said. 'And let me do the hot water.' She grabbed the kettle before Lewis could.

Lilah drifted over. 'This is amazing. I've always loved this shop because I love books, but I haven't been in for ages. It looks much better than I remember.'

Warning bells rang in Scarlett's mind. Would Lilah know that Lloyd's mum had owned and worked in this shop? Lilah hadn't mentioned that she recognised her when they were on the tour in the summer, but what if she put two and two together? Did it even matter?

Scarlett handed both Aidan and Lilah a hot chocolate, keeping half an eye on the stairs, just in case Lloyd thought the coast was clear.

'Do you know Scarlett?' Lewis asked like they were old friends.

'She's my sister,' Aidan said. 'Well, half-sister.'

'Which half?' Lewis grinned. 'Top or bottom?'

'You're a character.' Scarlett laughed. 'We have the same mum but different dads, that's why we're half brother and sister.'

'That's like my friend Robbie, but his brother and him have the same dad and different mums.'

'It happens quite a bit,' Aidan said. 'It's all good.'

'My mum died,' Lewis said. 'So I might one day have a half-brother, or a sister. If my dad has a new wife.'

'Sorry to hear that, buddy,' Aidan said.

'We were all sad too, but she was very sick, so now she's not suffering. Eve doesn't want Daddy to get a new girlfriend. She thinks it'll be horrible for us, like a wicked stepmother, you know?'

Scarlett's insides contracted.

'But I don't really mind.' Lewis shrugged. 'I don't think Daddy would like someone wicked, so if he did have a new girlfriend, she'd probably be nice. Daddy only likes nice people.'

Aidan nodded, and he sipped his drink, looking like he wanted to laugh, but also rather impressed.

'You should wish on that tree,' Lilah said to Lewis. 'Wish for your daddy to get a new girlfriend. Someone who's nice that you and your sister will like.'

'Ok... And Harry. I have a brother too.' Lewis came around the counter and lifted a pen.

Scarlett watched from the counter as he concentrated on what he was writing.

Lilah and Aidan grinned at her.

'He's a cutie,' Lilah whispered.

'Yeah.' Scarlett glanced at the clock, silently begging them to leave in case Lloyd got fidgety and came down.

'You coming to the lights switch-on?' Lilah asked.

'Yeah.'

'Then she's going to watch Tavern play in the pub.'

'Tavrach,' Scarlett said. 'And yeah, I'm meeting some old school friends.'

They browsed for a bit, then left saying they might bump into her later.

Lewis went to the door and waved to them, and Scarlett took the opportunity to go to the bottom of the stairs and call Lloyd.

'What was that all about?' he asked quietly.

'It was Aidan and Lilah.' She shot a look over her shoulder, but Lewis was still at the door watching a train. 'They would have recognised you and I didn't want them to think... Well, you know.'

'Yeah, I do.' Lloyd put his hand on her shoulder very gently. 'Are you ok?'

She nodded.

'Daddy.' Lewis ambled over. 'I just met Scarlett's half-brother – the top half, just kidding – and a lady. Who was she?' He looked at Scarlett.

'Lilah. She's Aidan's wife.'

'His whole wife or his half wife?'

Scarlett laughed. 'His whole wife.'

'They got me to make a wish,' Lewis said.

'And what did you wish for?' Lloyd asked.

Scarlett wished the floor had a trapdoor she could tap and jump through.

'For a new girlfriend.'

'Aren't you a bit young for that?' Lloyd raised an eyebrow.

'Not for me. For you.'

'What?'

'And someone that we all like.'

'Right.' Lloyd rubbed the back of his neck. 'Well, we'll see about that.'

Scarlett went back behind the counter, feeling the heat in her neck and hoping to god Lloyd didn't think she'd put Aidan and Lilah up to it.

The bustle of the morning lulled, and Lloyd went into the side room with Lewis. Scarlett heard them chatting. After a moment, Lloyd came out and moved in behind the counter to boil the kettle. 'Sorry about his nonsense,' he whispered.

'I don't mind. He's sweet, and he's got a great sense of humour.'

'Yeah, he does.'

The wild bell rang again, and Scarlett looked up only to almost faint.

Elise Reid swept in wearing an elegant coat, her long dark hair perfect. She was so intrinsically linked to Scarlett's life that seeing her about didn't normally elicit such a strong reaction... apart from in the summer when she'd stepped off the coach and they'd discovered she was to be their tour guide. Pretty awkward considering she was Aidan's ex. And now she was dating his best friend. But worst of all, Elise knew all about Lloyd.

Scarlett had confided in her when she was at rock bottom... what the hell would she make of this? There was nowhere to hide Lloyd this time.

Gabe had breezed in behind Elise.

Scarlett cringed as Elise scanned the shop in slow motion until her eyes landed on Lloyd. Her pupils expanded. Gabe clocked what she was looking at, grinned wider, and raised his eyebrows.

Scarlett's insides fell down an elevator shaft. She chanced a quick glance at Lloyd, who had turned, recognition dawning like he'd been slapped. For a second, he seemed to forget how to work his face.

Scarlett moved around from behind the counter, intercepting the two.

'Hey, strangers. What brings you here?' she managed, voice only slightly strangled.

Elise gave her a quick, searching look.

'We met Aidan, and he said to come in,' Gabe said.

'You kept quiet about this job.' Elise furrowed her brow.

Scarlett caught the questions, the calculations, the mounting curiosity.

'What's really going on?' Elise dropped her voice.

'Come in here.' Scarlett pulled her into the other room as Gabe meandered towards the adventure books shelf.

The rumble of the trains and a faint Christmas playlist from the shop speakers was an almost soothing backdrop, contrasting with the turmoil in Scarlett's brain.

'This isn't what you think,' Scarlett muttered. 'I mean, yes, it's Lloyd, but we're not...'

'Scarlett.' Elise put a hand on her arm, eyes narrowing. 'You told me you'd never see him again.'

Scarlett chewed the inside of her cheek. 'I honestly didn't expect to. I didn't even know he was moving here. The job was a total accident. I mean, yes, it's... weird, but—'

'Is it?' Elise's tone softened. 'Because you were pretty cut up about losing him... and now he's here.'

She looked at her boots. 'I swear it's a coincidence... We both got such a shock when we saw each other. But there's nothing going on. His mum owned this shop and now he's taken over. I got the job here and... well, that's it.'

Elise searched her face. 'Just be careful. Please.'

Scarlett let out a sigh. 'I'm trying.'

Elise hugged her, quick and fierce. 'If you want to talk, you know where I am. Don't disappear this time, ok? You have friends.'

'Thank you,' she whispered.

The shop bell broke the spell. Scarlett wiped her eyes.

'You'll be ok,' Elise said. 'You always are.'

Scarlett didn't answer. She wasn't sure she believed it.

Everything felt overwhelming and out of her control.

Chapter Twelve

Lloyd

Lloyd greeted the new customers who'd entered the shop in a flurry of snow, half-listening to Lewis but keenly aware of the muffled, urgent voices from the reading nook. Scarlett and Elise had vanished in there and had obviously found a deeply interesting subject to discuss – him.

'Watch this, Dad. If you squish the marshmallow, it sticks to the side – see? And if you do it like this, you can actually build a wall, like in Minecraft.'

'Impressive,' Lloyd said, still tracking the line of sight between Gabe, who was standing by the travel shelves, and the door to the nook.

A moment later, Scarlett emerged from the other room, her eyes a little glassy, followed by Elise. Lloyd's heart gave a lurch, and he straightened, not entirely sure what to do or say.

The last time he'd been close to these people was on the tour where, by the time it ended, everyone was looking at him suspiciously, thanks in part to his own mother, who had been one of the rumourmongers. His name had been linked to Scarlett, and it seemed now that she'd told her friends and family about him – her choice, of course, but it didn't exactly make moments like this easy.

Elise smiled at him. 'Hello,' she said, voice cool but not un-friendly. 'Isn't this an odd coincidence?'

'It is, yes.' Lloyd's mouth had gone dry.

Gabe sauntered over, hands in his pockets. He gave Lloyd a once-over and then a brief smile.

Elise looked around the shop. 'This place is so…' She hesitated, searching for the word. 'Nice.'

'Scarlett's doing,' Lloyd said. 'She turned up at the right place at the right time.'

'Wow, yes. How did that happen?'

'I don't know. Apparently, the universe works in mysterious ways.'

Scarlett stood beside the counter, glancing between Lloyd and Elise as if she were an umpire at a tennis match.

'Are you Scarlett's half-sister?' Lewis asked, and Lloyd ruffled his hair.

Elise shook her head. 'No, but we've known each other for ages.'

'He met Aidan a moment ago,' Scarlett said. 'Who introduced himself as my half-brother.'

'Though we still don't know if it's the top half or the bottom half.' Lewis shook his head with a shrug at Lloyd.

Lloyd took off his glasses and pinched the bridge of his nose.

'Someone on the tour told me your mum owned this place,' Elise said. 'But I didn't gather that you had anything to do with the business.'

'I didn't at the time,' Lloyd said. 'I only recently took over, and I had no idea you all lived in Glenbriar.' Something he now wasn't sure was a good thing – for him.

The air between Lloyd and Elise remained taut. He wanted to apologise because he felt like she was looking at him in an accusatory way. Possibly she was annoyed with him for being here, for ruining the trip, for hiring Scarlett, or for a combination of them all.

'Well, we'll let you get back to your day,' Elise said. 'It was good to see you.'

'You too,' Lloyd replied.

Gabe and Elise said goodbye to Scarlett, then left, the doorbell screeching on their way out. Lloyd winced at the noise.

'I need to dismantle that bell and get something quieter.'

'It's quite good fun,' Lewis said. 'Didn't that man who was just in here used to be on YouTube? I think I watched him when I was little.'

'You're still little,' Lloyd said.

'He's a podcaster, so yeah, you've probably seen him,' Scarlett said.

'Wilder at Heart,' Lloyd said, remembering how many of the people on the tour had crowded Gabe looking for autographs and guided walks. He'd even given in at one point and done a walk around a local woodland. Rita had gone on it, but Lloyd hadn't. He'd told her he was off on a more strenuous hike, which had been true, but he wasn't alone. Scarlett had gone with him, and they'd hidden from the others, using the time to kiss and make love in ways that Lloyd still couldn't believe. It was like that life belonged to a different man – and yet sometimes he longed to be that man again.

Scarlett caught his eye, and he had a weird sense that she was thinking about the same thing. Perhaps remembering how he'd found her upset, and they'd walked together up a barely there trail. At first, he'd just listened to her, allowed her to let off steam. But her way of doing that had also involved lots of physical activities. They'd left the path and found a desolated spot, sheltered by trees and rocks, dropped their backpacks, and slumped down with their backs to a boulder. Moments later, they'd kissed like their lives depended on it, and one thing had led to another. It had been so damn risky. So hot. So unforgettable.

And that was a really big problem.

Scarlett opened her mouth as if to say something, but Lewis piped up first.

'Is it time for the lights to go on yet?' he said.

'Not quite.' Lloyd replaced his glasses, then met Scarlett's gaze again. She was watching him with an expression he couldn't quite read, but she seemed to be trying to give him a secret message. 'Hey, Lewis.' Lloyd tapped his shoulder. 'Can you go see what your brother and sister are doing upstairs? See if they're ok yeah?'

'Ok-dokie.' Lewis grabbed a handful of marshmallows and bolted for the staircase.

Scarlett ran her hand through her hair, left it standing up for a beat, then dropped her arms to her sides.

'Sorry about all that.' She fixed her eyes somewhere on the floor between them. 'I had to tell people about... us. I was in a bad place after the trip.'

Lloyd nodded. 'It's ok. I mean, ok that you told people. Not that you were a bad place. I'm sorry about that.'

'Yeah, well, I wasn't exactly in a great place on the trip,' she added. 'It just got worse after we got back...' Her shoulder twitched. 'I didn't want them to hear the rumours about us and think you'd hurt me or made the situation worse. I actually don't know how I would have survived that trip without you.' She picked at the hem of her jumper. 'But none of them really understand that. They're all on edge about me after the summer.'

'I know how it was for you. I said at the time it wasn't a good idea.' He swallowed, unable to say 'hooking up' was a bad idea. Because he still didn't see himself as the kind of guy who did hookups.

'But I insisted. I know. And I suppose you regret it?'

He shook his head. 'No. I don't regret it. It's more like... I'm detached from it. You see what my life is really like.' He gestured towards the stairs, where his kids' voices were audible. 'What happened on that tour was something so different for me. An escape. But I hate the thought that people think I took advantage of you somehow.'

Scarlett shook her head. 'They know you didn't. I told them you were kind to me.'

He reached out and touched her arm, then took hold of her wrist. 'People want to look out for you. And god knows, I get it.' He tried to imagine what he'd be like if Eve was in Scarlett's position.

'Yeah. I just don't want them being angry or weird with you. You didn't do anything wrong.'

'Neither did you.' Lloyd held her gaze, gently rubbing a circle on her wrist with the pad of his thumb. 'Maybe what we did wasn't completely sensible, but it wasn't a crime.'

She gave a crooked smile. 'And it was kind of fun, wasn't it?'

'A lot of fun.' His chest ached at the memory. Sometimes joy only existed for a short time before it was confined to memories.

Lewis's voice echoed from the stairs. 'Harry's on his phone, and Eve called me a muppet.'

Lloyd let go of Scarlett's wrist, and she stepped back, wrapping her arms around herself. 'I better deal with that.' He let out a sigh. 'I'll send them out to the car to get those cushions and throws. Then I can live in hope that they'll set them up nicely upstairs.'

By the time the short December afternoon started to sag towards dusk, the bookshop had seen more customers in one day than it had in weeks. Through it all, Scarlett was on top form, gliding between the till and the tables and restocking the wishing tree.

Lloyd clocked the time – ten to three – and saw Lewis already waiting by the stairs, yawning.

'I should get going,' Lloyd said to Scarlett. 'I promised Lewis we'd do a tour of the town before the lights go on.'

'Ok,' she said.

'Lewis, call the others, will you?' Lloyd said. 'Tell them we're heading off.'

A few moments later, Harry and Eve came down, Eve trailing at the rear with her headphones on, Harry still gaming on his phone, not looking where he was going.

Lewis sidled up to the counter. 'Do you want to come too?' he asked Scarlett.

Lloyd smiled at her as she reddened and shook her head. 'Thanks for asking, but I can't. I'm meeting my friends to watch the switch-on. Then we're going to see Tavrach play at the pub.'

Lewis pulled a face. 'Oh yeah... you told me that. Did you know my friend's dad is a singer in that band?' he said to Eve.

'Yeah, you've told me like seven-hundred times.'

Lewis shrugged. 'I think it was only six-hundred actually.'

Scarlett laughed and shook her head at Lloyd. He half-rolled his eyes and then smiled back at her. 'Are you ok, locking up and finishing in here today?'

'Yeah, fine.'

'You did a great job today,' he said. 'Seriously. All of this was a great idea, and your social media posts have clearly worked to bring in the punters.'

Scarlett gave a lopsided shrug. 'I enjoyed it.'

A sharp tug registered in Lloyd's chest. He wanted to hug her, maybe even kiss her, tell her how much her existence brightened his days, but he was heavily aware of his kids watching him.

'See you later then.' He still couldn't look away.

'Yeah. See you later,' Scarlett replied, her eyes bright and un-blinking. 'And nice to meet you all.' She waved to Eve, Harry and Lewis.

Harry muttered, 'Yeah.'

And Lewis gave a huge grin. 'You too.' He held up his hand, and she high-fived him, then she glanced back at Lloyd.

He held her gaze a beat too long before turning away.

The kids piled out onto the platform, Eve already several paces ahead, Harry and Lewis chatting about something.

Lloyd looked back through the frosty window. Scarlett was still there, watching him go. She gave a tiny wave, then disap-peared behind the counter.

The air bit like dry ice, all the moisture crystallised into a faint, icy drizzle that powdered the pavement and dusted the top of

Lloyd's hair as soon as they stepped off the platform into the car park. From there it was a short walk to the High Street, which glowed with Christmas lights from the shops and heaved with people all wrapped up in winter woollies. Lloyd's heart cracked a little as he saw mums and dads with their children. His own dysfunctional group seemed completely disinterested in his presence. Even Lewis was more interested in talking about some kind of strategy game with Harry.

Eve strode ahead, hood up, hands jammed deep in her pockets, her boots punching holes in the thin crust of snow. She didn't look back.

Halfway down the street, Lewis asked if they could go into one of the cafés and get a cake. They all trooped in and waited in a short queue.

'Is Scarlett going to work at the shop forever, or is she just there until that old lady comes back?' Eve asked, not meeting his eyes.

'It's just temporary, while Eunice is off, though she's a really good worker. I kind of wish we could keep her.'

'Really?' Eve muttered. 'She's weird.'

'Eve.' Lloyd frowned. 'Don't be mean.'

'I'm not. She was being like really over-familiar and asking me all kinds of stupid things.'

Lewis pulled a face. 'What like?'

'Like what music I like, blablabla,' Eve said.

'And how is that stupid?' Lloyd asked. 'She was just being polite, which I don't think you were being all the time.'

'What did I do?' Eve held out her hands. 'Her hair makes her look kind of trashy.'

Heat pricked up Lloyd's neck. 'You shouldn't say that about someone you hardly know. And it's really not fair to judge someone on their appearance.'

'Whatever,' Eve said.

Lewis looked up at Lloyd. 'I liked her hair. Kinda cool.'

Lloyd managed a smile. 'Yeah.'

Eve narrowed her eyes at him.

What was she really objecting to? Was it just the change – new town, new people, everything raw and unfamiliar – or had she picked up on the undercurrent between him and Scarlett? Was that why her dislike was so strong?

Once they'd had cakes, they went out again and made their way to the fountain, a large Victorian structure in the centre of a paved public garden just off the main street. Darkness had fully descended, and a crowd had already packed in. At the centre of it all stood the Christmas tree, and a plywood platform in front of it with speakers, decorated with a plastic garland and twinkling lights. Some official looking people milled around in Santa hats and hi-vis jackets.

Lloyd and the kids found a spot near the fence. A burger van was on the other side and the generator hummed steadily. Lewis squirmed with anticipation, asking Lloyd a hundred questions but not waiting for any answers. Harry hovered, eyes on his phone, while Eve planted herself against the fence, earbuds jammed in.

A crackle of microphones got people's attention. There was a flurry of speeches – thank yous to the council, the local police, the businesses who'd sponsored the event.

'Now, without further ado,' the speaker said. 'We have a local celebrity here to do the honours along with our young winner of the Best Christmas Card Design. Let's first welcome to the stage Glenbriar born former tennis pro, Georgie Porter, who has helped a highly successful campaign for a multi-use games area in the town this year and who has agreed to help switch on the lights today. Up you come, Georgie.'

A young woman in a long-padded coat, with her hair pulled back in a ponytail, got up on the stage and waved. Lloyd remembered seeing her on TV during Wimbledon but hadn't realised she came from Glenbriar.

'We also have the winner of the Best Christmas Card Design.' Everyone clapped as a girl in a rainbow puffer jacket joined them on the stage. She looked terrified, but Georgie took her hand. After a countdown that was entirely off beat, they jammed the big red button, and the lights exploded into life – red, white, green, and blue, blinking in whorls up the tree.

'Wow.' Lewis clapped.

The crowd cheered.

'Now, let's celebrate with our wonderful local band,' the announcer said. 'If you'll please welcome to the stage, Tavrach!'

The crowd cheered as the band took the stage. Lloyd's eyes widened as Lewis pointed out his friend's dad. Never was he ever going to be able to compete with that. This guy was proper rockstar material with long dark hair, leathers, studs, and ripped jeans. His guitar broke through the still night air as the band launched into a rock version of "Ding-Dong Merrily on High".

'He's cool, isn't he?' Lewis shouted.

'Very. Does Robbie look like that too?'

'Na. He's normal,' Lewis said casually, and Lloyd laughed.

Tavrach powered through a set of Christmas songs, half of them traditional, some of them their own. People clapped and stomped, and Lewis did some ninja moves. Even Eve had pulled out her earbuds and was tapping her toe in time with the music.

They finished their set with "I Wish It Could Be Christmas Everyday", and it earned a huge cheer. Robbie's rockstar dad waved, then gave the pronged rock gesture to the crowd before he left the stage.

As the crowd dispersed, Lloyd herded the kids to the burger van as both Harry and Lewis were apparently starving.

They queued for a bit, stomping to keep warm in the freezing air. When they finally had burgers, chips and drinks – and Lloyd's wallet was severely depleted – they stood back and tucked in.

Across the road was The Stagger Inn, and Lloyd saw a rather rough looking gang at the door shouting and laughing. Some of them didn't look much older than Eve, and he bristled at the thought of her being part of a group like that. Like any parent, he wanted to protect but also knew he couldn't be everywhere with her all the time.

As he stared, his eyes landed on a familiar face.

Scarlett.

His insides twisted painfully. Of course she would be part of groups like this. She was young and spirited. When she'd said she was meeting friends, this was what she meant. What had he imagined?

Perhaps he envied her a little. The energy, the chaos, the sense of being young and alive, not tethered to a routine of obligations and failed expectations.

But more than envy, he felt protective. Not in a patronising way, but in a helpless, terrified way that came when you saw someone you cared about on the edge of something unpredictable. He wanted to text her. Or go to the pub and make sure she got home safe. Or maybe he just wanted an excuse to hang out with her.

Instead, he threw their empty wrappers in the bin, wiped Lewis's face with a napkin, and glanced up at the snow, which was getting heavier.

'Let's finish up and get back. Gran will have the fire on.' He took a last look at Scarlett. Maybe he was imagining it – it was hard to tell after all in only the street lighting with the snow falling thick and fast now – but she looked uneasy. Her smile was a little too fake, and she was picking at her gloves.

Screw it. It wasn't his business to notice, interfere, or even care.

But he did. And as he walked up the hill, his mind kept going back to The Stagger Inn.

'I made a wish on the tree for Dad to get a new girlfriend,' Lewis announced as they turned into Sweetwater Lane, which looked more like a Christmas card than ever with the dusting of snow. Lloyd wanted to grab his youngest and silence him, but the damage was already done.

'You what?' Eve glared at Lewis and then threw Lloyd a filthy look. 'Mum's barely been gone two years. And we… We don't want anyone else butting in. We're fine like this. Don't make stupid wishes like that.'

'It wasn't stupid,' Lewis said. 'It's not up to you. Dad might want a new girlfriend.'

'No, he doesn't.' She stopped dead. 'You don't, do you?' She framed it as a question, but it sounded more like a statement.

'I-I don't know. It's not something I've really thought about. But I can't promise I won't ever have… someone again.'

'Why not? It's not exactly fair on us.' Eve's cheeks were noticeably red even in the dim streetlights.

'Why isn't it fair on you?'

'Because you'll… well, what about Mum?'

'Eve.' Lloyd shook his head. 'Me staying single forever won't bring Mum back. And if I dated someone else…' He took a deep breath, wishing he knew how to put this. Not just for Eve but for himself. 'It's not like I'd stop loving you. Or Mum. Like when we had Harry, it didn't mean we stopped loving you. And when we had Lewis, we still loved you and Harry too. It doesn't mean the love that's already there will stop.'

'Yeah, but that's all just romantic nonsense. Because in real life it'd be horrible. We don't want some stranger coming along and trying to be our mum.'

Lloyd reached out to her, but she pulled away and stormed for the garden gate. 'Eve,' he called. 'It wouldn't have to be like that.'

'So... does that mean you've got a girlfriend?' Harry asked.

'No,' Lloyd said.

'Would you like Scarlett to be your girlfriend?' Lewis asked. 'She's nice.'

Eve turned back and glared at them. 'No way. She's not that much older than me.'

'She's at least ten years older than you,' Lloyd said as heat rose in his neck.

'Please tell me you're not going to ask her out. That would be mad and so wrong.'

Lloyd nodded, his jaw stiff. 'I don't have any plans to ask her out. Now, let's get inside. It's freezing out here.'

But not as cold as inside his chest.

Eve's words had cut like a knife, but it wasn't just that. His mind kept drifting back to The Stagger Inn, to Scarlett's face.

A strange, unsettled feeling crept over him. Maybe it was just the row with Eve...

But no – this was more than that. A tug deep in his chest. Like something was *wrong* with Scarlett. Like she needed him.

Or maybe something was wrong with *him*. Maybe *he* needed *her*.

Which might be the truest thing he'd felt in months.

But even if it was... what the hell was he supposed to do about it?

Chapter Thirteen

Tinsel garlands were strung from every rafter in The Stagger Inn. The famous old stag's head – that changed its look depending on the season – now wore a flashing Rudolph nose and had candy canes hanging from its antlers. This place was a favourite with locals of all ages. Scarlett had been coming here since before she was officially allowed in, dressing up to the nines and sneaking in until one of the locals had clocked who she was and had her chucked out. But it wasn't the kind of place where people held a grudge, so thankfully she hadn't been banned for life.

In the usual spirit of the place, they'd gone full on festive, serving mulled wine and hot mince pies along with snowballs and every other Christmas themed drink imaginable. Last Christmas in this exact place, Scarlett had started seeing Leon. The beginning of that disastrous six months. As she jostled her way to the bar with her group of old school friends, a whole reel of past Christmases in this place played in her mind, none of them good

– they ranged from getting so drunk as a teenager she'd blacked out to being pushed about by one of her exes.

She shuddered, wishing she'd been drunk enough that time to erase the memory. But it wasn't an isolated incident. Her previous boyfriends all seemed to think that kind of behaviour was acceptable.

Tavrach were already on stage singing a slow, almost melancholic tune that gave Scarlett a rush of shooting pains in her heart. Despite being part of a large group, a lonely, empty sensation of profoundly missing something – or someone – clawed at her.

It was a complete scrum at the bar, and everyone in her group had invited their own tagalongs, so she was being crushed by a group of people she barely knew. Even the ones she did were wrapped up in chats with others about subjects she didn't know much about or had missed how the conversations started and didn't want to butt in.

She tilted her head, tried to tune out the babble, but the PA system was already starting to fry her ears. Once they finally had drinks, they managed to get a booth in the corner, taking it over completely with some people sitting on the edge, the windowsills, even each other's knees.

'Since when is Lilah Clarke married to your brother?' Carli leaned over to ask Scarlett. Carli had been her actual best friend in high school, but these days they'd drifted apart to the point where Scarlett saw more of her on social media than in real life.

'Earlier this year,' Scarlett said.

'I saw them today. She looked a lot cleaner than she used to. Remember she was so scummy at school.'

Scarlett nodded. 'She's actually really nice.'

'You've changed your tune. Remember when she knocked your tooth out?'

'Like I could forget.' She still had a crown. 'But it was an accident, and we've made friends.'

Carli grinned. 'Cool. Anyone want shots?'

Everyone agreed, and Scarlett checked her phone. Zero notifications. She went straight to the camera and snapped a selfie, making the world's fakest duck face, then deleted it instantly. She missed the time when she and Carli would have been posting these to social media every five minutes. Doing that tonight seemed completely pointless.

Carli returned with a tray of fluorescent shot glasses. 'Down in one!' she yelled, and the table obliged. Scarlett knocked hers back. It was sweet, with a harsh bubble-gum aftertaste. She immediately regretted swallowing. Her insides already felt loose and hot, like everything was unspooling.

Chatter around the table seemed to be nothing more than noise and blended with the Tavrach duo – both men – singing "Fairytale of New York" in a humorously unironic and kind of sweet way.

Scarlett's now alcohol addled mind decided to wander back to the bookshop and run through the day's events, making her want to wince about every interaction with Eve, then feel sick about every interaction with Lloyd. It was like the universe was baiting her – dangling possibilities before her, then setting up a row of roadblocks to keep her out. What kind of idiot got attached to someone whose life was so different from her own? And why was she attached to him anyway?

Someone returned with trays of spiced rum shots. Scarlett lined them up in front of her, remembering the joke she and Lloyd had had about Christmas spirits, and started working through them, one at a time, a ritual for exorcising the day.

First shot: Eve. Scarlett had been a teenager once and knew exactly what it was like to see every adult as an invader. Still, Scarlett had managed to make herself even less likable than the average stepmum candidate. Maybe Eve saw her as a threat, or maybe she saw through Scarlett's skin and found all the places that still hurt. Either way, it was a fuck-up.

Second shot: Lloyd. Every time she looked at him, it was like someone was tugging her inside out. How did he manage to be so normal and so... hot? The worst part was that he wanted her too. Or he had done. Now he was probably regretting the whole summer, wishing she'd vanished forever.

Third shot: Lloyd's mum. No matter how much Scarlett liked Lloyd, his mother would always be an obstacle – like she'd ever forgive Scarlett for what happened on the coach trip.

Fourth shot: Herself. For being the kind of idiot who still wished for a miracle, even after all this time.

Carli's laugh rose above the crowd, and the world wobbled, then steadied. But Scarlett had had worse nights.

Far worse.

Tavrach launched into "Last Christmas" and the whole bar started singing along. The frontman's voice was raspy, but also smooth, and kind of hypnotic. Scarlett closed her eyes, trying to lose herself in the music, but her brain wouldn't shut up.

Someone handed her another shot. She drank it. The liquid burned her lips, then her throat. She started to laugh, then stopped herself. This was the point where she usually did something wild, something stupid, but maybe she'd used up her quota of stupidity this year.

The hours blurred. She lost track of time. At one point, she found herself outside on the smoking terrace, breathing in the ice-cold air, hands jammed in her pockets. A guy handed her a cigarette.

'I don't smoke.' The smell always made her sick, reminding her of her dad, who'd puffed away constantly. Whenever he decided to come home, the atmosphere in the house shifted. Her mum was on edge, the routine was shattered, and every time Scarlett smelled cigarettes it took her right back, unsettling her.

Back inside, Tavrach had upped the tempo. The bar was pure chaos: people dancing on chairs and shouting to be heard over the music.

Scarlett found her seat again, but it was occupied by a stranger who had clearly decided she was going to sleep there, and the rest of her group seemed to have disappeared. She hovered near the table and scanned the room, looking for anyone she half-knew.

In answer to her wish, her eyes landed on Leon. A fresh wave of panic started in her chest. She knew him alright, but she didn't want to see him or be alone anywhere near him.

For a split second, she considered texting Lloyd. But what would she say... And why would she assume he would come? Like how could he leave his kids to rescue a stupid damsel in distress? How had she let herself get so wasted?

She pushed through the crowd to the bar, ordered a lemonade this time, and sipped it slowly.

'You ok there, kid?'

She looked around and blinked as her eyes met with the Tavrach frontman. What the hell? Should she be starstruck?

'I, um, yeah.'

'You just looked a bit lost.' He scanned around. 'You got friends you can go to?'

'Um... Yeah. But I don't know where they got to.'

'There's someone over there waving to you.' He nodded his head towards the scrum, and Scarlett saw Carli.

'Aw, cool, thanks.' She almost knocked over a barstool as she made her way over.

'Was the rock dude hitting on you?' Carli asked, grinning.

'Na.' Scarlett shook her head, instantly regretting it as the whole bar spun. 'He seemed just... I dunno, quite friendly.'

Carli laughed and pulled her over to another table and another round of shots.

Scarlett was almost on her knees when people started talking about leaving and heading for the train.

Outside, the cold was so sharp it made her head whirl even more. The group walked down the main street, boots crunching the thin layer of ice on the pavement. Scarlett had no idea where she was going.

Carli squeezed her arm. 'Great night, huh?'

'Yeah.'

The newly lit street decorations twinkled on every lamppost, and Glenbriar looked so cute Scarlett wanted to cry.

She wasn't sure how she got to the station, but she'd lost her gloves, and her feet had started to go numb. The old-fashioned lamps on the platform made everything look like something out of a movie.

A train rumbled in, and the gaggle of Scarlett's friends climbed straight on. Scarlett followed them, but Carli pushed her off, almost causing her to fall.

'You're not coming with us,' Carli said.

'Why not?'

'Because you live here. You need to go home.'

Scarlett stepped back, wrapping her arms about herself and watching as the doors hissed shut and the train pulled away.

The world rocked and pitched.

I need to go home...

But where was that? Scarlett flopped onto a bench like a rag doll. The seat was metal, cold as a meat locker.

Her home was a long way from here, and she wasn't sure she remembered how to get there. The bookshop was shut up and dark. She pressed her face into her hands, felt the skin go icy against her palms.

What was she doing here? Why wasn't she on the train, or at home, or anywhere but here?

She tried to remember the reason. Maybe she'd left her bag. Maybe she was supposed to meet someone. But her brain was in pieces, each memory floating somewhere out of reach. Every time she tried to pin one down, it wriggled away.

Pulling her knees up, she wrapped her arms around herself and started to cry. Not the nice, movie-star kind, but a snotty, ugly, hiccupping cry that made her chest hurt. She kept her face hidden, hoping the wind would freeze the tears before they fell. It was so cold it hurt to breathe.

Somewhere in the village, a siren went off, and she wondered if it was people looking for her. She didn't remember how she got here. She didn't remember why she stayed.

She only knew she was alone and very cold.

CHAPTER FOURTEEN

Lloyd

'Seriously!' Eve stomped into the living room and Lloyd winced.

'What's the matter?'

'The charging case for my earbuds.' She lifted the cushions on the sofa, then tossed them back, not caring if they were squint or if they missed entirely and landed on the floor.

At eleven-thirty at night, Rita's house felt like a submarine at crush depth. Every door thud or heavy footstep vibrated through the thin walls, and the longer Lloyd stayed up, the more he felt the pressure building. His mum had got the tree and decorations out while they were at the light switch on. It was a sweet gesture and should have added to the festive feel, but now everyone was overtired and no one seemed to want to go to bed.

'Eve.' Lloyd put his hand on her back. 'Stop destroying Gran's living room and tell me what the problem is.'

'I think I've left my charging case at the shop. I put it on the table when we were there today. I need it. They've got hardly any charge left.'

'It's not the end of the world.' He kept his voice calm. 'You don't need to listen to anything this late, and we can nip down and get them in the morning.'

'But then it'll take ages to charge,' Eve shot back. 'Can't you go and get them now?'

'No, I can't,' he said firmly. 'It's time for bed, for everyone. The longer you stay up, the more annoyed you'll get. Rest will help.'

'I really need them.' She marched off.

'You don't *need* them.' But it was too late. She was halfway up the stairs and the door slammed a few seconds later.

'What is going on now?' Rita looked out from the kitchen.

Lloyd shook his head. 'Harry! Lewis! Upstairs now. No more excuses. Everyone is going to bed.'

Harry rolled his eyes but unexpectedly stopped at the bottom of the stairs and put his arms around Lloyd's waist. After the initial shock disintegrated, Lloyd held him for a moment.

'Night Dad. Thanks for the chips and stuff.'

'Love you, son.' Lloyd kissed his tufty hair, frowning after him as he went up the stairs. Lewis traipsed up after, yawning widely.

Lloyd said goodnight to his mum, who was switching off the lights before they both headed up the stairs.

After another ten minutes, everyone was in bed, but Lloyd suddenly felt wide awake. He was supposed to be winding down, but his brain was stuck in "background processing" mode. He went back downstairs and had a glass of water. As he was sharing a room with the boys, it was easier sometimes to let them fall asleep first. Otherwise, Lewis would ask him hundreds of questions.

A noise on the stairs caught his attention, and Rita appeared in the kitchen door.

'I forgot my glasses,' she said. 'I thought you were in bed.'

'I'm letting the boys get to sleep first. And... well, I don't feel tired anymore.'

Rita looked at him. 'It's grief. I was the same after your father died. It's in the night hours that the mind wanders to all the dark places you'd rather keep it well away from.'

'I might nip down and get Eve's earbuds just now. Then she'll have them first thing. And it might tire me out.'

Rita raised an eyebrow. 'Are you sure? In this weather and this late?'

'I'll take the car. It won't take long. You go to bed and don't worry.'

She shook her head. 'If you say so.' From the counter, she lifted her glasses. 'Night-night, and don't stay out too long.'

'I won't.'

As he got into the car, his thoughts drifted to Scarlett outside The Stagger Inn. Was she ok now? The shop was closed on Sundays and Mondays, so he wouldn't see her there for another couple of days. Should he message her?

It was a bit late now... and what would he say?

Maybe come morning he could think up a good reason.

The drive to the station was five minutes, and as the streets were dead, he had no issues getting there quickly. The car park was empty. He locked the car and zipped his coat to the chin. The platform wasn't gated or fenced off, so he strolled onto it, the air so cold it stabbed his nose. It too was empty at first glance, but he jumped out of his skin when he heard a muffled sound. On a bench in front of the shop was a huddled-up shape.

It took a couple of seconds to register that it was a person, and then another heartbeat to recognise Scarlett. She sat curled up tight, knees drawn to her chest, head bent so her face was almost hidden in the tangle of hair. Her boots were braced on the edge of the bench.

Lloyd's stomach plummeted. What the hell was she doing here?

He bent down in front of her, keeping his voice low. 'Scarlett?'

She didn't move at first, then raised her head. Her makeup was smeared, and her eyes glistened in the pale light.

'Hi,' she whispered. Her breath came out in clouds, heavy with alcohol and something sweet.

'What happened to you?' He eased onto the bench beside her and put a careful hand on her shoulder. 'Why are you here?'

'I don't know.' She slumped, tipping into him like a ragdoll with all the stuffing wrung out.

Lloyd put his arm around her, and she shuddered, letting out a little sob. He held her tight for a minute.

'You're freezing,' he said.

'And pathetic,' she muttered, burying her face in the collar of his coat. 'Only you know how pathetic I really am.'

'No, you're not.'

'Look at me.' She hiccupped. 'I fucked up. I always do.'

'How?'

'I drank too much, and I missed the train.'

'Do you need a train to get home?' He'd seen her address on the contract, and it was somewhere in Glenbriar – though he didn't remember exactly where.

She shrugged. 'Don't know.'

'Ok.' He just held her. She was a mess, but how did she always end up alone? He knew she had family and friends, but she didn't seem to have people looking out for her. Not in the right way anyway. Everyone had been quick to give him the judgemental stares, but where were they now? Where were they when she fell apart in the summer?

He saw the shivers tearing through her arms.

She looked up at him, eyes unfocused but pleading. 'I'm really cold. And I need a pee, but I don't know where to go.'

He rubbed her back. 'Ok. We'll go into the shop.'

She let him pull her upright. Her legs almost folded, but he caught her, arm around her waist, steering her to the shop door.

He fumbled with the keys and helped Scarlett inside. The heating timer had long since shut off, and it wasn't much warmer in here than out on the street. He locked the door behind them and used his phone torch to get them across the main room before switching on the light at the bottom of the stairs.

Scarlett blinked up at the ceiling. 'It's like a haunted house in here.'

'Come on. Upstairs.'

'Ooh la la,' she said, then giggled, then nearly tripped on the bottom step.

He steered her up the narrow staircase, hand braced on her back. At the top, she leaned against the wall and pawed at the bathroom door.

'I really need to—' she started, then made a beeline for it.

He got the door open just in time. She crashed inside, pulling the light cord and half shutting the door behind her.

Lloyd retreated into the main upstairs room and put on the side lamp. He took a deep breath, trying to re-centre. On the little coffee table was Eve's charging case. He pocketed it. The room looked much nicer now that it had been cleaned and tidied. The battered sofa was draped with the throws and cushions from Rita's house.

He heard a flush, then the sink tap, then Scarlett emerged, face puffy and a little green. She looked around the room, gaze landing on Lloyd. For a moment, she was the old Scarlett – bright eyes, mouth set in that self-deprecating half-grin.

She shuffled toward him, then leaned into him.

'Sorry,' she said, voice hoarse. 'You probably think I'm a complete embarrassment.'

'No.' He put his arms around her. 'You're not the first person to get a bit wrecked at Christmas. Or the last.'

'Did you get wrecked at this age?'

He shrugged. 'No. I had a new baby. Getting wrecked was never really my thing.'

Rita had told him he was born an old man. He and Amy had got together at university and got married as soon as they left. People praised him for always being responsible and reliable. Such a sensible guy... and how lucky Amy was to have found someone so steady.

God, if those people could see him now. Or discover what he'd got up to in the past few months... with this woman.

Scarlett rested on his shoulder. For a minute he let her, just listening to her breathing, feeling the heat of her against him.

Then she jolted and, putting her hand over her mouth, she ran for the bathroom.

He followed, catching up as she barely made it to the toilet. She heaved, tears streaming down her face, hands shaking as she clung to the cistern.

Lloyd pulled her hair back, held it in a loose ponytail with one hand, and rubbed her back with the other. He didn't say anything; just let her get through it.

When she was done, she leaned against the wall, arms limp at her sides. Her makeup was smeared, and a line of drool trailed down her chin. She tried to wipe it away with her wrist, missed, and started laughing hysterically.

'I'm so fucking classy,' she said. 'Bet you're glad you escaped me.'

He found a clean towel in the cupboard and dabbed her mouth. 'You'll feel better in a minute.'

'Doubt it.'

'You need water.'

'I need a new life.'

He took her hand. 'That's tomorrow's job. For now, just water.'

After helping her up, he got her a glass from the kitchen. She sipped the water, swished it around her mouth a bit, then looked at him with bleary, mournful eyes.

'What am I doing?' She leaned heavily on him, letting herself be half-carried back to the sofa.

'Just sit down. You'll feel better if you rest.'

He sat down with her and brushed her hair out of her face. His mind skipped back a few months to their fling and everything he'd seen then. Someone bright. Spirited. And even though she was a little lost, a little broken, and kind of sad, she'd laughed with him on that canoe trip, scrambled up a hillside with him to see the view, and pushed both of them out of their comfort zone.

Christ, he'd never have had a fling if she hadn't persuaded him, and it had been worth it. The sex had been great, the aftermath serene. She'd curled in against him and melted the edges of his loneliness. She listened too – really listened. Let him ramble about books, about the kids, about things he hadn't said aloud in years, and never once made him feel like a burden. He still saw it now. In the shop, with the way she'd poured herself into making it warm and welcoming, with the care she took over the wishing tree, the gentle way she spoke to customers, the way she somehow made him smile even when she didn't mean to. She did have a lot to give. Maybe she couldn't see it yet, but he could. She seemed more together now than she had been in the summer, but something had made her relapse. Maybe something that had happened with her friends. Or something else…

Me? Meeting my kids?

Had that upset her? He couldn't change the fact that they existed.

Scarlett reached for his hand, squeezing it tight. Her grip was strong. 'I missed you. Stupid, isn't it?'

'No,' he said, voice gone rough.

She finished the water, set the glass down, then slid closer, searching his face. 'I mean it. I've missed you since the trip. I keep thinking about it. About you.'

Lloyd went still. He felt her breath, the tickle of her hair. She was looking at him the way she had in Skye – unguarded, hungry, knowing exactly what she wanted.

He started to pull away. She was still half-cut, but she just leaned in, caught him by the shirt, and kissed him. It wasn't gentle. Her mouth was warm, tongue insistent, hands tangling in his hair. He almost let himself go with it, almost fell back into what had been such a fine time, but he couldn't.

'Come on, Scarlett. Where do you live? I can take you home.'

'I'm sorry. That was...' She closed her eyes. 'That was probably not ok. I just wanted to remember how it felt. I don't get to feel good very often.'

He swallowed, wiped a stray tear from her cheek. 'You deserve to feel good, but this isn't the right time or place. I have the car. I can take you home.'

'You're so nice. Too nice.' Her words slurred again. 'I wish you weren't. Then I could forget you.'

'Really, Scarlett, just tell me where you live.'

'I can't even remember.'

'Well, I can go and look for your address on your contract.'

'Can't I just go to sleep?' Her eyes were closing, and she yawned.

He let out a sigh. 'Ok, take your coat off and your boots, and we'll get you lying down here.'

She seemed too paralytic to move, so he helped her off with her coat, then leaned down and unlaced her boots before pulling them off. He was all too aware how they'd done stuff like this a few months ago without any constraints, knowing where it would lead, and embracing that. But this was completely different.

When he sat up, she leaned in, nuzzled his neck, and then, before he could stop her, started unbuttoning his shirt.

'Scarlett...' He held her wrists.

She grinned, eyes glazed. 'I remember how good it was. I want it again.'

He shook his head, gently, but she kissed him again, hands moving to his neck. 'Please,' she whispered. 'Just let me. Please.'

He gathered her up, held her tight, let her bury her face in his shoulder.

'Not tonight,' he said softly. 'You just need to rest.'

She made a sound halfway between a laugh and a sob, then melted into him, arms limp.

He lay her down on the sofa, wrapped the fleece blanket around her. She pawed at the edge, then found his hand again.

'Don't leave?'

'It's ok.'

He sat beside her, her head at his lap and he stroked her face, smoothing her hair out of her eyes, and kept watch.

There was a strange peace in just watching her breathe. A tear rolled down his cheek as he remembered Amy's last breath. What the hell would she make of this? He didn't know what to make of it himself.

He stayed on the sofa, one arm draped across Scarlett's shoulder, the other holding his phone as if he might absorb some comfort through the plastic.

At three A.M, his body threatened to shut down. He thumbed a quick message to his mum.

In case you're awake and wondering where I am, I'm fine. Had to help someone at the station. Will be back soon.

He leaned back on the sofa, shoes kicked off and let his eyes close for a minute. Just a minute.

He woke with a jolt at half five. It was still pitch black, and Scarlett was curled up under the blanket, snoring softly. Stretching, he got to his feet quietly.

As he crouched to put on his shoes, he watched Scarlett, tracing the curve of her cheek with his eyes, remembering how it had felt to have her want him so badly. His chest hurt, and he didn't have words for the kind of ache it was.

How long before Lewis told his gran about Scarlett? He groaned. Rita was going to find out at some point.

Would she understand? Why did he think not?

He reached over, tucked a strand of red hair behind Scarlett's ear, and leaned in to kiss her on the cheek. She didn't wake, just sighed and wriggled deeper under the covers.

Quickly, he scribbled a note on an old envelope.

You're safe, but if you need anything, just message me. I'll drop in later to see if you're ok. Lloyd x

He left it on the table next to her, then padded down the stairs to the freezing world outside.

The drive back was a blur. The radio played a festive playlist, but the lyrics barely registered. Sweetwater Lane was bathed in the glow from the streetlamps, the snow now turning to ice crystals in the freezing air. Inside, the house was silent. No one was up.

Lloyd set the charging case on the kitchen table, took off his shoes, shirt and trousers, and crept up to his room, getting into the bed next to Lewis in just his boxer briefs and socks.

He closed his eyes, listening to both his sons breathing deeply, but he didn't sleep. Not for a long time.

CHAPTER FIFTEEN

She was standing outside Lloyd's house.

The wind tugged at her hair, and sleet fell like confetti, but she wasn't cold. She stepped closer, peering through the front window.

Inside, Lloyd sat slumped in an armchair, elbows on his knees, staring blankly at a pile of unopened boxes. One was labelled *Christmas Stuff*, and beside it sat three more boxes – slightly crumpled, one with a corner torn. The tree was up but bare, a skeletal shape by the window. Not a single bauble on its plastic limbs.

Lewis knelt on the rug with a glittery garland tangled around him like a snake. He was poking at it without enthusiasm. Harry sat on the edge of the sofa, scrolling on his phone. Eve had earbuds in, arms crossed, her expression thunderous. They looked like a painting of family dysfunction.

Scarlett pressed her hand against the window. 'Oh, no, no, no,' she murmured. 'This won't do at all.'

And then, quite suddenly, she was *singing*.

'*Deck the halls and clear the gloom,It's time to sparkle up this room!*'

With a theatrical flourish, she flung open the front door – though it made no sound – and twirled inside like she'd blown in on the wind. The moment she entered, her clothes shimmered and transformed: her hoodie vanished, replaced by a red velvet cape and glittery skirt that swirled as she danced.

'*Tinsel trails and fairy lights,*
Fa-la-la-la-la, la-la-la-la,Mince pies, cocoa, starry nights,
Tra-la-la-la-la, la-la-la-la...'

As she spun, the decorations lifted themselves from their boxes and whirled through the air like enchanted props. Garlands leapt to the banister, lights tangled up the stair rail, and baubles floated like bubbles to the waiting tree.

Lloyd blinked at her. 'Scarlett...?'

She shimmied across to him, took his hands and pulled him to his feet mid-verse.

'*Come on, Mr Miller, get out of your chair,*
Fa-la-la-la-la, la-la-la-la,
Put that star on the tree if you dare!'

He gave in – helplessly, bashfully – and soon he was dancing too, awkward and shuffly at first, then twirling her with surprising grace as the decorations kept levitating around them.

Lewis laughed and clapped to the beat, spinning under a rain of snowflake stickers. Even Harry looked up from his phone, a smile playing at the corner of his lips.

Eve remained seated… but Scarlett pirouetted toward her.

'Don't be grumpy, don't be mean,
Fa-la-la-la-la, la-la-la-la,
There's magic here you haven't seen.'

Eve rolled her eyes but let Scarlett tie a ribbon in her hair, and for a fleeting moment, her scowl softened. The music swelled, filling the house with warmth and wonder, and then—

It all shimmered and melted like a snowflake on her tongue.

Scarlett opened her eyes, and her head threatened to split along the seam. She was cold, then hot, then cold again.

Where was she? Not in bed, though she had a blanket over her. And her clothes… Why did she have on clothes?

Christ alive. The sparkly dream faded, and the night came back – shots at the Stagger, her friends, the world spinning like a dodgy merry-go-round, and then… Lloyd, Lloyd helping her up, steering her, making her drink water and holding back her hair as she threw up.

She rolled onto her back, wincing some more. A glass of water on the coffee table caught her eye, and a note, too, written on a torn-off envelope:

You're safe, but if you need anything, just message me. I'll drop in later to see if you're ok. Lloyd x

She stared at it for a long time. How humiliating was this? Just when she'd thought she couldn't get any worse.

Her mouth tasted like something had died inside it. She made herself sit up, shuddering as the fleece blanket slipped off her shoulders, and drained the water in slow, painful gulps. Then finally she braved her phone. It was almost out of battery, but the notifications hit like a sledgehammer.

Six missed calls and thirty texts from her mum. Then, in quick succession: Aidan, Lilah, and Elise. All of them, panicking because she hadn't come home, hadn't replied, hadn't even left a trail of disaster to follow.

She sat, paralysed, as the phone kept buzzing. Her hands shook so much she had to set the phone down on the cushion just to read the screen.

Scarlett. Where the hell are you? Are you ok? Please answer.

Please tell us you're safe, I'm worried sick x

Everything was frantic, repetitive, heavy with that note of dread: What if she'd done it again? What if this time, she didn't come back?

Because she'd done this before. When she'd been at rock bottom, she'd run off with plans to hurt herself, but ended up hiding in the local church overnight. Everyone had been so scared, and Elise had eventually been the one to pull Scarlett around. She'd suggested counselling, and it had made things better for a while, but not enough to make her immune to this sort of mess.

A full-body cringe ran through her. Why did she always do this? Did she have no sense? No filter?

She curled up on the sofa, knees to her chest, and replied quickly to her mum.

Scarlett: I'm alive. Sorry. Got drunk and crashed at a friend's. Will explain later. Let the others know please. My phone's nearly out of charge.

She pulled the fleece over herself and stared at the ceiling. There were so many ways to ruin a perfectly decent life, but she seemed to add some new ones every time she tried to start over.

The headache rolled in again, pounding at her temples. She pressed her hands to her eyes, hard enough to see stars, until the need for a wee overwhelmed her desire to be a blanket burrito. She staggered upright, clutching her stomach, and shuffled to the tiny bathroom off the landing. The light in there was criminally harsh, spotlighting her streaked mascara and puffy eyes. She looked like a crime scene.

Splashing water over her cheeks, she rinsed her face, then her mouth.

With her hands shaking, she rewrapped the blanket shroud around her shoulders and shuffled to the top of the stairs. The shop below was dead silent. As she put her foot on the top step, a clatter like someone knocking on the door made her stop dead. The front door rattled. Her heart thumped double time.

This old place always creaked and groaned. Was it haunted? Eunice probably liked that idea.

Scarlett pressed her back to the wall and listened harder. Another noise. This time a scrape.

For a split second, she panicked, wanting to run, as the wild bell screeched, cutting her already fragile head in two.

She shrank back. Maybe it was an actual ghost, and this was her penance for every stupid thing she'd ever done. But when she peered down, it wasn't a phantom, but Lloyd.

He came in, fiddling with his car keys, then looked up and saw her frozen on the stairs.

His face transitioned through various expressions – first surprise, then relief, then a sort of soft focus that made her heart do a nervous somersault.

'You're still here,' he said.

'Yeah,' she croaked.

'I hoped you would be. I wanted to check you were ok.'

'Sorry, I didn't mean to be in such a bloody state.' All the mortification bubbling up inside her made her feel worse than the hangover.

Lloyd shook his head. 'Don't be daft. You were having a fun night out. It's not a crime.'

She stared at the floor. She couldn't look him in the eye after last night – after everything she'd said and done, the tears, the puking, the desperate attempts at a kiss.

'It's a shame you were left on your own. That wasn't exactly safe.'

She let out a huff. 'I've never been great at looking after myself. Even when I don't mean to, I end up doing stupid stuff.'

He ran a hand through his hair, then came over, keeping a polite distance. 'How about I give you a lift home?'

Scarlett shrugged, her whole body shrivelling under the blanket. 'I'm so sorry, Lloyd. I keep making such a spectacle of myself. What the hell must you think of me?'

'I've told you before what I think of you.' He gave her a little smile.

She looked at his face. He was serious. No hint of annoyance, no judgement, just a quiet sort of care. 'You're too nice.'

'Don't let it get around.'

She almost laughed, but it got stuck in her throat. She hugged the blanket tighter. 'I should get out of your way and never darken your door again.'

'Don't say that.' He cut her off, the gentle edge in his voice hardening for the first time. 'You work here now. You can't... just leave.'

She blinked. 'You want me to keep working here, even though you know how irresponsible I am?'

'Of course I do. You're allowed to get drunk on a Christmas night out with friends.'

'I'm never doing it again. Honestly, that was my farewell to shots. I'm officially too old for them now.'

A low chuckle rumbled from him, and he glanced at the window. 'Don't be too sure. My mum had quite a few the night she... well, on Skye.'

Scarlett knew what he meant. The night Rita had marched up to her and accused her of seducing Lloyd. 'She was drunk when she said that stuff?'

'She'd certainly had one too many gin liqueurs.' He shoved his hands into his coat pockets. 'Listen, I can't hang about. I told my mum I'd get some bits from the shop, and if I'm not back in twenty minutes, she'll send the search party out. But if you need a lift somewhere, I'm happy to take you. I'd prefer not to leave you here alone. I mean... Do you live alone? I'm sorry, I don't even know.'

He was so earnest it made her want to cry and punch him, both at once. It would have been easier if he was cold or dismissive, if he'd just made a joke and left her to the shame spiral. But Lloyd wasn't like the other men she'd let herself fall for. He was just... good. Too good.

'I've been living with my mum since the breakup. And yeah, I'd appreciate a lift. Let me get my stuff.' She dashed up the stairs, face burning, and jammed her feet into her boots, then yanked the blanket off, and made herself look in the mirror just to see how bad it was.

Not as bad as it could be, but bad enough.

She went for another pee, then brushed her hair with her fingers until it mostly covered the hangover face, then tramped back down. Lloyd was leaning by the counter, rolling his keys between his fingers and glancing at his phone.

He looked up as she appeared, and something in his eyes made her almost flinch.

'You really don't have to do this,' she said. 'I can walk.'

'What if I insist?' he replied. 'I can't in good conscience leave you here alone. You should be with someone.' He looked away with a pained expression. 'I'm sorry it can't be me.'

Scarlett exhaled, feeling empty. Raw.

'It's not up to you to look after me,' she said. 'And I shouldn't have put you in that situation. Again.'

'You don't need to be sorry. In fact, I wish you'd messaged me; I... I would have been happy to help.'

She felt a spike of anger, but it wasn't at him. 'Why do you have to be so kind?'

He huffed out a laugh. 'Maybe it's a flaw.'

'It's definitely not a flaw.' She looked up, and he was so close she could see the deep-sea blue in his eyes, the little flecks around the edge of his iris, and the way his lips trembled, just a little.

She felt her own face go soft, her mouth quiver. 'Thank you,' she said.

He didn't answer, just wrapped his arms around her. She went to pieces in the hug, pressing her face into his shoulder, hands grabbing at his jacket like she'd fall through the world if she let go.

He was warm and solid and smelled so wonderful – his sandalwood cologne that brought back so many memories and made her insides clench with need, desire, and a sense of absolute peace.

'It's ok,' he murmured. 'You're ok.'

She shook her head against his shoulder. 'I'm not, though. I'm really not.'

He pulled back just enough to look at her. 'Then let's get you some help.'

'I have a counsellor. I guess that's a start, right?'

'Definitely.' He stroked her hair. 'I did too... after Amy.'

She put her hand on his cheek and ran her thumb under his eye. 'You miss her?'

'Yes.' The word came out on a breath. 'And that makes me feel so guilty.'

'Why?'

'Because I've also missed you.' He shook his head and looked at the ceiling. 'I'm so confused about how I feel... I've tried to explain to the kids that it would be ok for me to see other people, but part of me can't reconcile myself to it. How can I expect them to get it if I don't get it myself?'

Still holding his face, she gazed at him. 'I don't know,' she whispered.

His eyes met hers, and for a moment, they just looked at each other, then she leaned up, caught his lips, and held them in a soft, tender kiss.

Lloyd froze for a moment, then he kissed her back with a firm gentleness that broke her even more. There was nothing hurried, nothing cheap about it; it was so strong and powerful. The kind of kiss that told the truth, even when the words couldn't.

She pushed deeper and their tongues met, causing an electrical current to tear through her. This level of heat was surely a fire hazard in a shop with so much paper in it.

Then slowly, Lloyd pulled back. Scarlett was breathless, staring at him, tears starting in her eyes.

He wiped one away with his thumb, then smiled, sad and warm at once. 'No matter what happens, you're a very special person to me. And what we had this summer... it meant a lot to me.'

She held her breath, afraid of what might come next.

'But I can't go back to it. Not like before. I have three kids who need me more than anyone ever has. And... I'm not young, not really. I'm forty, for god's sake, and you... you're—'

'Don't.' She held her hand to his lips. 'Don't give me the age thing. I've never cared about that. I care about how you treat people. How you treat me. And you're... the only person who's ever made me feel good... and safe.'

'And you make me feel alive,' he said softly. 'But I don't want to hurt you, or give you false hope, or... or pretend I can give you everything you need.'

She shook her head. 'I don't need everything. I just want something that's real.'

He drew her closer, his arms tight around her, and she burrowed in, breathing in the smell of him. They held each other for ages. Nothing felt awkward, just right.

She pressed her cheek to his chest, felt the thump of his heart, until he pulled back.

'Come on. We should go.' He opened the door for her, and the two of them walked together into the brittle morning towards the car park.

They reached his car, and he unlocked it with a beep. She got in, pulled the seatbelt tight, still processing his words.

He started the engine, then looked at her with a little smile. 'Do you remember where you live now?'

She grinned. 'Yeah. It's in Oakfield Road. Do you know it?'

'No, I'm not from here; you'll have to direct me.'

After he pulled out of the car park, she guided him up a steep side road.

'Where do you live?' she asked. 'Or where will your new house be?'

'It's on Golf Course Road.'

'Ooh, the houses there are all very posh.' Was it like the house she'd dreamed he lived in? She almost laughed at the memory. That dream had been insane.

'It's a nice house anyway. I just wish we could get into it soon.'

'When will that be?'

'I'm supposed to get the keys next week. I'm hoping we can move in at the weekend.'

'Golf Course Road isn't that far from here.' Scarlett showed him where to stop outside her mum's house, an old Victorian semi with a large bay window. 'Thanks for the lift... and for everything.'

He nodded, then reached out and took her hand. 'This may be crazy, but... would you like to go somewhere sometime? Just for coffee, or hot chocolate and a Christmas cake, or whatever. No drama, no strings, just... a chat.'

She nodded. 'Yeah. Ok. I'd like that.'

'Good. I'll see you on Tuesday at the shop and we can decide where and when.' He squeezed her hand, then let go.

She leaned over and gave him a quick peck on the cheek before she got out the car, shivering again, and waving as she went up to her mum's door. There was a strange, brittle happiness in her chest, and it hurt, but it was the best thing she'd felt in months.

As she stood at her mum's door watching some fairy lights twinkling in a window across the street, she thought about Lloyd's kids and the dream. About how Eve hated her, and how Harry was indifferent, and how Lewis was the only one who she'd made a connection with.

A stupid idea popped into her head, one so deranged she almost laughed: What if she could win them over? Not in quite such a theatrical fashion as she'd dreamt about, but what if she could make Eve and Harry and Lewis fall in love with her, just enough that they'd want her around? What if she could make herself fit into Lloyd's weird, messy family – no, what if she could make herself like the idea of fitting in at all?

Maybe she could do it to prove she was better than her exes, her dad, or all the ghosts of the past who'd assumed she'd never amount to anything.

Christmas had been crap for her recently, but what if she could flip that script? What if she became the person who made Christmas less crap for someone else? Maybe that's how you fixed yourself – by helping others.

Even if it was the last good thing she ever did, she was going to make this Christmas count.

And if she could manage to make three kids smile at least once before New Year, maybe that would be enough to fix the whole sad, broken mess that was Scarlett Finch.

Or at least give her something better to wish for.

Chapter Sixteen

Lloyd

Lloyd pushed open the door of his mum's cottage, kicked off his boots, and dropped the shopping bag onto the kitchen table.

Rita appeared at the threshold in her dressing gown, a hot-water bottle clamped in both hands, and a steely frown on her face that made guilt bubble up inside him – though he wasn't sure exactly what he'd done this time. Or perhaps he was all too aware, but how could Rita know about it?

'Is everything ok?' He loaded the milk and bread into the fridge. 'Are you having a flare up?'

She let out a huff. 'I suppose so. The cold weather always gets to me.'

'Why don't you just go and relax?'

'How can I?'

He tensed, cold creeping up his neck. 'Why? Is something else wrong?'

Rita leaned against the counter. 'Lewis has just finished telling me that the person you hired to work in the bookshop is a girl with bright red hair by the name of Scarlett.'

'I see.' Lloyd crossed to the sink and filled the kettle, not looking at his mum. This was his own fault, and he'd always known she would find out sooner or later, but it didn't ease the level of cringe. She literally had him backed into a corner.

'Please tell me this is not the same one from the summer. The one you—' She made an ambiguous gesture, like she was twirling a lasso. 'You know who I mean.'

'I know who you mean, yes,' Lloyd said, voice steady. 'And yes, it's the same person.'

'Christ above, Lloyd, what are you thinking? Have you been seeing her all this time? Is that why you moved here?'

He lifted a mug from the cupboard. 'Of course not. I had no idea where she lived.'

'You expect me to believe that this is a coincidence? You—' She stopped, biting back whatever was next. 'You can't let yourself be taken in by her again. She's ridiculous. She wrecked that coach trip for everyone.'

'No, she didn't. And I wasn't taken in by anyone. I'm not a child.'

'Maybe not, but what's she? A teenager?'

'No, she's twenty-five.'

'Which is far too young for you, and I don't want to see you making a fool of yourself. Your children need you to be responsible, not tearing around after some young thing.'

'Don't call her that. And really, it's not like that.' Though something raw gnawed at his gut. He knew he was too old for her. She'd said she didn't care, but for Christ's sake, she was closer to Eve's age than his. 'It was Eunice that employed her first,' he said, deflecting.

'What?'

He explained about the sign on the door and then the coincidence of her needing a job and being in the right place at the right time.

'Oh really, Lloyd. You believe it was a coincidence? She must have known. She sounds like a stalker.'

'No, she isn't. I could tell she was just as shocked to see me.'

'So, assuming that's true, what's happening now? Are you and her still...' She pulled a face. 'Doing whatever you were doing on the trip?'

He shook his head. 'She's working in the shop until Eunice comes back.'

'And this is strictly a professional relationship?'

'Well...' He raked his fingers through his hair. A frown slipped onto his face. 'I consider her a friend.'

'A friend?' Rita's voice was high-pitched. 'After the trouble she caused?'

'She didn't cause any trouble. Stop saying that. I didn't know at the time that you were hurting so bad with the ankylosing spondylitis, and I know it's hurting you now, but please don't let that sour your judgement. She was in a lot of pain too. She still is. What that man did to her was horrific.'

Rita let out a huff and sat down next to the cat. 'I just don't want you doing anything silly. You're the one who told me you weren't going to get tangled up again after Amy. That you needed to focus on the children and rebuilding your family before you even considered it.'

His jaw clenched at the mention of Amy, that sudden, sledgehammer guilt always ready to drop. 'I *am* focused on the children. Nothing I've done has harmed them.'

Rita raised an eyebrow. 'You think they'll appreciate you being friends with someone like that?'

'They might if they get to know her. You might too. Because right now, you don't know her at all,' he said quietly. 'Not really.'

'Look.' She folded her arms. 'If you want to start dating again, I'm not going to stand in your way. You're a grown man. I only ever wanted you to be happy, but I don't think it's a good idea to involve that girl with your children. I know she wasn't to blame for what happened to her on that coach trip with her boyfriend, but even after that, she did some stupid and childish things.'

'Haven't we all when we're not in a good place?'

'Hmm. She just doesn't seem like the kind of person the kids need in their lives right now.'

He tried to keep his tone measured. 'I said she was my friend. I'm not asking her to raise my kids. I'd never ask anyone to do that, let alone—'

'But you let her into the shop with them. You let her around Lewis, and he's already obsessed.'

'And how is that bad? If he liked her and got some happiness from the day, then so what?'

Rita gave a tight, pointed laugh. 'You're blind when it comes to her. She's not good for you. Look at the spectacle she made of you on the trip.'

'*She* didn't do that.' Lloyd's voice rose before he caught himself. 'Gossipy people caused the spectacle.'

Rita's eyebrows shot up. 'Are you blaming me?'

'I'm not blaming anyone. She and I struck up a rapport on that trip, and there was no harm in it. The drama only happened because other people made a big thing out of it. God knows, I wouldn't have, and neither would she. You don't really think she wanted all that, do you?'

'Oh, Lloyd.' She sighed. 'I can see you're determined to go down this path. I just wish you'd listen.'

He let out a breath, feeling the words like sandpaper in his mouth. 'I am listening, and I'm not determined to do anything. Nothing harmful anyway. But cutting her out of my life now isn't going to help. I'm allowed friends no matter what age, sex, colour, etcetera. So please, no more. She's not perfect, but she's not a villain. She's been through enough without us piling on.'

Rita pressed her lips together, apparently fighting the urge to say more. For a moment, she seemed to shrink, and the lines around her eyes deepened. 'Just... don't get hurt again.'

He wanted to promise, but how could he? 'There are no guarantees in life, Mum.'

'Sadly that's too true.'

He crossed the kitchen and gave her a brief hug before escaping into the living room with his coffee. He collapsed on the sofa, rubbing his temples. It was like fighting a war on two fronts – against his own head, and against his mum.

His eyes met Eve's across the room, and she scowled at him... Make that three fronts.

On Tuesday, Lloyd let himself into the shop, the bell at the door giving its usual spasm of rage. He didn't see Scarlett at first, just a stack of books on the counter.

'Morning,' Scarlett said.

'Oh, you're there.' He smiled at her. 'You've literally been covered by books.'

'Yeah. This is me doing everything I can to show I'm a good and responsible worker after Saturday night's disaster.'

'No harm done. You got home safe; that's the important thing.'

'I still feel a total idiot though.'

'You don't have to.'

The corner of her lip quirked up. 'Thanks, but I'm not sure my brain will let me off the hook that quickly.'

He slipped off his backpack and put it on the floor, then took off his coat and draped it over his arm. 'Well, I should tell you, you've been rumbled. My mother discovered that you're working here.' He raised an eyebrow. 'From Lewis.'

Scarlett froze for a second, hand clamped to her mouth. 'Oh god.'

'Yup.' Lloyd mirrored her helpless look.

'Does she want me to leave?'

He gave a little shrug. 'To be honest, that's irrelevant. It's not up to her.'

'But I bet she's not happy about it.'

'Well, she'll just have to deal with it. Because I'm not firing you.'

The air between them shimmered. Scarlett reached out and touched his arm – just a brief, friendly squeeze – but it zinged all the way to his heart. 'Thank you,' she said.

He didn't answer, just watched her.

'Does this mean you don't want to go somewhere with me now? I mean... like we talked about on Sunday.'

He reached for her hand and held it. 'Of course, I still want to. It's my life and I can do what I want with it.' If anyone knew how important it was to seize moments of joy when they arose, it was him. Because love could be snatched from you at anytime. Grief came in many ways – large and small. The loss of his wife was huge; a cutting look from Eve was small, but it still hurt.

So, stealing some moments of happiness was necessary. And being next to Scarlett gave him a sense of being loved, whole, and wanted. Even if it was only temporary and wouldn't last. So what?

She wrapped her arms around his neck and hugged him. The world tilted on its axis for a second, but she pulled away just as fast.

'Sorry,' she said, breathless. 'I'm just so happy that I get to see you again.'

Placing his hand on her upper arm, he leaned in and gently pressed a kiss on the shell of her ear. 'Let's shut the shop at lunchtime on Friday and we'll go out for lunch.'

'Ok.' She trembled a little, but he increased the pressure on her arm.

His focus landed on the wishing tree, and he smiled. If he closed his eyes, he could almost believe all his wishes had come true.

Chapter Seventeen

Scarlett

The kitchen table at Patricia's house was almost completely hidden beneath crafting supplies, scraps of material and assorted glittery shapes. Although she owned the Crafty Bee Barn, which was all done up as a studio, come winter, she preferred to work a lot in the house.

Scarlett sat down and tugged her ankle boots on over her skinny jeans. The radio was tuned to a music station that seemed jammed on Slade, and Patricia was multitasking, making coffee, gluing sparkly stars on Christmas cards, and glancing at Scarlett every few seconds.

'This job seems to be doing you a world of good.' Patricia smiled, laying another card on top of the radiator to dry. 'Is it a long-term option? Or will it stop completely when the injured lady comes back?'

'I think it'll stop,' Scarlett said, and a lead weight dropped in her stomach. Even though she couldn't lie that she'd taken the job initially to be close to Lloyd, she was enjoying it so much she would keep it on anyway. No other job had appealed to her this much or made her want to get up every day and go back. 'Seems typical, doesn't it? I find something I like, and then it comes to an end too soon.'

'Don't start with the negative thinking already.' Patricia set down a mug in front of her. 'You need positivity. People respect you more if you look on the bright side.'

Scarlett sipped her coffee, then nodded.

'I'm really hoping they'll find a way to keep you on. You've been smiling ever since you got it.'

'It's just nice to have somewhere to be,' Scarlett said. 'And the shop's kind of amazing. Almost magical.'

Patricia raised an eyebrow. 'That's not something I ever thought I'd hear you say.'

'I don't mean it's full of wizards or anything. It's just cute, and it has a good vibe.'

'I'll need to pop in and see it sometime. Do you think the owner would stock my cards there?'

'Maybe. I could ask him.'

'If you didn't mind. But only if you feel up to it and make sure it doesn't put you in a bad position. This job is good for you. I wouldn't want to jeopardise it. I haven't seen you this happy for... a long time.'

Scarlett bit the inside of her cheek. Everyone knew the mess Scarlett had got herself into after the summer.

Was she doing it again now?

'Listen, Mum,' she half-mumbled it into her mug. 'You remember the guy I met on the coach trip?'

Patricia's eyes widened. 'I never met him, but obviously I remember. You weren't right for months after that. In fact, this job seems to have done what none of us could and stopped you moping about him.'

Scarlett took a deep breath, not looking at Patricia. 'That's because he's the owner.'

'What?' Patricia almost shot herself with the glue-gun. 'He's the owner of the bookshop. And you knew this?'

'No. I didn't. It was all a weird coincidence. But... Well, he's nice. Like really nice.'

'Oh, for god's sake, Scarlett. Isn't he married?'

'His wife died like two years ago.'

Patricia blew out a breath. 'I don't even know where to start. So, what's happening with him now?'

'Nothing really. We're just... being friends. He's got three kids and, well, they're his priority.'

'Sensible.'

'But I can't lie. I like him. A lot.'

'Isn't he in his forties?'

She gave a little shrug. 'Yeah, he's forty, but I really don't care what age he is. He's a nice guy, and he's never been anything but polite and kind to me.'

'Even when he decided it was a good idea to get up to all sorts with you on that trip?'

'If you must know that was my idea. He would never have suggested it. He only gave in because I pestered him, and he admitted he was lonely. We both were. I'd been in a relationship with Leon, but it didn't stop me from feeling lonely. Because I was. He was so horrible to me, but I couldn't see a way out, and I didn't know there was anything better. Lloyd showed me that there is.'

Patricia went quiet, sipping her coffee like she was thinking about something. 'You know you were the result of a one-night stand, right?'

'Yes, Mum. I did know that.' Her mum had never made a secret of the fact.

'It wasn't even one night. It was one hour. But I chased after him. I thought maybe we could be a thing. That was when he decided to go along with it. Because I pestered him. Just like you did with this guy. And look what happened. He turned out to be a shit who drifted in and out of lives just as he pleased for fifteen years.'

'I know that.'

Patricia looked away. 'You remind me of me, sometimes. And that terrifies me. Because I don't want you to get hurt the same way. Or worse, to keep making the same mistakes. It's like there's some family curse that means we always fall for the ones who are no good.'

It hurt, but she knew it was true – or it had been up until now.

'Lloyd isn't like that.'

'How do you know?'

'Because if he really didn't give a shit, he wouldn't have given me the job. He wouldn't have helped me the night I was drunk.'

'What are you talking about?'

Scarlett didn't elaborate. 'He could have cut and run if he'd wanted. And it would be much easier for him to do that. But he hasn't. I know he has a good heart.'

Patricia let out a sigh, then picked up the mug and drank deeply. 'Well, if you say so. But I can't help feeling it has disaster written all over it.'

Scarlett laced her boots tighter, even though it hurt her toes. 'I don't know how you can say that when you thought Leon was a nice guy when you first met him. And look what he turned out to be.'

'Fair enough. I'll give this man a chance, but please be careful.'

'I will be.' Though she didn't know exactly how. She'd never been someone to stop and think. Most of her life choices were made on impulse, and it seemed to be a trait she couldn't switch off.

She grabbed her bag and the scarf from the banister, then zipped up her leather jacket.

'Love you, Mum,' she said.

'Love you too, darling.'

Scarlett went out into the cold air. It bit her cheeks, making her feel raw and awake. She breathed it in, then started the walk to the station.

It was just long enough for her fingers to go numb and her thoughts to go haywire. Today was the day Lloyd was taking her out for lunch. Maybe that was the kind of thing her mum meant when she said to be careful. She paused outside the bookshop entrance and checked her reflection in the glass. Would it be more sensible if they just stayed here for lunch? Perhaps being seen out together wasn't sensible.

Lloyd was already inside and looked up as she entered. 'Morning.' He smiled. 'Your coffee's ready.'

She managed to return his smile, despite her face being mostly frozen. 'Thank you.'

He handed over her mug, then nodded at the window. 'It's a cold one today, isn't it?'

'Freezing.' She cupped her hand around the mug. 'This is better than the one my mum made. I had to leave it. No matter how often I tell her, she always makes them too strong. You know just the way I like it.'

He gave a half cough, half snort, and she laughed.

'Is that where your mind went?'

'Sorry.' He flashed her a look. 'Did you decide on a place you'd like to go for lunch?'

'Not yet.'

He looked at her, then at the clock. 'Well, you've got until noon to decide. Then I'm kidnapping you.'

'Promise?' She raised an eyebrow.

'One hundred per cent.' He took her hand and gave it a gentle squeeze. 'I better do some work. See you at lunchtime.'

Scarlett moved behind the counter, still wondering where she'd like to go for lunch. Every time her mind thought of Lloyd though, all she could think of was cuddling up next to him or kissing him in ways that were not appropriate for a café.

The hours crept past, each customer bringing a brief blip of interaction. A man with a beard and a huge book stack. A mum and daughter who were interested in the wishing tree. Scarlett made small talk, rang up sales, and in between, she kept running through possible lunch venues in her head. The Italian place was nice, but too fancy. The Drip Drop Café had good food, but she knew people who worked there, and she wasn't sure she wanted them to see her out with Lloyd – not yet.

At five to twelve, Lloyd reappeared at the bottom of the stairs, hair slightly mussed, glasses halfway down his nose.

'So, where have you decided on?' he asked.

'Um, I'm still not sure. I don't know if I'm even hungry yet.'

He went to the door, flipped the sign to CLOSED, and locked up. 'Well, let me think.' He took off his glasses and ran his hand through his hair.

He always looked super-hot when he did that, and Scarlett's tummy fizzed.

They stood facing each other in the hush of the closed shop. Lloyd looked down at her lips, still fiddling with his glasses. 'Maybe we could go to the deli and get a takeout.'

She stepped forward until their faces were only a few inches apart. Her heart battered her ribs, but she didn't care.

'What if I don't want to go anywhere?' She swallowed, bracing herself.

For a second, he didn't move. His eyes searched hers. 'You want to stay here?'

'I'd like to go upstairs and have you do unspeakable things to me.'

He cupped her cheek, and the warmth of his palm and the tick of his thumb along her jaw were soothing. But they also started little tingles all over her.

'It certainly sounds like the most exciting dinner offer I've had since... well, since we were on Skye, but I'm not sure it's sensible.'

'Probably not.' She glanced away. 'I'm a bad influence on you. I led you astray on the trip and now I'm trying to do it again. Seriously I should learn how to control myself.'

'I didn't say I didn't want to,' he murmured. 'Maybe I've got no restraint either.'

'Is it something you'll regret, do you think?'

'I'm not sure. I know that being with you before made me feel a whole lot better.'

'Same.'

'Then maybe we could help each other out... as friends.'

She grinned. 'The kind that have benefits?'

'Yeah. That kind. Though I never thought I'd hear myself agreeing to anything like that.'

'You never thought you'd hear yourself agreeing to half the stuff we did on Skye.'

A laugh escaped him, and he shook his head. 'You're not wrong.' He reached out and took her hand. 'I can't deny how much I've missed you.'

With a smile, she kissed him. A full-throttle, needy press of mouth to mouth, every bit as intense as the first time in Skye. He kissed her back, arms around her waist, pulling her tight.

When they broke apart, they were both out of breath. Lloyd's hand found her hair, stroking the back of her neck, and his voice was a low rumble. 'You do things to me.'

'Same things that you do to me.' Her knees wobbled with relief and excitement. Lloyd steadied her.

'No need to rush.'

'I don't know about you, but I'm desperate.' She grabbed her bag, and they made it halfway up the stairs when Scarlett stopped, spun, and pushed Lloyd against the wall, crashing her mouth to his. He groaned, the sound vibrating through his chest and onto her lips. Her hands clung to his collar, her feet on tiptoe. He pressed back, gripping her hips like he was terrified she might vanish if he let go.

'Careful,' he said. 'We'll fall.'

'I know you'll keep me safe.'

He held her tighter, half carried her the last few steps, and somehow they made it to the landing. The whole time, they couldn't stop kissing, couldn't stop hands wandering – her fingers raking through his hair, his slipping beneath her jumper to stroke her back.

By the time they reached the office, Scarlett was alight with the same sparkling joy she'd felt in the summer. Lloyd kicked the door shut, then turned to her, eyes burning with blue fire.

She backed him towards the sofa. 'Sit,' she ordered.

He obeyed, sinking into the worn cushions, and she climbed straight onto his lap, straddling him, hands on his shoulders, daring him to move. He didn't. He just looked up at her.

'You really are very beautiful to look at.'

'You say the sweetest things.' She cupped his jaw, ran her thumb along the stubble, then kissed him. It started slowly, but the urge to go hard and fast nearly overtook her. She wanted to eat him, to dissolve into him, to live in this moment for the rest of her life.

She broke away and reached for the hem of her jumper, yanking it over her head and tossing it across the room. Her hair was no doubt standing up in all directions, but she didn't care. Lloyd stared, mouth slack, at the sight of her half-naked on his lap.

'I can't lie... I missed this.' He ran his hands up her arms, over her shoulders, to her neck. 'What we did on Skye was special.'

'I know. But no one else believed me.'

'Well, you don't have to convince me because I was there.' He kissed her collarbone, his tongue flicking warm and careful. His hands moved to the clasp of her bra, fumbling for a second before she arched her back to help him, and the bra was off, tumbling to the floor.

She'd picked this set because it made her feel confident, but now she felt brave for an entirely different reason – she didn't care what she looked like, because with Lloyd, she felt invincible.

'You're looking again,' she said.

'Yeah,' he replied. 'You know I like to do that.' She did. It had made her a little unsure at first. Guys didn't normally look her in the eye when they were doing their thing, but Lloyd's eye contact had made everything even more intimate.

He stroked her breasts, thumbs circling her nipples until they peaked hard. She shuddered, grinding her hips into his. She was already tingling, and the simple pressure of his thigh beneath her made it worse, or better, or both.

She got the first few of his shirt buttons open before losing patience and just yanking the shirt out of his waistband, her hands searching the skin underneath. He was solid – abs flat, chest broad – and she ran her hands up and down, feeling the heat of him.

He kept kissing her, sometimes her lips, sometimes her neck, sometimes a slow trail down to her nipple.

'You're cruel,' she whispered, but she meant it as a compliment.

He reached for her jeans, looked at her for approval, then popped the button and slid the zip down. She raised up on her knees so he could work them over her hips. She tried to help by wriggling, but they stuck around the boots. She laughed, half embarrassed, but Lloyd just said, 'Let me,' and bent down to tug them off. He was so gentle that when he finally got her jeans and boots off and she was sitting on his lap in just her knickers, she wanted to cry and laugh at the same time.

He ran his hands up the backs of her thighs, then traced the line of her underwear, thumbs dipping low in the front.

'You're trembling,' he said.

'I'm desperate,' she replied.

He kissed her again, slower this time, but with more weight. One hand cradled her head, the other moved down to stroke the thin cotton between her legs. She moaned, pressing herself into his palm, breathing more and more heavily as sensations built quickly. With a flash of white light behind her eyes, a fast and hot burst of pleasure tore through her. 'Oh god,' she murmured. 'I didn't expect that to happen so quickly.'

He kissed her neck. 'You make me feel so alive, so happy.'

'Now you.' She unbuttoned the rest of his shirt, then pushed it off his shoulders. Her hands ran over his chest, and she flicked her tongue across it just to make him squirm. He gasped, caught off guard, then pulled her close, both of them skin to skin.

'Scarlett...' he breathed, his voice gone shaky.

She reached for his belt, unfastened it, and opened his trousers. He was so ready, straining against his underwear. She stroked him through the cotton, loving the way his whole body arched into her touch.

He groaned. 'If you keep that up, this is going to be over very quickly.'

She liked the power of that. She liked the way he lost his composure, the way he let her take charge.

'I want you to know,' she said, 'how much I missed this.'

She slid off his lap, down to her knees, and pulled his trousers and pants down enough to free him. He was breathing hard, both hands on her head, not guiding but gripping her. She loved it. She loved the rawness, the urgency, the fact that she could do this to him.

'Scarlett, I can't... please.'

She stopped, pulled her mouth away, and looked up at him. He was so handsome it hurt – flushed, hair all wild. 'I'm not used to being this happy, and I love being with you.' She crawled back up onto his lap and kissed him.

'Likewise,' he whispered.

'Let me get a condom.' She moved off him and grabbed her bag. 'Then we can get you where I need you.'

Gently stroking her thigh, he smiled at her. 'I love how you just say it as it is.'

'Blunt and no filter, yep. I've been called that many times.' She pulled a condom from the box, then watched him, her pulse jumping, as he took off his boxers, and sheathed himself.

'Just the way I like you.' He looked up and smiled. 'Ready?'

'I've been ready and wishing for the last few months.' She pulled off her knickers, climbed back over him, and slowly and carefully he guided her down, filling her inch by inch. They found a rhythm, rocking together, and enjoying the ride with kisses, smiles and eye contact.

He held her hips, letting her set the pace, and she ran her hands over his chest, down his arms, over his stomach. She wanted to remember every detail so she could keep him with her even when they were apart.

Soon the pressure built in her again. From the look on Lloyd's face, she knew he would soon fall apart, but he was still looking at her with his adoring eyes and gently touching her everywhere she needed it. Her body was ready to burst with ecstasy, and so was her heart. This was why sex was sometimes called making love – because this felt like love – both physical and emotional. Her mind blanked out as pleasure hit her like a lightning bolt, then she was floating in endless, languid heat. She melted into him, face buried in his neck, arms around his shoulders, and his body shuddered. He let out a low groan, then fell back onto the sofa, panting and spent.

Neither said anything, but Lloyd stroked her hair, gently. A huge wave of emotion surged through her, and Scarlett let out a few tears, then more, until her face was wet. *Fuck.* She tried to turn away. He'd think she was unhinged.

'Hey,' he said. 'Are you ok?'

She nodded, unable to speak.

He wiped her cheek with his thumb. 'You're sure?'

She let out a wobbly laugh. 'I'm sure. I'm just overwhelmed. How do you make it this good?'

He kissed the tear tracks on her face with a featherlight touch. 'You deserve it to be good.'

'You really think that?'

'Of course, I do.'

They didn't move for ages. His arms stayed around her, strong and sure. She felt safe, as she always did with him.

'I think you just made one of my wishes come true.' She smiled into his shoulder.

'And you did the same for me.'

She nuzzled into him. Maybe the spontaneous choice of lunch venue had been the right one after all.

CHAPTER EIGHTEEN

Lloyd

Lloyd threw a blanket over Scarlett and stroked the bare line of her back, drawing little spirals with his thumb. It felt so natural with her lying on him like this, like she belonged here, their bodies tangled and content. He could have stayed this way forever, but of course, forever wasn't a thing that happened in real life. In real life, people got their hearts cracked open and spent years patching them up. Yet with Scarlett, it was like the last two years of being a half-man melted, leaving him almost whole.

'I meant what I said earlier.' He nuzzled his nose into her hair.

She snuggled closer, squeezing her arms tighter around his neck. 'Which bit?'

'All of it... You make me feel more alive than I have in years.'

Scarlett's lips moved on his shoulder, and he felt her smile. 'I'm glad.'

'And you did make my wish come true.' He tried to grin, but it went soft at the edges. 'Because I wished so hard after the summer that I could see you again. It was such a regret for me that we didn't stay in touch.'

Pulling back, she looked at him. 'Me too... though I assumed you wouldn't want to.'

He kissed the bridge of her nose. 'That's exactly how I felt. I convinced myself our reasoning was sound. That what we had for a few days could never translate into something real.'

'And now?' She toyed with the line of the throw blanket, not meeting his eye. 'I know you have kids and a million things going on.'

'I can't lie. I care about you. I wouldn't have let you in if I didn't think you were worth it.'

She snorted, but the sound was more sad than funny. 'I'm not worth much.'

'That's not true.' He gently cupped her face. 'You're worth a lot to me. An awful lot. Even in the summer, you scared me a bit at first, but it didn't take me long to realise how special you were. You listened to me. You didn't judge.'

'I'm not exactly in a position to judge, am I?'

'You reminded me how to have fun. And now... you're doing the same. You make me smile. And I love what you've done to the shop. You've brought it to life. Just as you've done to my heart.'

She sucked on her lip and looked away. 'You're going to make me cry again, and then you'll have to deal with another mascara emergency.'

'I can handle that. Because I've seen it before. Just like you've seen me raw and hurting. But it hasn't put us off yet.'

She searched his face. 'Do you worry that we're just trauma-bonded or something?'

He gave a little shrug. 'Maybe it was like that – in the beginning – but we can work with it. Happiness isn't guaranteed. We need to take it while we can.'

Scarlett went quiet again. This time, her hand wandered down his chest, circling his ribcage. 'I don't want to lose you again,' she whispered.

'I don't want that either. But the path is so unclear.'

She curled in tighter, pressing her face into his shoulder again. 'There's no rush, is there?'

'No, that's true.' Lloyd rubbed more circles on her back. He remembered her loving this in the summer. Her dreamy intake of breath and the way she went boneless in his arms told him she still liked it. 'Do you want any food? We didn't actually get lunch. I've got some cheese and crackers – the edible kind, not the ones with party hats and silly jokes.'

'You really do look after me.' She dipped in and kissed him, softly and still with a slight sadness in her eyes, but she smiled when they parted.

'I told you, I care about you and what happens to you. You're a special person to me.'

All she needed was someone to nurture her. And while he wanted to give her everything, he also didn't want to give her false hope. He wasn't a free man who could jump into a relationship – especially one that would bring so much external judgement.

Scarlett moved her hand to his, interlacing their fingers. 'I know you won't hurt me.'

'Not intentionally. Never. But I have to be honest with you. I don't know what happens now. I have no idea how I could even... fit someone else into my life. My kids, they're not going to be ok with it. Especially Eve. And they'll always come first. They have to.'

'I know that.' Scarlett nodded. 'And you should put them first. That's not even a question.'

'But you...' He tilted his head and met her gaze. 'You deserve to be with someone who can give you all their time and attention. Not just the scraps.'

Scarlett leaned in, pressing her forehead to his. 'I'll take what I can get.'

Lloyd cupped her cheek. 'But you shouldn't have to. I don't want you to settle for anything when you deserve everything.'

'No one deserves everything. I'm happy just to have you in my life again... for anything. Being your friend is enough.'

'With the extra benefits.' Lloyd raised an eyebrow.

'Well, I'm not going to lie, I like the benefits, but I don't want to force you into anything awkward that might harm your family life.'

'We can keep the two things separate for now... though that's not to say I don't want you to see the kids again or anything like that. I'm happy for them to know we're friends, but they don't need to know about the benefits thing.'

'Ok. I'm cool with that.'

'Good.' He gave her a bracing hug. 'Because you're awesome.'

'And so are you.' She kissed his jaw.

'Let's see if I'm awesome enough to find us something to eat before I have to do the school run.'

Scarlett shuffled off him, and he wrapped the blanket around her before he got up and sorted himself out, searching for his discarded clothes.

A sharp, metallic clicking echoed from the shop below. Lloyd quickly pulled up his boxer-briefs and glanced at Scarlett.

'What was that?' she whispered, eyes wide.

'I don't know.'

He listened, heart thumping. The sound came again – like a key turning, then the juddery rattle of the stubborn lock, and then the mad shriek of the bookshop bell. Adrenaline hit him hard, and he grabbed his jeans. 'Shit,' he hissed. 'Someone's coming in.'

'Who has a key apart from you?'

'My mum. Eunice. Oh Christ, it's probably my mum.'

Scarlett's face went pale. She grabbed her clothes.

Lloyd scrambled for his shirt and tried to flatten his hair. He almost tripped over his jeans in his panic to get them on.

The sound of a voice drifted up from downstairs. A woman's voice – definitely not Rita's.

'I think it's Eunice.' He tiptoed to the door, then walked down as casually as he could.

'Lloyd, ducky. Is that you up there?' Eunice said.

'Hello, Eunice. How are you?'

'I'm much better, thank you. I missed this place. And Clarence did too.' She waddled over to the counter, pug trotting behind, and looked around. 'I see you've made a lot of changes. The wishing tree is very festive.'

'It was all Scarlett. She's done a great job.'

Eunice's face lit up. 'I knew she'd be wonderful.'

'Hi.' Scarlett waved as she came down the creaky steps.

'Ah, you're here too,' Eunice said.

Lloyd ran his hands through his hair, trying to look innocent.

'Well...' Eunice beamed. 'My physio said I can start working again. I'm happy to start tomorrow. I find weekends deadly dull, so it would be good to get out.'

Scarlett's face flickered with what might have been panic, even sadness. Lloyd gave her a reassuring smile.

'That's great to hear you're better.' He nodded at Eunice. 'I remember you mentioning before that you were finding the workload a bit heavy though. Maybe we could come to an arrangement that means both you and Scarlett could work here. You could go back to only working weekends, and Scarlett could do the weekdays.'

Eunice beamed. 'Oh, that would be perfect. Weekends definitely work best for me. The weekdays are so busy, and if I need time off for appointments, it's very inconvenient.'

'Great… So, if you could do that, and if Scarlett still wants to work five days, we could open every day instead of closing two days a week.'

Scarlett nodded. 'Sounds ideal.'

Eunice looked between them, glasses sliding down her nose. 'You're keen to stay on, dear?'

'Yeah. I really love it here. It's… the best job I ever had.'

'I hope this is what Rita wanted.' Eunice patted Lloyd's arm. 'She called me and said you needed me back pronto. Sounded pretty desperate too. I thought you must be in trouble.'

Lloyd's stomach dropped. His meddling mother. Honestly, she didn't know when to stop sometimes – in fact, most of the time. She was great with the kids, and he appreciated all the help she gave him, but he hated the way she took that as a free pass to interfere in his business.

'No, no trouble.'

'I was worried when I came in and you were closed.' She looked around the shop, hands on her hips. 'It seems early for a Friday.'

Scarlett shot Lloyd a sideways glance.

'We were having some lunch and doing a stocktake,' he said.

Eunice's eyebrows went up. 'A what?'

'Counting the books. Making sure the numbers match up.'

'Oh dear,' she said. 'I hope you don't expect me to do that when I'm back. Those were the kind of jobs I was never any good at.'

'No, you won't have to worry about anything like that.'

'Thank goodness.' She turned back to Scarlett, taking her hand and giving it a squeeze. 'I'm so pleased you're staying, ducky. The place needs a bit of your sparkle.'

Scarlett's face went pink. 'Thank you.'

Eunice released her and let Clarence waddle off, then turned to Lloyd, suddenly businesslike. 'Right. So, I start tomorrow, do I?'

'If that's ok with Scarlett.'

'Yeah, sure. I'll do Monday instead.'

'I'll drop in tomorrow at some point and check you're ok, though it's a busy one for me. The removal vans are bringing the furniture to my new house. If I get a minute, I'll nip down.'

'I can do it,' Scarlett said.

'Oh, really, you're a pair of fusspots,' Eunice said. 'I'm sure I'll manage. Now, I better go and tell Captain Beaky the good news.' She air-kissed them both, then shuffled out, Clarence in tow, the bell screaming after her.

The second the door closed, Lloyd sagged against the wall, laughing with relief.

Scarlett looked at him, grinning. 'That was close.'

'Yup. But no harm done... And you get free weekends from now on.'

'Nice one. Thanks.' She high-fived him.

'Poor Eunice. I think she's really lonely. I suppose during the week she busies herself with appointments, but weekends are too quiet in the house.'

'And the daytime TV isn't as good.'

Lloyd huffed out a laugh. 'Probably. Though most people stream whatever they want, when they want these days, but she's probably of a generation that likes the comfort of TV at certain times.'

He put his arm around Scarlett's shoulder, and she rested her head on him.

'You know...' His lips brushed her hair. 'I'm starting to think we have a gift for being caught out.'

Scarlett tipped her head back, laughing. 'It definitely spices things up.'

He grinned, then sighed, letting the weight of everything settle on his shoulders for a moment. 'I wish I could give you more than this. More than stolen minutes in the back of a bookshop.'

She pulled back and looked up at him, straight and unblinking. 'You've already given me so much. You treat me like I matter. You make me feel...' She trailed off, struggling for words. 'Just so good. Like you actually want me, and not just for a quickie, though I'm not denying I like that side of things too.'

He pressed a gentle kiss to her forehead. 'So do I. I want you and I care about you.'

She leaned into him, wrapping her arms around his middle. 'Then we can work with that, yes?'

He stroked her hair. 'Yes.' Though he still couldn't see an easy way forward – not with the new house, the kids, his mum, and memories of Amy blocking the path in every direction. But he was used to life being tough, so if he wanted this, he knew what he had to do.

Keep fighting for it.

CHAPTER NINETEEN

Scarlett

'Do you want a lift home?' Lloyd asked as Scarlett locked up the bookshop. 'It's sub-zero out here, and I'm already numb in places I'd rather keep warm.'

'Yeah, thanks.'

They crossed the platform together, feet crunching over old grit, and Lloyd put his hand on the small of her back. She glanced up at him, and they shared a goofy grin. Everything about him made her insides brim to bursting point with happy bubbles. If she kept her eyes focused on him and didn't let her mind stray, it was easy to imagine nothing – or no one – could pop those bubbles.

Lloyd's car was a large charcoal coloured people carrier with roof bars and thick tyres. A sensible family car but still kind of sexy, though she couldn't really explain why.

'You ok?' He popped the central lock.

'Yeah, fine.'

The car smelt faintly of something nice – maybe the fragrance tree, or maybe just him. He looked good in the dusky light as he started the engine, hair all soft and mussed from the day.

'So, tomorrow's the day you get into your new house,' she said, remembering what he'd told Eunice.

'Yeah, the kids and I went to see it yesterday.' He reversed out of the slot. 'But I thought it was sensible waiting until the weekend before we move in, when we get the furniture delivered. Then hopefully they'll all muck in and help.'

'I hope it works out that way.'

He huffed out a dry laugh. 'Well, nothing about this move has so far. So, I don't have high hopes. The house itself is stunning. The flat we had in Edinburgh was in a great location. But more suited to single people or couples. It was too small for a family, and it had no garden. Also, the parking situation was dire. This house is a palace in comparison. Lewis has decided he wants a football net and a trampoline and a pet rabbit, all in the first week. Harry is pleased to have a bigger room, and he doesn't have to share anymore, but Eve – well.' He sighed. 'She's just not happy about any of this.'

'I feel your pain. But only because I was just like that at her age – probably worse. Ask Lilah.'

'I'd like to hope it's just a phase, but I feel so powerless to help her.'

'She probably doesn't want to be helped. I know I didn't. I thought I was the centre of the universe and that everyone else was in the wrong.' She hid her face. 'I'm not sure I got any better... Even in the summer I was being a drama queen.'

Lloyd put his hand on her thigh. 'You were in a terrible place in the summer. That ex of yours was an abuser. He treated you like shit and messed you up. But you got help. You got through it.'

'Has Eve had counselling?'

'Yes. All the kids have. And me. Eve's new guidance teacher is great too.'

'The one I overheard you talking to?'

'Yeah. Miss Morgan. She's a very kind person and has a natural warmth about her.'

'I noticed that. She helped me work out where to clean because I didn't have a clue what I was doing. Hopefully she'll help Eve too.'

'I'm sure she'll do her best.' They turned onto the main street. Every shop window had gone full Christmas with the lights and fake snow.

'Would you like to see the house?' Lloyd glanced over, his blue eyes flicking back and forth between her and the windscreen. 'I could give you a quick look before I take you home.'

'I'd love that.'

They coasted through the traffic lights and up the hill towards Golf Course Road, a well-known 'posh' street where Scarlett could only dream of living. With very little money and even fewer prospects, she couldn't afford a one-bedroom flat above the baker shop, never mind a property on a street like this. For now, she was stuck living with her mum, a fact that got more and more embarrassing the older she got. The two times she'd moved out were to move into dreadful shared accommodation with her exes – first Zeb, then Leon. A shudder ran through her at the thought. Never again.

She pressed her nose to the window. The houses were a mismatch of old and new, but all large with gardens and driveways decorated with twinkling fairy lights and outside Christmas trees. A couple had light-up reindeer and sleds on the lawn.

Lloyd pulled into the drive of one of the older houses, which had no lights or décor, and turned to her. 'This is it.'

She followed him up the path, crunching gravel, and did a slow three-sixty. The house was a neatly kept, well-proportioned Victorian house with large bay windows at the front. Not flashy in a show-home way, but impressive and very smart.

Fumbling with the keys, he found the right one and opened the door onto a small porch. The hall had a large staircase, a wooden floor and high ceilings.

Scarlett stepped in, closing the door behind her. With no furniture yet, just the smell of paint and floor cleaner, the place had an echo and an energetic aura... Like it was hovering on the verge of a new adventure.

She drifted through to the front room. Bare floorboards, plain walls, and a stunning real fireplace. From the bay window, she could see the wintery garden.

Lloyd watched her, hands in his pockets. 'What do you think?'

'It's beautiful,' she said, the word sticking in her throat.

'Yeah. I liked it. Though it'll be better once we have furniture.'

'And a fire with stockings on it… And a real tree, right here.' She gestured around the space in front of the window. It reminded her of the dream she'd had the night she'd had too much to drink, when she'd imagined she was standing outside a house like this, watching through the window, seeing Lloyd and the kids, all miserable and lost, until she'd run in and started singing at them like some deranged Christmas fairy.

'Exactly.' Lloyd ran his hand through his hair. 'Assuming I can get everything unpacked and in situ. It's been a struggle even to buy gifts this year. Last year was bad enough, but I was kind of on autopilot then. Now, it's like apathy. I need a firecracker up my rear end to get me into the spirit.'

'Yeah… This must be painful for you.' She wandered into the kitchen, which was even bigger, with a window overlooking the back garden. 'What's through there?'

'That's the utility room. And there's a basement down the backstairs, which I'm not sure if I like it or if it just creeps me out.'

'Still, you could have a workshop down there. Or store bodies, depending on how things go.'

He laughed. 'I knew you'd see the upside.'

She wandered back to the hall, trailing her fingers along the wood panels.

'This is where Lewis wants the other tree.' Lloyd pushed open another door. 'The first thing you see as you walk in. Though I think it would be better in here.'

Scarlett followed him into another large, empty room.

'The dining room.'

Her insides ached so badly to be part of this world with him. Or at least to help. Even if it was just for a week, or at Christmas, or one afternoon.

'You ok?' he asked, voice gentle.

She nodded. 'I really, really like it here.'

He smiled. 'Me too. Thank you for coming to see it.' Closing the door behind him, he crossed to the stairs.

'Thank you for showing me,' she replied. 'Is there anything I can do to help? I mean without intruding.' For a moment, she imagined what it would be like to spend Christmas here, to see the tree in the bay window, to fill the house with music and laughter.

He headed up the stairs. 'Well, I'm going to take Monday and Tuesday off to sort the place out. I might order some of the presents tonight and try to force myself into wrapping them. Would you want to help me with that?'

'Definitely. We could leave the shop closed on Monday and Tuesday and start the new opening hours next week. I could help you wrap, or unbox, or anything... if I'm not in the way, that is.'

He blinked, then grinned. 'You're serious.'

'Well... only if you want.'

He shook his head in disbelief, like he was trying to figure out why anyone would volunteer for such a job, then he reached out and pulled her into a hug. Wrapping his arms around her, he squeezed so tight his heartbeat thudded against her. 'I really would love that.'

She hugged him back, her face pressed into the side of his neck, and he exhaled into her hair, then he pressed a kiss to her cheek.

'You just answered another of my wishes.'

She kept her arms around him. How many of hers had he answered just by existing in her world and giving her moments like this?

He gave her another kiss. 'Let me take you home. I need to get Lewis from school.'

The drive to her mum's was quiet. Not the heavy kind, just amiable and comfortable. She glanced at him in the dim glow of the dashboard, watched his hands on the wheel, and smiled when he took her hand for a moment.

When they pulled up outside her mum's house, Lloyd cut the engine and looked over at her.

'I hope you know how much you matter to me. Even if...' He stopped.

'Even if what?'

He pressed his lips together. 'Even if I don't know how to do this right.'

She rubbed his thigh and squeezed it. 'It doesn't have to be right. You make me happy. Even sharing a little bit of that is good.'

He let out a breath, smiling like he might cry or laugh or both. 'I'm so glad we found each other again.'

After giving him a brief kiss, she opened the door.

'Good luck with the van tomorrow. I'll make sure Eunice is ok in the morning.'

'Thank you.'

She shut the door and stood in the dark, watching as he pulled away. The car turned the corner, taillights fading. How could a person be so happy and so sad at the same time?

Scarlett turned up at the bookshop the next day to find Eunice behind the counter like she'd never left. She wore a scarf patterned with dancing Santas looped around her neck, and it had an actual bell attached to it. Her arm was still tucked in a chunky grey sling. She was in her element, fussing over the wishing tree display.

'I love reading these.' She peered at one of the wishes. 'Though far too many people wishing for useless electronics. They need to stop being robots and get outside into the real world.'

'I just hope no one is disappointed if their wish doesn't come true,' Scarlett replied, unpacking a box of graphic novels.

'I have great faith in the wishing tree, and for everything else, there's Mastercard.'

Scarlett snorted, but before she could reply, the doorbell shrieked like it had been stabbed. A gust of cold air hit them, followed by Lloyd and Harry, both looking windblown and a bit sleep deprived.

'Morning.' Lloyd smiled at them both.

Harry trailed behind, his hood up, hands stuffed in the pockets of his black jacket.

Eunice brightened. 'I didn't think you were coming. And who is this young man?'

'Harry.' Lloyd put his hand on his son's shoulder. 'He's come to look at the manga section and get some peace.'

Lloyd leaned on the counter as Harry went around the corner.

'The removal van's delayed. Lewis is hyperactive and going wild in the empty space. Eve's barricaded herself in her bedroom and won't come out. My mum wants me to phone the removal company every five minutes even though we know they're running late, so Harry and I decided to take a breather.'

'That's the spirit!' Eunice cheered. 'Kids need to see adults carrying on, no matter what chaos is happening.'

'Someone's definitely carrying on, but I'm not sure it's me.'

Scarlett grinned at him.

Eunice was in full flow, chatting about her various medical appointments, the lack of anything worth watching on daytime

TV, and how she'd crocheted three hats for Clarence just out of boredom.

Lloyd took a step back and craned his neck to check Harry was ok in the other room. 'I can't stay too long in case the van arrives. Leaving Mum and Lewis in charge of that is not a good idea.'

'Well, everything's fine here,' Scarlett said. 'Eunice is doing great, and I was about to go myself.'

Eunice nodded. 'Yes, yes, I can manage perfectly well, though it was nicer when Captain Beaky was here.'

'Hmm... best to leave him at home.'

Harry returned with a book and showed it to Lloyd. Lloyd nodded, and Harry took it to the till, where Eunice fussed over him.

Lloyd edged closer to Scarlett, then leaned in and whispered. 'He needed an escape from his siblings. He likes his own company sometimes.'

Scarlett looked over at Harry and realised he was watching her and his dad.

As soon as he had the book, he came over and Lloyd ruffled Harry's hair. 'Come on, mate. Let's get back and see if the van has shown up.'

'Yeah.' Harry's eyes strayed to Scarlett for a second. He didn't look hostile, just a little puzzled, like he was trying to figure something out.

'See you.' Lloyd waved to them and headed for the door. Harry followed, but paused before he left, glancing back at Scarlett, his face still unreadable, stuck somewhere between shy and curious.

The bell screamed in protest.

Scarlett watched them go, something tight and hot twisting in her chest. What did Harry's look mean? Maybe he'd clocked the close way Lloyd had whispered to her and was unhappy about it – though he didn't look angry or sad.

'You alright, dear?' Eunice asked, breaking her reverie.

Scarlett nodded. 'Yeah. Just... thinking about stuff.'

Eunice patted her good hand over Scarlett's. 'Well, if you need to talk, you know where I am. I'm never short of things to say myself.' She started up again about her ex-husband and the parrot.

Scarlett's train of thought was broken, but an uneasy sense lingered, and she couldn't pinpoint it for bad or good... or what to do about it.

CHAPTER TWENTY

Lloyd

Harry sat in the passenger seat, flicking through the manga he'd picked at the shop as Lloyd drove back to the house.

'Weird how they go backwards,' Harry said. 'Like sometimes I don't get which speech bubble goes first, and it mucks up the story. At least the drawings are cool.'

'Yeah, I remember trying to read one to you when you first got into them, and I got confused too.'

Harry twisted in his seat to face him full on. 'One of the boys in my class has a collection of like fifty of these books.'

Lloyd turned onto the street. 'Wow. Lucky kid. Is he a new friend?'

'Kind of, yeah.'

A small weight lifted from Lloyd's shoulders, hearing Harry chatting about kids in his class. He was the quietest of Lloyd's kids, so to know that he'd made some connections was good.

'I'm glad you've made a friend.'

Harry's face flickered. 'I've made more than one. I play chess in the library at break with some others.'

'Chess?' Lloyd grinned. 'Well, you were always good at that.'

'I'm not that good, but I sometimes win. We usually just have a stalemate.'

'Sounds normal.'

'And...' Harry hesitated, twiddling the corner of his book. 'Is it ok if I join rugby? Not now, but after Christmas.'

Lloyd blinked. 'Absolutely. Of course it's ok.' Things were looking up. This had to count as a win. And he'd take it.

'Cool. There's a form you have to sign. And they do practice on Saturdays, but only for an hour.'

'We'll make it work.' Lloyd pulled up in the driveway and saw Lewis running full speed down the icy garden path, arms churning like a windmill. At the porch, Rita stood clutching her mug and shaking her head.

'What's he doing?' Harry frowned at his little brother.

Lloyd got out of the car and Lewis barrelled into him. 'Dad, can I show you something? It's super-important!'

'Sure.' Lloyd locked the car. 'What's up?'

Lewis led him inside, never breaking pace, narrating as they went. 'Right, so when you come in, this is where the first tree goes. The real tree. But in the living room, you have to see this, I measured it – there's room for two!'

'So, we've upped the total to three trees?'

Lewis pointed at the bay window, where a rectangle of winter sunlight landed. 'See? If you put the green tree there, and then the black tree in the corner, it's like an ambush. A Christmas trap!'

Lloyd blinked. 'I thought the black tree was for the hall?'

'Yeah, but it's a ninja tree, remember? So, it would look cool if it was sneaking up on the other tree.'

'Right. I'm not sure two trees in the one space will work. We don't even have one yet.'

'The vans have arrived!' Rita called from the hall.

'At last.' Lloyd headed out to greet the removal crew, and soon the driveway was a flurry of movement. Boxes piled up in the hall, furniture was ferried into various rooms, and the stairs creaked as people shunted up and down.

Eve came out of her room and sighed as Lloyd started fitting her bed together. He didn't exactly expect a thank you but come nighttime she might appreciate it if she didn't have to sleep on the floor.

As he worked, he let his mind wander. The old flat in Edinburgh had been suffocating, every room haunted by the memory of Amy. She'd been a bright, kinetic force, never still, always making plans. When she was gone, the place felt like a mausoleum. Maybe that was why he'd pushed for the move – he wanted the kids to have a shot at happiness somewhere that wasn't flooded with old ghosts. Was that just selfishness on his part?

Stop with the old arguments!

We're here now.

The headboard slipped and bumped his shin. 'Shit.'

'Dad?' Harry poked his head in.

'Sorry. Just fighting the bed.'

Harry hovered in the doorway, then padded in and sat on the floor. 'Can I help?'

'Sure, if you want.' Lloyd passed him the Allen key.

Harry tightened the bolts in silence, then said, 'I like this house.'

Lloyd tried not to look too eager. 'Yeah?'

'It's big, and the garden looks cool. And I don't have to share with Lewis. No offence to him, but he talks a lot and gets up at six.'

'No offence taken,' Lloyd said. 'I completely understand.'

Harry smiled, and it was beautiful to see. 'Maybe if the beds are up, we could all watch a movie tonight. I mean, some of the Christmas films are funny, right?'

'Of course. Sounds great. If we can find the TV and get it working. The broadband isn't connected yet, so we'll have to see if my phone works as a hotspot.'

'Wouldn't it be cool if we could project a movie onto the big wall before we hang the pictures up?'

Lloyd nodded. 'That would be brilliant. Only we don't have a projector.'

'I know.' Harry shrugged. 'The TV's fine. It just seemed like a cool idea.'

'Maybe I could order one.' He tightened the last bolt. 'If I remember. You might have to remind me.'

'Ok, Dad.'

Lloyd put his arm around his son and gave him a tight hug. 'You're a good lad.'

Harry ducked out of the embrace but didn't look angry. 'Whatever you say.'

By four o'clock, the house resembled a shipping depot on the losing end of a postal strike. The hall was grid-locked with boxes; the kitchen overflowed with crockery, and Lloyd's hands were two shades grubbier than when he'd started the day.

He flopped onto the bottom step, scrolling his phone with a thumb that barely bent anymore. A message from Scarlett blinked at the top of the screen.

Scarlett: Hope everything went well with the move!

Smiling, he typed back.

Lloyd: Yeah, not too bad, though I might retrain as a joiner at this rate.

He thumbed through the next few boxes, locating the bag of screws for the final bed – the one that mattered least, because it was his, and he doubted anyone would care if he slept on the floor. The removal crew had put the mattress in the master bedroom, but it still felt echoey and empty.

He'd invested in a new bed. Silly maybe, but the old bed would always be full of images of Amy. And many of them sad images. Ways he didn't want to remember her. Not yet. Maybe never. It hurt to think of the years she'd been ill. How she'd faded away. How hope had gone up and down, until eventually it was lost, and they could do nothing but wait for the inevitable.

He laid out the slats, then sat down on the floor to read the instructions. Halfway through, he stopped. The room felt too big, too bright, and in a few hours he'd be alone in it, listening to the wind rattling the sash windows.

His phone vibrated. Another message from Scarlett.

Scarlett: I forgot you were so god at DIY. Hope you have a good first night in the new house.

He grinned at her typo.

Lloyd: I'm not a god at DIY... but thanks anyway.

After he hit send, he bent over the bed, screwing each slat into place.

'Dad, can we get Wi-Fi?' Eve stood at the door, arms folded.

'I'll set up a hotspot on my phone.' Lloyd sat up, brushing dust off his jeans. 'Have you run out of data?'

She frowned. 'Yeah, because I needed to message people. We're trying to learn lines.'

'Lines?'

'For a play,' Eve said, like this should have been obvious. 'At school. We're doing *A Christmas Carol*. I'm the Ghost of Christmas Past.'

He blinked, then smiled. 'Did you audition?'

'I was forced into it.' Eve tucked a loose strand behind her ear, refusing to look at him. 'It's not a big deal. That Miss Morgan made me do it.'

'She's really nice. I don't see her forcing anyone. I'm sure she was just encouraging you. And you must have been good to get the part.'

Eve rolled her eyes, but there was a smile fighting its way out. 'I guess I was ok.'

'So... who were you messaging about it?'

'Like the other people in the play.' She held out her hands as though it was blatantly obvious.

'I see.' He didn't push it, but surely that meant she had friends. 'So... when is it? Do I get to see it?'

'Obviously. It's just before we come off for the holidays. You have to buy tickets.'

'I'm sure I can do that.' Lloyd grinned, his heart lighter than it had been in months. He remembered what Miss Morgan had said at the meeting about trying to encourage Eve to do drama. Silently, he thanked the lovely lady.

Looking around the room at the half-assembled furniture, he yawned. But the bone deep tiredness was slowly ebbing away, and something else was seeping in.

Hope.

If he could just hold on to it.

CHAPTER TWENTY-ONE

Scarlett

By the time Scarlett reached Lloyd's house on Monday morning, her toes were so frozen she couldn't feel them inside her boots. It wasn't too far from her mum's house to Golf Course Road. Standing on the doorstep of a house like this may as well have been part of a dream. Scarlett Finch had no business being here.

But why not? Since the summer split with Leon, the fling with Lloyd, the counselling, and now the job in the bookshop, Scarlett felt like a new woman. Drawing attention to herself in whatever crazy ways she'd done before didn't feel like something she had to do now. Because she wasn't with a guy who didn't care. She was strongly aware that even if she and Lloyd got together, she'd have to share his attention, but it was ok. Sharing the attention of a man who loved his kids was a lot more appealing than trying desperately to get the attention of someone who loved getting high or going out to get smashed.

The whole horror of her past relationships flared before her. How, at twenty-five, had she already done so badly? One thing was certain, she had to break the pattern. Her hand rose to knock. But the door opened.

'Hey!' Lloyd's hair was in maximum disarray, his eyes bright. He pulled her in with a hug, not even hesitating, and held on a few seconds too long. 'You made it. I'm so glad you're here.'

She grinned, letting herself soak in the warmth of his body, his smell, the general Lloyd-ness of him. 'I'm looking forward to whatever work you have for me.'

He pulled back but didn't let go of her. 'Thank you. I've made soup for later, and bought plenty of food. The heating's working, so we'll be nice and cosy.'

'You're so sweet.' She wrapped her arms around his neck. He really was such a thoughtful man.

He finally released her. 'Come in.'

She followed him in. Boxes formed weird little cities across the hallway. The living room was half empty, but the fire was on and the window seat had a cushion and a blanket draped over it. It looked cosy already.

'If we can unload these boxes first, that would be great.' Lloyd pointed to the boxes nearest the door.

They set to work, unpacking books, cushions, lamps, and photos in frames. Lloyd put together a bookshelf and Scarlett tried not to get distracted as he rolled up his sleeves and nailed the shelves into place. But her eyes hadn't got the memo and kept straying up to see what he was doing.

Once the shelf was up, he started organising the books, every now and then having to get up as deliveries came, bringing the gifts he'd ordered for his kids.

He and Scarlett chatted a lot of the time. Sometimes about the house, sometimes about the kids, occasionally about Skye. Even when they weren't talking, the silence was easy, and Scarlett's body was warm with a deep sense of wellbeing and safety.

'Objectively, this is so much better than our old place. The size, the garden, the proximity to schools and grandparents.' Lloyd stared at the window from his place on the floor among a pile of books. 'The flat was... full of ghosts, I guess. It was hard for all of us. I wanted a proper home for them. But this is hard too.'

Scarlett shuffled over and took his hand. 'Maybe there wasn't one good choice and one bad choice. You weighed up what was needed and made a tough decision.'

He nodded. 'Exactly, but it means I'll never know if it was the right one.'

'Give it time.'

Lloyd put his arm around her shoulder. 'I really am glad I found you again.'

'Me too.' She leaned into him.

'I'm a bit more hopeful after the weekend that the kids are coming around. Harry asked to join the rugby club after Christmas, and Eve's got a part in the school drama. *A Christmas Carol*. She's the Ghost of Christmas Past.'

'Oh, wow. That's great.'

'Yeah. She's downplaying it, but she wouldn't have done it unless she wanted to. We know how stubborn she can be.'

'As most teenagers can.'

'Well, it's the most Christmassy thing she's done for a while. Unlike Lewis, who still wants a black Christmas tree for the hallway but now wants another one to ambush the other tree… or something like that.' Lloyd rubbed his forehead. 'I kind of lost the thread of what he was talking about.'

'How could you?' Scarlett laughed and prodded him. 'I think I still have a black Christmas tree in the cupboard at my mum's house. From when I went through my goth phase. If I find it, you can have it.'

'You just made his year. You'll be the hero of the house.'

Maybe not quite that, but if she could make his wish come true, that was what she was all about.

Later, they finished up the boxes in the dining room and Lloyd's office, then sat on the window seat with mugs of hot chocolate, watching the world outside.

'It's almost three.' Scarlett checked her phone. 'Should I make myself scarce before you have to get Lewis from school?'

'If that's ok.' He looked at her, then at his phone. 'But we've got a few minutes left.'

She set down her mug. 'For what?'

He stood, went over to a side table and put his phone into a newly unpacked speaker. Soft Christmas music drifted from it. 'Do you want to dance?'

She laughed. Was he joking? The look on his face was dead serious and a bit shy. 'Um... ok.'

She let him pull her up, and he tucked his hand around her waist. He was tall enough to make her feel like she was being twirled by a proper ballroom pro. The Christmas music in the background was slow, and he moved her around the space in the living room.

They didn't speak, just danced, and she looked into his bright blue eyes. The feeling in her chest was so big she couldn't even process it.

When the song ended, he didn't let go. He leaned in and kissed her gently but firmly.

'Thank you.' He broke the kiss but not the embrace. 'You make it all feel possible.'

She buried her face in his neck, laughing and nearly crying at the same time. 'Why am I so happy with you?'

'I know. But I feel the same with you.'

'Don't say stuff like that unless you mean it.'

'I mean it.'

She pulled away, just enough to see his face. 'Go get Lewis.' She shoved him lightly.

'See you tomorrow, yeah?' he asked.

'I'll be here,' she promised.

Nothing would keep her away, and if she could, she wouldn't return empty-handed. The cupboards at her mum's house were stuffed full of craft supplies and things her mum had kept 'in case they might be useful'. She rummaged through the one under the stairs until she found the ripped cardboard box containing the black Christmas tree.

Upstairs in her room, she got it out and dusted it down. It was only a small four-foot tree, but still, if it made Lewis happy then he was welcome to it.

The following morning, Patricia stared at Scarlett as she propped the tree by the door ready to take with her.

'What are you doing with that? You're not planning on putting it up, are you?' Patricia set down her mug and gaped.

Scarlett shook her head. 'Not here, no.'

'Not at the shop. It'll ruin the place.'

'Nope. It's for Lloyd's son.'

Patricia's eyebrows shot up, but she didn't say anything for a long moment. 'His son? Are you seeing this man now? For real?'

Scarlett shrugged. 'Not exactly. But we're friends, and I want to help him if I can.'

Patricia got up, came over, and brushed the hair off Scarlett's shoulder with a gentle hand. 'Just... be careful, ok?'

'I know, Mum. I really do. But being with Lloyd doesn't feel anything like being with my exes. I know it's going to be hard no matter what happens. He's got baggage – lots of it. But he's worth it.'

They stood in silence for a minute, then Patricia nodded. 'He sounds like a good guy. Maybe I'll get to meet him one day.'

'You will... I hope.'

Half an hour later, Scarlett lugged the tree across Lloyd's front garden. A bitter wind whipped down Golf Course Road and tried to strip her face off.

The door opened as she was halfway up the path. Lloyd stood in the frame. When he saw the tree, his face lit up.

'What's this?' He took the box from her as she came inside.

'The black Christmas tree.'

'Oh, wow.' He pushed his glasses up his nose and grinned at the box. 'Lewis is going to lose his mind.'

She kicked off her boots and left them next to Lloyd's in the porch. 'Shall we put it in the hall?'

He put his hand on her shoulder. 'Thank you so much for this.'

'It's really nothing. Like I'd be using it again.'

'Come in and warm up.' He helped her out of her jacket, then without even thinking about it, she reached up and kissed him on the lips. It was warm, and so delicious it got her hot inside, and she nearly forgot to breathe.

'Nice way to start the day.' He grinned and propped the box in the hallway. 'Maybe we should let Lewis set it up. He knows the vision best.'

'That's sensible.'

'Most of the presents are here, and I printed off some labels, so we can unbox and wrap if that's still ok.'

'Sounds great.'

He led her through to the living room, where he'd stacked a pile of delivery boxes, with scissors, tape and sheets of printed labels nearby. Soft Christmas music played from the speakers again.

They sat side by side, the presents forming a barrier between them. Lloyd started with a Nerf gun, a Pokémon plushie, and some books. The labels he'd printed were on an A4 sheet divided into eighteen. There was a sheet for each child with their name in fancy script in a Christmassy border.

'This was Amy's idea,' he said. 'And it works really well. Not only can we make sure the presents don't get muddled, but it means everyone has the same amount. eighteen presents. It sounds like a lot, but most of them are just silly stocking fillers really.'

'Wow. So organised.'

'Some are easier than others. Finding eighteen presents for Eve is getting trickier. I'm not attuned to what teenage girls like. I kind of wish there was an easy-buyer's guide or something helpful.'

'Do you want some suggestions?'

'Yeah.'

'Ok... make-up, hair products, false nails, perfume, a tennis bracelet or a charm bracelet, earbuds, a waffle maker, gift cards for coffee shops, candles, string lights, fluffy slippers... I'm sure I could think of more, though she might not be happy if she knows it's me who picked them.'

'Well, if you could write them into a note on my phone, I'll use the ideas to choose things, so she doesn't think I haven't put in any effort at all.' He handed over his phone.

Grinning, Scarlett took it and added ideas to a new list.

'She'll start believing in Santa again when she sees all this,' he said. 'Because she'll know it wasn't me.'

Scarlett laughed, adding aromatherapy candles to the list. 'You do a good job.'

For a second, the lightness in his face dimmed. 'Sometimes I feel like I'm barely keeping it together. Like I'm just pretending to be what they need.'

She set down the phone, reached over, and touched his wrist. 'You're amazing. You care so much even when you want to shut down and hide yourself away. But you show up and you keep going.'

He let out a sigh. 'I'm trying. I just hope the kids see it and don't dwell on the negative stuff. It would kill me to think that in a few years' time, when they're adults, that they don't want to come back, or they blame me for giving them a traumatic childhood.'

'They've had a traumatic childhood anyway, Lloyd. There's no escaping that.'

'And have I made it worse?'

Scarlett leaned her head on him. 'You could be sitting in your flat in Edinburgh wondering exactly the same thing.'

'I guess that's true.'

They kept going, Scarlett wrapping, and Lloyd adding labels. On the mantelpiece was a family photo. Lloyd, his kids, and his late wife. The kids looked similar to how they did now, so it must've been taken shortly before Amy died. She had on a beanie hat, and her eyes and skin looked drawn, but she was smiling. Scarlett's heart cracked, and a tear fell down her face. How must the poor woman have felt knowing she wouldn't be around to see her kids growing up?

Lloyd followed her sightline then reached up and wiped the tear from under her eye. 'Hey, what's up?'

'Just so sad about your wife, which I know is stupid, because I didn't know her... and now...' She looked at Lloyd. Now, she was in love with the woman's husband.

'Yeah. I get it.'

'She was beautiful.'

'She was. I still don't really know how to do this. Moving on. I want to, but no matter what I do, I worry: is it fair to the kids? Or to her? Or to you?'

'Or you.' She squeezed his hand, then let go, and returned to wrapping.

'Yep, it's messy alright. I like the idea of us being friends... but I also like the idea of us being more. I just don't know how to make that happen.'

'I don't think there's a right way. I just know I feel good when I'm with you, and surely that's a good start.'

'Yes, it is.' He glanced at the clock. 'Shall we eat? There's still soup.'

Scarlett got to her feet, and they went to the kitchen. Together, they set up the table, and Lloyd heated the soup.

'I've got an idea for the shop.' Scarlett leaned on the work surface next to him.

'Yeah?' His face brightened.

'There's this Icelandic tradition called Jolabokaflod. It means Christmas Book Flood. Basically, everyone gets a book on Christmas Eve, and then they just spend the night reading, with snacks and hot chocolate and whatever. I thought maybe we could do a thing at the shop. Put together gift packs, or even just tell people about it and get them excited.'

Lloyd stared at her for a second, then a slow, amazed smile spread across his face. 'That is the most perfect idea I've ever heard.'

'Really?'

'Absolutely. It's so right for the shop, for the town. And for you. You're a Christmas fairy after all.'

She rolled her eyes, but she couldn't stop herself from grinning. 'Can I run with it, then?'

'Run wild. Whatever you want. You're the boss now.'

'Don't say that. You know what happens when you let me take charge.'

He cupped her face in his hands. 'I love it when you do.'

Heat rose from her core to her cheeks.

'And I think you're wonderful.' He kissed her, a lingering, hungry one this time. When he broke off, he hugged her, arms tight around her back, and she buried her face in his shoulder, inhaling the warm, safe smell of him.

They held on for a long time, rocking slightly, the kind of hug she never wanted to end. She shifted and felt him pressed against her. She giggled into his neck. 'Do you want to use the "benefits" card now?'

He groaned, but it was a happy one. 'I've been trying to be good. But you're making it impossible.'

'You really shouldn't say "impossible" around me. It's like a dare.'

He loosened his grip just enough to look her in the eyes, blue and shining and very, very needy. 'Let's have lunch first. We might need the energy.'

They made eyes at each other all through lunch before stacking the dishwasher.

'Maybe you'd like a tour of the bedroom now?' Lloyd winked at her.

'You bet I do.'

The bedroom was still half-unpacked, with a duvet flung wild across the mattress and a tower of cardboard boxes in one corner. None of it mattered. Lloyd pulled Scarlett close, and they toppled onto the bed, still in their clothes, laughing into each other's mouths. For a few seconds it was just hands – her fingers tangled in his hair, his thumb drawing lines down her spine, both of them smiling.

Physical contact brought so much joy, and Scarlett's insides were warm and fuzzy already.

He nuzzled into her neck and whispered, 'This feels so depraved on a Tuesday afternoon, but I really enjoy it.'

'Me too.'

He kissed her again, deep and determined, and slipped his fingers beneath her top. She let him, even though her hands shook so much she could barely undo his buttons. The energy inside her pulsed so hard she might burst.

When she was down to her bra, he paused, sitting back on his heels, just looking in the way that said, *you are exactly what I want.*

'You're staring again,' she said.

'You know I like looking at you.'

'And what do you see now?' She reached behind, flicked the catch open, and tossed the bra away. His hungry eyes travelled over her, and his breath caught.

'I see someone thoughtful, kind, and helpful. Someone who's been through a lot of pain this year, but who's still willing to help another broken soul.' He ran his warm palm down her shoulder, skimming the curve of her breast, and she gasped.

'I wish I'd brought the edible underwear.' She raised an eyebrow.

'I don't think we need it... Let's do a taste test.' He leaned down, mouth brushing the sensitive skin on her breast, then her stomach, then lower, his hands steady as he shimmied her jeans off. Tossing back her head, she moaned as he pressed his mouth to her thigh, breathing her in, then kissed his way up. When his tongue brushed over her, she jerked, shocked by how good it felt. He moved so carefully, so methodically, and so lovingly.

She bit down on her hand, trying not to shout, but the more he did, the more impossible it got. She locked her thighs around his head, and he hummed in pleasure, the vibration sending her over the edge. The sensations were so strong they almost hurt.

When she caught her breath, he crawled up beside her, smiling that soft, secret smile of his.

'You're magic.' Her eyes rolled back as aftershocks hit. 'There's no one like you.'

'It's all for you.'

'For us.' She pulled him on top of her and kissed him, loving the way he seemed to need her as much as she needed him. 'In my bag...' She reached her arm out, scrabbling to find it. 'I have condoms.'

'Ok.' He found one, tore it open, rolled it on, and lined himself up against her. For a second, he paused, stroking her cheek, making sure she was ready. 'You've shown me how to feel again. So much of me was dead inside until I met you this summer.'

She pulled him in, wrapping her legs around his hips, and he sank into her.

'And you showed me how this should really feel. How good sex can be with a caring partner.'

'I'll always care about you.' He started moving slowly, kissing her everywhere – her lips, her nose, her collarbone. Her heart pounded so hard she thought it might break through her ribs.

Soon she was lost in the sensation, the heat and the pressure and the knowing she was safe, adored, exactly where she wanted to be. When she felt herself starting to coil inside again, she looked him straight in the eye and kept looking. Her insides flooded with love. This was the physical manifestation of how her heart felt. So much love.

Holding her tight, he murmured her name, and moved faster, the intensity building until she couldn't hold it anymore. She cried out, her hands clawing at his back.

He followed her over the edge, groaning into her neck as he went rigid in her arms, and then they both collapsed, a tangled mess of limbs and laughter.

His hand stroked over her hair, down her back, and she snuggled into his chest, completely content.

'You ok?' he whispered.

'Never better.'

He kissed the top of her head. 'I think I'm in real danger.'

'Of what?'

'Falling for you so hard I might break bones when I hit the bottom.'

She swallowed. 'Do you mean that?'

'Of course I do.'

The smile wouldn't leave her face. Maybe it never would.

They lay half asleep until an alarm on Lloyd's phone started vibrating against the bedside table.

He groaned. 'That's the school pickup.'

She giggled. 'You have to go be Dad now.'

'I do. But I don't want to let you go.'

'Just for now. I'll see you again tomorrow. At the shop.'

'Yeah. Definitely.'

She reached up and kissed him. 'And I'll start advertising the jolabokaflod.'

He got up and started searching for a shirt.

After lying on the bed for a minute longer, Scarlett wriggled into her clothes, her body still humming from everything that had happened.

They went downstairs together. Lloyd kissed her at the door.

'Thank you for today. For the tree. For everything.'

'Thank you for letting me in,' she said.

She walked home with a smile so wide not even the biting cold wind could blow it away. As she crossed the road to go down to her mum's house, she saw a woman trudging up, head down against the wind, face screwed up like she was in pain. Scarlett's insides squirmed. That was Lloyd's mum. Even the brief sighting made Scarlett's heart pound. Rita Miller did not like or approve of her. And that wasn't likely to get any better if she discovered where Scarlett had just been and what she'd been doing.

Dropping her chin into her scarf, Scarlett rounded the bend, hoping against hope that Rita hadn't seen her.

Chapter Twenty-Two

Lloyd got back to the house with Lewis, who hadn't stopped talking all the way home from school, even when Amanda Reid had walked partway with them and told Lloyd about some church events that were happening for Christmas. Lloyd hadn't mastered listening to two different conversations despite having three kids, and his head felt like it had been put through a wringer.

The door wasn't locked, which made him frown. Maybe he'd forgotten in the muddle of saying bye to Scarlett. But when he heard someone moving inside, his pulse leapt. Had Scarlett come back?

'Who's in the house?' Lewis asked.

'It's only me.' Rita appeared in the hall.

Lewis ran to greet her, but a bubbling acid burnt the insides of Lloyd's chest. 'I didn't know you were coming.' Lloyd hung up his coat, then closed the porch door behind him. 'You should have given me some warning. I thought you were a burglar.' He appreciated everything his mum did for him – and hell, he moved here partly so she could help him out – but he wasn't sure he appreciated her just coming in like this unannounced.

She fixed her gaze on him, eyes narrowing behind her glasses, as Lewis ran off up the stairs like a baby elephant.

'I went down to the shop earlier. And there was nobody there. It was all closed up,' she said.

'Today's Tuesday,' Lloyd replied. 'It's always closed on Tuesdays.'

'I know that.' Rita pursed her lips. 'But Eunice told me she was working weekends now and that Scarlett was doing the weekdays, but she wasn't there either. The place was all closed up. And when I was coming up the road, I saw her wandering about. She clearly hadn't been to work.'

'Scarlett's starting full-time next week. Yesterday and today, we were closed as usual.'

Rita scowled and shook her head. 'I need to sit down. My back's giving me hell.'

'Then why did you walk all the way to the shop?'

'I had to go into the town anyway. I needed to post my Christmas cards. Then I met a friend of mine. I mentioned that Scarlett was working at the shop, and, my goodness, did she have a lot to say about that girl!'

Lloyd counted to five. 'So what? Give her a break. She's done a good job so far, and she has some really great ideas.'

Rita huffed out a sigh, and Lloyd folded his arms before continuing. 'Whatever she's done in the past, she's a nice person, ok... And I happen to—'

Lewis came thumping back down, and his eyes landed on the box with the black tree in it. 'What is *that*?' His eyes widened.

'A black Christmas tree, just for you.'

'Where did you get it?'

He could lie. With Rita watching him like this, it would be far easier. But that wasn't fair. Lewis should know exactly who had made this wish come true.

'Scarlett brought it over for you.'

'She was here?' Rita gaped at Lloyd.

'Wow.' Lewis ran to the box and started pulling out the tree. 'This is so cool. I can decorate it with my ninja cats.' He ran off up the stairs again.

Rita shook her head. 'Lloyd.' She sighed. 'What are you playing at with this girl? She's far too young for you. It's blatantly obvious what she wants from you.'

'Which is what?' Lloyd gripped the edge of the doorframe.

'Your money. A house like this.'

'No.' Lloyd shook his head. 'It's nothing like that. She's not like that. It would be crazy of her to think like that. I come with a lot of baggage.'

'Exactly. Too much for someone of her age. So don't play around with her. You'll both end up getting hurt.'

'I've already been hurt in so many ways. And...' He swallowed. Divulging to his mum that he felt happier with her than he had in ages felt too dangerous an admission.

'Yes?' Rita watched him closely. When he didn't continue, she said, 'You need to be sensible. For your kids' sake.'

'I will always do what's best for my kids,' he muttered.

The front door banged open, and Eve and Harry came in chatting. They slung their bags and coats up in the porch, then came into the hall.

'Hi, Gran,' Harry said. 'I didn't know you were coming.'

'You need to check your emails,' Eve said to Lloyd.

'Why?'

'There's something about tickets for the school show.'

Rita leaned in, all attention. 'What's this?'

Eve fished out her phone, tapping through screens. '*A Christmas Carol*. It's the last week of term. I'm in it. The teachers made me do it.'

'Made you?' Rita raised an eyebrow.

'Well, Miss Morgan said it would be "good for me"—' she air-quoted '—so I did it. She came to the audition with me and said I was really good, but it wasn't up to her who got the part. But I did anyway.' She smiled, and Lloyd almost fainted at the sight, then she added in a spooky voice, 'I am the ghost of Christmas past.'

'This I must see,' Rita said.

'Then Dad needs to book, or you won't get seats.'

Lloyd opened his email and, sure enough, there was the school office message. 'Ok, I'll book us all a seat.'

His mind took a mini detour, wishing he could invite Scarlett, but that wasn't exactly going to work. Eve wouldn't want that, and neither would Rita. And if Lloyd wanted any kind of future with Scarlett, that was going to be a major issue. But how to find a way around the two women currently in his life?

On Friday at the bookshop, Lloyd was hiding out in the upstairs office with his laptop, doing banking work while enjoying watching the trains come and go from the window. Downstairs, the faint murmur of Christmas music drifted up, along with the knowledge that Scarlett was there. Not far away.

He glanced at the clock. Nearly lunchtime. This week, he'd behave and not close the shop early so they could do unspeakable things to each other, though he wouldn't deny the thought was a sweet one. They could close up for half an hour and have a sandwich.

As he reached the bottom of the stairs, he caught her mid-conversation with a customer, selling an obscure book about the secret life of eels. She had her hair up in a scruffy bun. Her red top looked very festive, but also very Scarlett when teamed with the short tartan skirt, knitted thigh-highs and thick chunky boots. In her ears were flashing stars Lloyd hadn't noticed earlier.

When the customer left, Lloyd followed him to the door and locked it. 'Were you wearing those earrings this morning?'

Scarlett beamed. 'Yeah, but I didn't switch them on until I opened the shop.'

'Very festive.' He winked at her.

'Just getting in the spirit.'

'What will you do for Christmas Day?' He ran his hand over the back of his neck. Of course he would love to have her around to his but that wasn't really something that could happen.

'Probably go to Aidan and Lilah's with Mum.' She gave a little shrug. 'I don't usually plan much, just gatecrash a party where I can.'

'Well, I hope it's a good one. It's not long now. Just a couple of weeks. We still haven't got the main tree, though Lewis is still loving changing the display on the black tree every day.'

'Eunice was talking about a Christmas tree farm on the side of Loch Briar where you can cut your own. I think she wanted to go, but she can't drive or lift a tree.'

'She could come with us if she wanted, but I'm not sure I'll succeed in getting all three kids to agree to that.' He slapped his hand against his forehead. 'Shit.'

'What?' Scarlett looked alarmed.

'I just remembered something. Harry asked last week if we could project a movie onto the wall. I was going to order a projector and surprise him with a Friday movie night. But I forgot.'

Scarlett chewed her lip. 'I think I have one. One of the things you connect to your phone. I bought it for Leon's birthday before we split. I think it's still under my bed. I was going to return it, but I don't think I did. I could look for it, if you want.'

Lloyd blinked. 'Seriously?'

'Yeah, I'll check tonight.'

'Wow. You really are the Christmas fairy who grants all the wishes. First a black tree, then coming up with all those gifts for Eve, and now this.'

'Happy to help.'

He gave her a little wink. 'Thank you.'

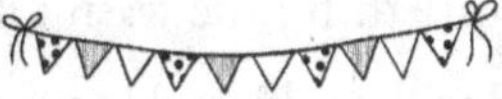

It was almost five, and Lloyd was in the kitchen with the kids, who were all constructing their own pizzas on pre-made bases.

'Guess what, movie night is on the wall. I've found a projector for us.'

Harry looked up. 'Seriously? Did you buy one?'

'I'm borrowing one.'

Scarlett had messaged to say she'd found one, and she was happy to drop it off. Lloyd hated putting her out of her way, but she was so determined. He loved her for it. So much his heart might burst. She cared about him, and she was really trying to make things easier for him.

He smiled, then caught Eve watching him.

'Who are you borrowing it from?' she said.

'Scarlett.'

Eve made a face. 'That woman from the shop?'

'Yeah. She really wanted to help out and make Christmas special for us all.'

'Right.' Her sceptical tone said it all.

Lloyd let out a sigh and turned away. This fight wasn't going to be an easy win. He took Harry and Lewis's pizzas and put them in the oven.

'Hey!' Harry ducked out of the room after Lewis, who'd grabbed Harry's tablet and run off with it.

Lloyd's insides strained under the tension of what he should do about Eve and Scarlett. But he wasn't doing either of them any favours by dodging the subject. He turned back to her.

'Can I ask you something?'

She raised one eyebrow in a perfect teenager move. 'What?'

'Do you honestly want me to stay on my own forever? No one else in my life except you, Harry and Lewis?'

Her face flushed red, and for a second he thought she was going to storm off. Instead she muttered, 'I just don't want someone replacing Mum.'

Lloyd's chest ached. 'No one could ever do that. Not Scarlett, not anyone. Your mum will always be your mum. I loved her. I'll always love her. But it doesn't mean I can't care about someone else too.'

Eve picked at her sleeve. 'Scarlett's nearer my age than yours. She doesn't... fit.'

'Fit how?'

'I don't know. Just... she's not us. She doesn't get it. She doesn't know what we've been through.'

Lloyd nodded. 'You're right. She doesn't. And that's why she's trying so hard. Because she wants to. Because she cares about me, and I'm sure she'd grow to like all of you. I wouldn't want her to be a mum to any of you. I wouldn't want anyone to do that. You could just be friends. But you don't have to like her overnight. All I'm asking is that you give her a fair chance.'

Her lips pressed together in a stubborn line.

'Listen,' he said, keeping his voice quiet. 'I don't expect you to approve of every decision I make. But you, Harry and Lewis, are the most important people in my life, and I want us to be honest with each other. I'm not going to hide Scarlett, or anyone else I care about, in the shadows. That's not fair on her and it's not fair on me. What I need from you is time. And maybe a little grace. Can you try that, for me?'

Eve didn't answer right away. The silence stretched, broken only by the muffled sound of Lewis laughing from the other room. Finally, she shrugged, her eyes on the carpet. 'I'll... try,' she muttered. 'But I'm not promising I'll like her.'

The tension eased a little, pushing a lump into his throat. It wasn't acceptance, but it was a crack in the wall. 'That's all I ask,' he said.

He reached out, brushing his hand lightly over her shoulder. For a moment, she let him. Then she shifted away, pulling out her phone like the conversation was over.

Lloyd lifted her pizza as she retreated into the glow of the screen. If only he could fix everything with a single talk... *I wish love worked like a switch you could flick on.* But it didn't. It would take time. Patience. A thousand small moments.

And as much as it hurt, he'd do whatever it took.

CHAPTER TWENTY-THREE

Scarlett

Scarlett paused outside the house, clutching the projector box under her arm. The December air clawed at her face. Just knowing his family were inside sent nervy jitters through her tummy. This wasn't only about Lloyd anymore. If things between them grew serious, there would always be more people in the room – his children, his history, his whole world. She couldn't assume a place in it, not when one of them clearly didn't want her there. But if she wanted a real chance with Lloyd, she had to try. She could show up, be kind, and hope they might one day accept her. Still, a cold thought prickled at the back of her mind: what if they never did?

Lloyd opened the door. His hair was at full mad professor level, but he smiled broadly.

'Come in. Quick, it's freezing.'

She stepped into the porch and kicked off her boots. The house was warm and smelled faintly of cooking. Lloyd led her inside, then closed the door with a gentle click.

'Thank you so much for doing this.' His gaze held hers. 'I feel terrible dragging you out on a night like this.'

She gave a shrug and a smile. 'I told you. I wanted to do it.'

'Scarlett's here!' Lewis came bounding out of the living room and screeched to a halt inches from her.

'Hi, Lewis.'

'Look at the tree.' He gestured proudly to where the black Christmas tree sat in the hallway, fully decked in ninja cats, tinsel, and one actual sock. Scarlett's heart did a small twist and she giggled.

'Wow, I've never seen anything like it.'

'It's the best tree ever.'

Lloyd ruffled his hair.

'And thank you for letting us use it,' Lewis added.

'You're welcome. I'll leave you to it then.'

'No, come and see.' Lewis took her hand and dragged her into the living room. Eve didn't look up from her phone, but Harry smiled faintly.

'Hi,' she said.

'Hi.' Harry gave a little wave, and Eve grunted something that could have been 'hi' but was maybe just a reaction to something on her phone.

Lloyd sat down and patted the seat next to him. 'Can you show us how it works before you go?'

Scarlett sat next to him, and Lewis plopped down on her other side. The same warmth she always felt around Lloyd radiated from him. The opposite of the icy vibes she was getting from Eve.

'Can I open the box?' Lewis said.

'Yeah.' Scarlett handed it to him, and he pulled off the round seal and opened it. 'It's new, but it's been in a box for several months, so I hope it works. I've never used it, so I'm probably not the best person to get it going.'

'Harry's very good with the tech,' Lloyd said. 'I'm sure he'll get it working.'

Lewis took out the white projector, which looked a bit like a camera lens, and the assorted cables. Lloyd lifted the instruction booklet, pushed up his glasses and studied it. Scarlett leaned in to look too, their heads close, knees touching.

Harry stood up and wandered over. 'I see how it works. Can I have your phone?'

Lloyd handed it to him.

'Is the black Christmas tree from when you were a kid?' Lewis asked Scarlett.

'No, I bought it when I was having a goth phase.'

'What's a goth?'

'It's a way of dressing – mostly in black and being interested in certain music, art, films. Usually quite dark stuff.'

'Is it scary?'

'Not really. I just like dressing in black stuff and doing the make-up styles. I wasn't heavily into the lifestyle.'

'Just means you dress like a witch,' Eve muttered.

Lloyd gave her a look and shook his head.

'Are you gonna stay for the movie?' Lewis asked.

'Probably not.' She didn't need to look at Eve to know she wasn't wanted.

'You should,' Harry said. 'You were the one who brought the projector.'

It was the first time he'd really spoken to her. 'No problem.' Scarlett blinked.

Harry took the projector from Lewis and pushed a cable into it.

'What are you going to watch?' Scarlett asked.

'*The Grinch*,' Harry said.

'We voted,' Lewis said. 'Eve wanted to watch *A Christmas Carol*, but she lost.'

Eve's prickly aura grew a few more spikes.

'She only wanted to watch it because she's in the play at school,' Lewis went on.

Scarlett smiled over at Eve. 'That's so cool that you got a part. I love *A Christmas Carol*. It's my all-time favourite Christmas story. That and *Love Actually*. Which I know is a crime to admit these days, but I love that moment where the guy comes to the door with handwritten signs... I just wish he wasn't showing them to a married woman. I'm always thinking up better endings for some of the couples.'

From the far side of the sofa, Eve muttered, 'Sounds like a load of crap.' She didn't look up.

'Really, Eve. Be nice, please,' Lloyd said.

Scarlett shuffled forward on the seat. 'Looks like Harry's sorted everything. I'll leave you to enjoy the family time.'

Lloyd touched her hand – just a feather touch, but enough to light up every nerve from knuckle to wrist. 'Ok.'

'I don't mind if you stay,' Harry said.

'Me neither,' Lewis chipped in.

Eve rolled her eyes loudly.

Scarlett got to her feet. 'I'll leave you to enjoy it as a family.'

'I'll walk you to the door,' Lloyd whispered.

Harry waved goodbye, and Lewis watched with a droopy expression. Tears pushed their way up Scarlett's throat at the look. Did he actually want her to stay?

In the porch, Lloyd slipped his hand into hers and held them.

'I'm so sorry, I'd like you to stay. I don't want you to feel… pushed out, or like you're not welcome. But this is my life. I don't want Eve to behave like she did, but I'm scared. Bloody terrified, in fact, that if I say anything too harsh, she'll explode, and I'll lose her. She's not someone I can control and…' He looked around helplessly.

Scarlett took both his hands in hers. 'Don't try to control her moods. She'll have to find her own way out of them – with mistakes along the way, like we all did. I know I lashed out at people when I was her age, but it didn't mean I had the right to. If you tell her off, she might bristle, but she also needs to hear where the line is. She can feel what she feels, but she shouldn't take it out on you or anyone else. That's not fair. But what matters is that she knows you're still here for her, even when she's angry. Your kids need you... more than I do. I get that.'

'It makes me feel sick,' he said as she opened the door. The wind had died, but the air was still edged with ice.

'Don't let it.'

'Are we still ok?' His blue eyes were dulled with an almost desperate look.

'Yeah. We're still ok.' She pushed up, kissed him on the cheek. 'Go be with your kids.' Her voice threatened to crack. 'They need you, and I'm not going to be the reason they don't get that.' Then she turned and walked into the night, letting the cold bite at her all it wanted.

'Text me when you're home?' he called after her.

'I will.'

The night was full of a silence that made her ears ring. As she hit the end of the path, she glanced back. Lloyd was still standing in the doorway, hand braced against the frame. He gave her a slow wave and a look that made her wish, just for a second, that she had no sense of decency or self-control at all.

She turned away, walking fast so the tears wouldn't freeze on her cheeks. She breathed deep, letting the cold burn her lungs, and forced herself to keep moving.

Halfway down the street, a few snowflakes began to fall, tiny white stings on her face. She stuck out her tongue and caught one, laughing through the tears because why not? She was Scarlett Finch, a crazy mess of a human being trying to fit herself neatly into a world where she didn't belong.

Lloyd was a sensible father of three with a lovely house, a garden, a good job, and a fancy car. She'd worked hard to get her own life back on track – therapy after the mess she'd made of things, real friends instead of drinking buddies, a proper job in the bookshop that she was actually good at. And still, standing here, she felt small and out of place. Why had she ever thought she could belong in his world?

She wiped her nose with the back of her mitten and kept walking, past the glow of the streetlamps and the ghost of her own shadow, towards whatever was next.

CHAPTER TWENTY-FOUR

Lloyd

Lloyd lingered at the door longer than necessary. The cold air stung his bare feet through the porch tiles, but he hardly noticed. All his focus was on Scarlett's retreating shape. A breath steamed from his lungs. He closed the door, locked it, and stood still for a moment. While he recognised how his eldest felt, he hated the thought of her being rude enough to scare Scarlett off – though Scarlett also had the right to choose for herself. And spending Friday night watching a film with his family maybe wasn't top of her list of activities.

In the living room, the projector cast a blocky menu onto the bare wall. The kids were ominously quiet, staring forward.

'Are we ready?' he said.

Eve shook her head. 'Why did you have to invite her in?'

A silence – loud as a foghorn – followed. Harry looked up, then quickly down, fiddling with a thread on his cuff. Lewis glanced between them, wide-eyed.

'Because it's good manners. She came around especially to loan us the projector. It would have been rude to take it and just send her away. It feels rude pushing her out like that, but she wasn't exactly getting a warm welcome.'

'I did,' Lewis said.

'Thank you.' Lloyd sat down next to him. 'We should be grateful for her going out of her way—'

'You don't even care how weird it is?' Eve cut him off. 'Having her in this house. It's disrespectful.'

The old guilt roused inside him, hungry as ever. But this time, he pushed back against it.

'Eve,' he said firmly, catching her glare. 'I know you're hurting, and of course you can be angry with me, but you still need to be polite.'

Her chin lifted, eyes bright and rimmed in pink.

'It's not meant to be disrespectful,' he went on. 'Least of all to your mum—if that's what you mean.'

'Really?'

'I told you before. I'll never replace her. I couldn't. I'll always love her. I think about her every single day.'

Tears trembled on Eve's lashes. 'You say that, but it doesn't look like it from here.'

Harry shifted on the cushions, pulling his knees up. 'Eve, Dad's just—'

'Don't bother trying to defend him,' Eve hissed.

'Harry's allowed to speak,' Lloyd said. 'We all are. In fact it's better if we do. This isn't easy for any of us, but you all need to understand something. I'm not trying to erase your mum or what she meant to us. But that doesn't mean I can't make new friends, or maybe new relationships. Just like you've made new friends at school. That's part of life.'

'So I'm just supposed to accept it?' she brushed away a tear.

'Not necessarily. But you do have to be respectful while we work through this. You can be angry, but you can't take it out on everyone else. That's not right.'

Eve's jaw trembled. 'It's like we're not enough for you.'

Lloyd reached over and took her hand. 'That's not true. You'll *always* be enough. All of you mean more to me than anything else in the world. But people can care about more than one person. If I grow to like Scarlett, it won't mean I love any of you, or your mum, any less. Not for a second.'

'You already do like her,' Eve said. 'It's so obvious.'

Lloyd drew in a breath. 'You're right. I do like her. She's kind, and she makes me happy. That doesn't mean she replaces your mum, and it doesn't mean I love you any less.'

'Whatever.'

'Life doesn't wait for us to be ready,' he murmured. 'I didn't plan this. I never thought I'd feel anything for someone again. But it happened. And I can't pretend it didn't. What I *can* promise is that your mum will always matter, and so will you. Both things can be true.'

For a moment, it seemed like Eve would explode, but instead she sat rigid, shaking, her eyes fixed on the wall above the projector's light that now showed the paused opening frame of *The Grinch*.

Lloyd moved to the sofa beside her. She flinched but didn't pull away.

'If you ever want to talk about Mum – or anything – you can. I'll always listen. I want this house to feel solid and safe for us. For you, for Harry, for Lewis. New people might be part of our lives, but they don't take away from what we already have. They add to it.'

Eve wiped her nose with the back of her hand. 'You don't get it.'

'I'm trying.' His voice stayed calm, but his eyes didn't waver from hers. 'I won't always get it right, but I won't stop trying. And I know a new person in our lives can feel like a threat. But I need you to trust that you and your brothers will *always* come first.'

'It's ok if you like her, Dad,' Harry said. 'I mean, we're all going to leave someday. For uni or whatever. I think it would be worse if you were just... on your own, moping. That would suck.'

Eve shot Harry a glare, but he only shrugged, and she let out a snort that was almost a laugh.

Lloyd gave her a hug and winked at Harry. 'Thanks, son.'

'Now can we put the film on?' Harry said.

'Of course.' Lloyd returned to his seat next to Lewis and hit play. The room filled with the opening bars of cartoon sleigh bells. Lewis, after a while, climbed onto Lloyd's lap, curling in close.

'I think Scarlett is cool,' he whispered. 'I hope she comes over again soon.'

Lloyd squeezed him tight, blinking furiously at the screen, willing the tears to hold until the lights were off and the kids were all asleep.

The next morning, Lloyd woke far too early for a Saturday – not that he'd been sleeping much lately. The house felt heavier somehow, as though last night's words had seeped into the walls. Would Eve take them onboard? Or would him confessing to liking Scarlett just make things even worse. Padding downstairs through the quiet dark, he caught a thin glow leaking from the living-room door. For a second, his stomach clenched – half expecting another confrontation – but when he pushed the door open, he found only Harry, cocooned in a blanket on the sofa, a manga propped on his knees.

Lloyd sat on the arm of the sofa, yawning. 'Morning.'

'Hey.' Harry flipped a page. 'Can I borrow your phone and use the hotspot?'

'Sure. The Wi-Fi should be on by Monday; otherwise, I'll have to ring them again. This is ridiculously long to be without it.'

Harry nodded, and Lloyd left him to it. In the kitchen, he put the kettle on, then stared blankly at the array of bread and cereal.

Footsteps pounded overhead, and Lewis appeared in the doorway, hair sticking up like a dandelion clock.

'Dad, are we getting the tree today?'

'Yeah. I promised, didn't I? We'll go after breakfast. I heard there's a tree farm out at Loch Briar. We can cut one ourselves if we want.'

Lewis whooped. 'Yes! With a chainsaw?'

'I think not.'

Behind him, Eve hovered at the threshold, pale and sullen, arms wrapped tight around her hoodie.

'Morning,' Lloyd said.

'Do I have to go and get the tree? Can I stay here?'

'You decide,' Lloyd said gently. 'It'd be nice to have you, but if you'd rather stay here, then fine.'

'Ok.'

They made breakfast together – porridge for Lewis, toast for the others. Conversation was thin but serviceable.

After breakfast, he shooed the kids to their rooms to get dressed and puttered around the kitchen, wiping the counter and tidying up. He was halfway through loading the dishwasher when the doorbell buzzed.

He wiped his hands on a tea towel and opened the door.

Scarlett stood on the step, breath clouding in the crisp morning. Her hair was wild from the wind, and she wore her leather jacket and a scarf knotted around her throat. For a second, Lloyd's heart stopped in his chest.

'Hey.' He frowned at her. 'What are you doing here?'

She stamped her boots and rubbed her hands together. 'I got your message about coming for the projector?'

He blinked. 'My message?'

'Yeah.' She pulled out her phone and showed the text.

Lloyd: We're done with the projector. Can you come for it now? x

'Sounded like you wanted rid of it ASAP.'

He hadn't sent any such thing.

Scarlett raised her eyebrows. 'If it's a bad time, I can just—'

'No, god, it's not a bad time. Come in. Please.' He moved aside, and she brushed past, trailing cold air and a quick, sweet scent. 'Listen, that message.' He pulled a face. The message had been rather blunt. 'I didn't send it.' Running his fingers through his hair, he thought around the house to where he'd even put his phone. 'Harry was using my phone for the Wi-Fi. Maybe he sent it, though I'm not sure why he would. And I'm sorry it was so direct and dragged you out of the house.'

'It's fine. I wasn't doing anything anyway. I very rarely am. You'd think at twenty-five I'd have a more exciting life.'

'Here.' He took her jacket and scarf, hung them on the hook. She let him do it, even though obviously she didn't need him fussing around her. 'Do you want a coffee?'

'Sure. If you don't mind? Though I don't want to impose.'

Lloyd smiled. 'It's not an imposition. It's a pleasure.' He poured her a coffee and handed her a mug.

She took it, their fingers grazing. Static snapped between them.

He cleared his throat. 'Let's go through and see if we can get to the bottom of this message.'

They went to the living room together. Harry and Lewis were on the floor, both with controllers, playing a game on the TV. Harry looked up, then away quickly. Lewis lit up like a searchlight.

'Scarlett!'

'Hi.' She gave him a wave.

'Do you want a shot of this game? I can't do it.'

Scarlett shook her head. 'I don't know how it works.'

'Me neither.' He ditched the controller and came and sat next to her on the sofa. 'We're going to get a big tree today.'

'Harry,' Lloyd said. 'Did you use my phone to message Scarlett to come this morning for the projector?'

Harry's lips twitched at the corners. 'Dunno what you're talking about.'

Lloyd arched an eyebrow and reached for his phone, scrolling through the messages. 'This one?' He showed the screen to Harry, who shrugged, but couldn't quite keep a straight face.

'Might have,' Harry said.

Scarlett snorted, then covered her mouth.

'And why did you do that?' Lloyd shot Harry a look that was supposed to be stern but ended up just affectionate.

'Thought you might like to see her,' he mumbled.

Eve appeared in the doorway, lips pressed together in a thin line.

Scarlett offered a tentative wave. 'Hey.'

'Hi.' Eve slumped onto the sofa.

'Are you coming with us to get the tree?' Lewis asked.

Scarlett shot Lloyd a glance, the faintest panic in her eyes. 'You can if you want.'

'That's sweet, but it should be a family thing. I'm not...' She trailed off.

'You could be.' Lewis grinned. 'Daddy fancies you.'

Lloyd's entire face ignited. 'Lewis.'

Harry bent forward like he'd been seized by silent giggles, and Eve rolled her eyes to the ceiling. 'Shut up, Lewis,' she said.

'It's true though,' Harry mumbled. 'He sent her a kiss at the end of his message.'

'That was you,' Lloyd snapped, though he caught Scarlett's eye and couldn't help smiling. Hopefully Harry hadn't looked back the whole message thread – while Lloyd was pretty sure there wasn't anything bad on there, he couldn't be a hundred per cent sure he hadn't sent her kisses before.

'Can you not?' Eve glared at them all.

Lewis turned to her. 'Why is it bad to like someone?'

Eve sighed. 'I didn't say that.'

'You kind of did,' Harry said. 'Just wait until you bring a boyfriend round. We'll all hate on him.'

'Shut up, you idiot.'

'Right, guys, be nice,' Lloyd said. 'No one's going to hate on anyone.'

Lewis looked at Scarlett, eyes huge and blue. 'Do you like Daddy too?'

Scarlett flushed, and for a second Lloyd thought she'd burst out laughing, or run for the door. But she didn't. She glanced up at Lloyd, their eyes meeting, and in that glance was a whole volume of unspoken things.

'I do,' she said softly. 'But I also know this is a really tough time for you guys. So I don't have any expectations.'

Eve's face twitched, like she was either going to laugh or cry but couldn't make up her mind.

Scarlett stood up, smoothing her skirt. 'Anyway, I should go. Let you all get on with your day.'

Lewis clung to her arm. 'Please come and see the trees with us.'

Lloyd caught her gaze again, and his heart filled with the warmth it always did when she was near. He wanted to tug her close, tell her he loved her, and welcome her into his life... But there was still a very large Eve-shaped obstacle in the way. And that was before he tackled his mother.

CHAPTER TWENTY-FIVE

Scarlett

'Let Scarlett decide for herself,' Lloyd said.

And she would, though her heart was torn. Lewis looked like he desperately wanted her to go with them to cut a Christmas tree. Harry too seemed fine about it, but a blinding flash of something glowed behind Eve's eyes. Was it worth the risk?

'It's really kind of you,' Scarlett said, keeping her eyes on Lewis. 'It's so sweet that you'd want me to be part of your family day.' She shot a glance at Lloyd, whose eyebrows were slightly raised like he wasn't sure exactly how he wanted this to play out. 'But you don't really know me yet. It would be a bit weird for me to muscle into your family fun.'

Harry gave a little shrug. 'Well, it's pretty obvious Dad likes you. So.'

Scarlett's stomach flipped. Harry had seemed so quiet at their first meeting, and maybe he was, but he was like his dad – caring.

Lloyd coughed into his hand, but his ears went a bit red. 'How about we invite Eunice too? You said she wanted to go but had no one to give her a lift.'

It was actually a decent idea. Eunice could fill any silence and probably start a fistfight with Eve's negative aura if it came to it. 'Ok,' Scarlett said. 'I can message her, but she'll be at the shop.'

'Tell her we could shut at two today as part of her Christmas bonus.' Lloyd winked.

'Ok. I'll text her.' Scarlett pulled out her phone and fired off a message.

While she waited for a reply, Lewis plopped down next to her and said, 'Do you want to play Uno?'

Scarlett blinked. 'Um. ok. I haven't played since I was about ten. You'll have to remind me of the rules.'

'Lewis just makes them up as he goes along.' Harry turned around from his beanbag. 'I'll play too. Eve? Dad?'

Eve didn't look up from her phone. 'No.'

'Ok.' Lloyd sat on the floor next to Harry. His head was close to Scarlett's knee, and she wanted to ruffle his hair, but she didn't.

Lewis brought the deck over and handed it to Lloyd, who dealt the cards onto a small table.

Scarlett checked her cards, and Lloyd glanced up and smiled at her.

Harry played methodically, Lewis with all the subtlety of a sledgehammer, piling on every plus-four card with manic delight; Scarlett and Lloyd just joined in, laughing when the chaos bubbled over. Was this a rose-tinted look at family life? Or was it real? If it was, she wouldn't mind a piece of it – even with Eve scowling at them. Scarlett let her be. She didn't need her approval.

'Want to play the next round?' Scarlett asked casually.

Eve glanced up long enough to flatten her with a 'Don't try to be my stepmum' glare, then looked away again. Scarlett shrugged and started a new hand, content to let the silence settle. No doubt she'd have been the same at fifteen.

Her phone buzzed.

Eunice: That sounds wonderful. Thank you so much for thinking of me! I'll bring Clarence if he's allowed.

Scarlett smiled. 'Eunice is in. She wants to bring the pug.'

Lewis clapped his hands. 'Cool. I love dogs. We're getting one after Christmas.'

'Are we?' Lloyd frowned at him.

Lewis waggled his eyebrows. 'Worth a try.'

Lloyd chuckled. 'You're a rascal.' He checked his phone. 'Ok, that gives us a couple of hours before we need to leave. I'll duck out this hand and make us some lunch.'

'Should I help?' Scarlett said.

'You don't have to.' He smiled at her, silently telling her with his eyes that if she wanted a break, she could come with him – but she was welcome to decide.

'Stay and play,' Lewis said.

'Unless you're scared of me winning again.' Harry gave her a sly grin.

'I'll stay,' she said to Lloyd, and he smirked. On the way out, he leaned over and patted Eve's head. She shrugged him off – but for just a fraction of a second, her eyes lingered on the cards, and a tiny, almost imperceptible twitch at the corner of her mouth suggested she wasn't as wholly engrossed in her phone as she was making out.

After lunch, they all piled into Lloyd's car. He'd popped the two seats in the boot. 'Harry, you and Lewis, you can go in there,' he said.

'Eve can have the front,' Scarlett said quietly. 'I'll sit with Eunice.'

'Ok.' Lloyd gave her a gentle rub on the upper arm

Lewis, already overexcited, yelled 'Race you!' and jumped through the side door, nearly flattening Harry. They shoved and giggled, boots banging on the seatbacks, until they'd both wriggled into the back seats.

Scarlett looked back at them, then caught Lloyd's eye in his rear-view mirror. He gave her an apologetic smile.

Glenbriar was busy with shoppers and tourists who came for pre-Christmas deals in the local hotels. In the station car park, Eunice was already waiting, and she waved enthusiastically as Lloyd pulled into a parking space.

'Does the dog have to wear the hat?' Harry muttered as Eunice got into the car.

'He loves it.' Eunice sat Clarence next to her. 'Don't you, pudding?'

Clarence's face suggested he did not.

Eunice turned to Scarlett and squeezed her arm. 'Thank you for inviting us.'

'It was Lloyd's idea.'

'And yours,' Lloyd said.

'Well, thank you both. It'll do Clarence good to see the world. He gets bored with my company.'

'How's Captain Beaky?' Scarlett asked as Lloyd pulled off and took the turn that led to the top of the town and onto the Loch Briar road.

'Oh, he's loving life,' Eunice said. 'I've given him full run of the conservatory. He can fly from the palm to the window ledge and back, but the place looks like a Jackson Pollock most mornings.'

Scarlett snorted, not wanting to imagine the sight.

Eve's gaze caught hers in the mirror, and for a moment they held it. Eve looked like she was trying not to burst out laughing.

Eunice filled the silence with stories about old Christmases, weird customers, her ex-husband's allergic reaction to pine sap, and the time she got locked in the Station toilets overnight at Glasgow Central. The kids contributed now and then, especially Lewis when a story involved blood or someone being sick.

As they pulled into the Christmas tree farm's mud-splattered car park, even Eve cracked a smile when Clarence farted and nearly knocked out the back two rows.

Lloyd cut the engine. 'We made it. Everyone alive?'

'Barely.' Lewis flapped his hand in front of his face to indicate he was dying from the smell.

Scarlett unbuckled, trying not to burst into a fit of giggles. This was what family could feel like. Not perfect, not even close, but alive and loud and absolutely worth showing up for.

She followed Lloyd and the kids out, boots crunching on frosty gravel, and grinned as Clarence stalked ahead on his long lead.

The Christmas tree farm was a cross between a Nordic fantasy and a Survivor challenge. The trees themselves ranged from legendary giants to tiny bushy little toy trees, lining the banks of a slushy, half-frozen loch. To get to the best ones, you had to pass through half a mile of mud, puddles, and toddler-grade booby traps – slick branches, icy dips, and half sunken boardwalks. That, or wait for the tractor and trailer that was ferrying people back and forth. Eunice, however, decided they should walk – Clarence would enjoy it.

'For a dog that's meant to be enjoying this—' Lloyd murmured in Scarlett's ear '—he looks very grumpy.'

Scarlett leaned into him, enjoying a brief moment of contact. Her boots were already caked and her jeans tattooed with wet grit. Lloyd took her hand and helped her over a muddy patch.

Eunice was in her element. 'You can really feel the oxygen up here!' She marched ahead, her coat looking like it had been cobbled together from retired snowmen – if she expected it to stay white, she was clearly deluded. Her injured arm was still in a sling, and she balanced Clarence on the other side, letting the pug lead the way. 'Don't pull too hard,' she warned with a grin. 'I've got one shoulder in a sling already – I don't want to injure the other one!'

'Could I hold his lead?' Eve asked. 'He's a cute wee dog. And maybe it would help you balance.'

'Yes, dear. Please do. That would be helpful. He's a menace though. If he smells a rabbit or a pigeon, he'll be off and we might not catch him before the sun goes down, so hold him tight.'

'I will.'

'If we cut down a tree, do we have to carry it all the way back?' Harry asked.

'We have to ask the people in hi-vis jackets,' Lloyd replied. 'They help us cut it and then they take it back on the tractor and net it up for us. All we have to do is strap it to the roof of the car and hope it doesn't fall off.'

Eve stalked along beside Clarence, hood up, hands stuffed deep in her pockets. Every time Clarence got tangled in a branch, she paused to gently free him, then scratched behind his ears. For the first time since Scarlett had met her, she seemed content – almost happy.

Scarlett lagged behind the pack, not wanting to step on toes – literal or metaphorical. She pretended to study the needles, running her hands over the scratchy blue-green branches. Her mum had a fake tree in the house, and Scarlett didn't have her own home to put one in. The black one had graced her room a couple of times, but this year she was much happier at the thought of it being in Lloyd's house.

'You ok?' Lloyd sidled up next to her, smiling.

'Yeah,' she said. 'You?'

'I'm glad you're here.' He glanced around. 'It might be easier to do this with just the kids, but easy isn't always right. And this feels right.' He pressed his hand to his heart, over his coat. 'In here.'

Scarlett looked at him, but he blinked and looked away into the woods ahead.

A few rows down, Eunice had stopped to survey the "Noble Firs." She raised her arm in the air. 'Here's a beauty!'

Lewis and Harry bombed over, nearly wiping out on a patch of ice. Lloyd and Scarlett wandered over to look too. Eve stayed a little way off with Clarence.

As Lloyd and the boys chatted to Eunice, Scarlett drifted towards the loch. The air bit her cheeks, but the water's surface glinted like a million sequins. It was beautiful. She took out her phone and snapped a picture.

A rustle in the trees made her glance over – Eve and Clarence were following a parallel path. Scarlett hesitated. Desperate thoughts nudged her to strike up a conversation. She wanted to forge some kind of relationship with Eve, but the memory of her own teenage moods warned her not to crowd her. She hovered on the edge, pretending to study the loch again.

'He's funny, isn't he?' Eve said, scratching Clarence's chin.

Scarlett edged a little closer. 'Yeah. Though he doesn't seem to know how that lead works.'

Clarence was merrily wrapping it around a tree trunk. Eve groaned and tugged at it.

'I just need to unclip him for a second.' She unclipped him, holding firmly to his collar as she unravelled the lead. 'Maybe you could hold him, so I can get this.'

Scarlett stepped forward, but before she reached them, a pigeon flapped up from a tree, and Clarence shot forward. Eve's fingers slipped on his collar, and he bolted.

'Clarence!' Eve yelled, but the dog was a blur of red and white, ears flapping, Santa suit trailing like a parachute. 'Shit.'

Scarlett was already running. Eve yanked the lead free then she broke into a sprint after them.

Clarence headed downhill straight for the lochside. He stopped at the water's edge and started snuffling furiously at a clump of reeds. Scarlett caught up, panting.

Eve appeared out of the trees on the other side like she was trying to ambush him. She crept up behind him, crouched, and reached for his collar.

In that moment, the dog jerked sideways. Eve lost her balance, arms pinwheeling, and would have gone face-first into the slush if Scarlett hadn't grabbed the back of her coat. Unfortunately, Scarlett's own boots hit a patch of ice, and her bum landed flat in the mud, dragging Eve on top of her like she was sitting on Scarlett's lap.

Clarence barked as Eve clambered back onto her feet very quickly.

Scarlett was stuck in a horrified trance, and braced herself for humiliation, laughter, a sneer, or maybe a photo for posterity. Instead, Eve turned and stared at her. 'You ok?'

'I think so.' Cold, wet mud oozed through Scarlett's jeans, up her back, in her socks. It was so comically horrible that she couldn't help it – she started to laugh.

Eve looked at her like she was mad, then started laughing too. It was sudden, loud, and way more beautiful than Scarlett expected. The more they tried to stop, the worse it got, until Scarlett had tears in her eyes and Eve was wheezing into the sleeve of her hoodie.

Clarence ran circles around them, snuffling and snorting like a miniature pig.

After what felt like years, Eve put out a mucky hand and helped Scarlett to her feet. 'This is so gross.'

'But we got the dog.' Scarlett took hold of Clarence's collar and Eve clipped him.

Eve shrugged. 'Thanks for helping me. If I'd lost him…' She swallowed.

They stared at each other's clothes, peeling mud off each other's sleeves. Scarlett tried to brush the sludge off Eve's jeans but only made it worse.

'Sorry,' she said, pulling a face.

'Doesn't matter. I don't even like these jeans.' Eve walked beside Scarlett along the path, Clarence trotting ahead, firmly clipped to the lead.

'We're going to get your dad's car in a right mess,' Scarlett said.

Eve shook her head, eyes fixed on her boots. 'Listen… Sorry I've been so… narky.'

'It's cool,' Scarlett said, a bit thrown. 'Honestly, I get it. I remember being your age like it was yesterday. My mum went through, like, five boyfriends. I gave every one of them hell. I used to hate the thought of someone stealing her away. But none of them ever stayed, and now I feel bad, because I think she'd still like to find someone, but she feels like she's lost her chance. I wish now I'd been more understanding.'

Eve nodded. 'But this isn't just about my dad. It's about Mum. I feel like if I'm nice to you, I'm betraying her or something.'

Scarlett nodded. 'Makes sense.'

'Yeah… Though I don't think my mum would really want me to be mean to anyone, so…' She gave a little shrug.

Scarlett patted her back. 'Being a teenager is confusing enough. You've had so much shit – excuse my language – piled on top of that, I'm not surprised you're upset.'

They walked a bit further.

'I just...' Eve started, then shut her mouth. She tried again. 'It's not that I hate you. And I guess I have to accept that Dad will see other people at some point. It's the change, you know. And we've had so much of that already.'

'Yeah. I know. That's why I'm trying not to muscle in too much. I don't want to rush in and make things worse for everyone. But...'

Eve glanced up, meeting Scarlett's eyes, and Scarlett saw the resemblance between her and her dad. 'Do you love my dad?'

The question was so sudden, so sharp, that Scarlett nearly tripped over her own boots. She tried to laugh it off, but Eve didn't drop her gaze.

'I... well, yeah,' Scarlett said. 'I do. But I've never actually told him, because I didn't want to make things awkward for him with you guys... or with his mum. Your gran. She doesn't like me.'

'Doesn't she?'

They crunched through a patch of old leaves. Scarlett looked down at her hands. 'She doesn't think I'm right for your dad. And maybe she's right. You're not the only one who's confused, believe me.'

'I didn't even know she knew you.'

'Well, she does.'

'Gran's not been very well. Not that I'm making excuses. She's got a back problem; I never know how to pronounce it. I just remember calling it spongilitis once and everyone laughing, so I've always called it that in my head. When she has flare-ups she can be a bit narky. She doesn't usually tell people when it's bad – doesn't want us to worry, I suppose. After Mum... we're all a bit on edge when it comes to people getting sick.'

'I didn't know... but then, I don't really know her that well.' And Scarlett wasn't sure even the illness excused the way Rita had spoken to her that summer. Even the thought of facing her filled Scarlett with dread – possibly humiliation. Shame welled inside her. Rita's opinion had been formed about her when Scarlett was at one of the lowest places in her life, and unlike her son, Rita hadn't sought to nurture her through this rough time, but to call her out on her stupidity and make her feel about two-feet tall. She, more than anything, was a reason for Scarlett to steer clear of this family, even if every part of her yearned so hard to be with them.

Chapter Twenty-Six

Lloyd

Lloyd saw Eve and Scarlett, both absolutely caked in mud, traipsing up the mucky path with a mortified pug and an expression on Eve's face that Lloyd hadn't seen for a long time – a real, actual smile.

He broke into a jog, Harry and Lewis right behind him. Lewis ran past, nearly taking Lloyd's knees out.

'Are you ok?' Lloyd called out.

Eve looked up, still giggling. 'We're fine. I slipped, Scarlett tried to rescue me, and then we both fell.'

Harry snorted so hard it was almost a sneeze. 'You look like you've crapped yourselves.'

'Language, Harry,' Lloyd said.

Scarlett pointed at her jeans. 'It's just mud.'

Lewis gave a whoop. 'Epic fail! Can you do it again? And let me film it?'

'Absolutely not.' Lloyd held up his hands. 'Let's get you all back up the hill before you catch pneumonia.'

Scarlett and Eve exchanged a glance, and Lloyd caught it – something had shifted. The tension had cracked.

As they started the squelchy trek back, Eve offered her sleeve to Scarlett, who pretended to wipe her nose on it. They both cracked up again, leaving Lewis to narrate the story of the Great Pug Chase for the rest of the climb.

At the top, Eunice stood sentinel by a row of firs, wagging an accusatory finger. 'That dog is a bloody menace!' she declared, but her eyes were twinkling. 'What has he done to the two of you?'

Clarence, seeing his owner, tried to bolt, but Eve held tight. 'Sorry. I unclipped him for a second to untangle his lead from a tree, but he saw a pigeon and bolted. I lost my grip on him.' Eve looked down at her hand. 'And one of my nails fell off.'

'He extracted a fingernail?' Eunice looked horrified.

'It's ok. It was fake. I've got spares.'

'Well, that's alright then.' Eunice took Clarence's lead, then patted Eve's mud-streaked back. 'If you'd lost Clarence, I'd have taken you as a replacement. Better manners and less drool.'

'Not so sure about that,' Eve muttered. 'Sorry, I let him go.'

'Oh, don't worry. No harm done... apart from the muddy clothes and the missing nail.'

Scarlett glanced at Lloyd, and in her eyes, he saw a thank you, though he hadn't done a damn thing. He just smiled, feeling a hot rush behind his own eyes. Nothing – absolutely nothing – compared to seeing his daughter acting like herself again.

'Maybe we should pick the tree,' Lloyd said. 'Before it gets dark. Or we have any more mishaps.'

Eventually, they agreed on a tree, and Eunice chose one for herself, asking for plenty of advice from Scarlett.

A farm worker came over to help them fell the trees, then told them if they wanted to get into the trailer, he'd take them and the trees back to the barn so they could pay while he wrapped the tree.

Lloyd helped Scarlett into the trailer, and she glanced down at herself and laughed.

Lewis clambered over the wood slats and immediately started a game of "Who Can Push Who Off First" with Harry.

'Behave, you two,' Lloyd muttered.

But the ride was good. For the first time in years, he felt like he was part of a slightly deranged but enjoyable family outing.

Back at the car, Lloyd paid for the trees while the farmworker netted them up. Harry and Lewis admired the netting machine and suggested at least three ways it could be weaponised for home defence.

'Let's get the trees on the roof before it gets dark.' Lloyd unlocked the doors.

'You'll get mud in the car.' Harry pointed at Eve and Scarlett.

'Dad's got towels and stuff in the boot,' Eve said.

'Who am I, Mary Poppins?' Lloyd opened the back, which was very small now that the extra seats were popped up, and fished out a bag of old supermarket carriers. 'These'll have to do. All right, Eve and Scarlett, you're demoted to the boot seats. I'll line them with the bags.'

'Why?' Eve moaned.

'You're both a biohazard.'

'I get the front, then?' Harry grinned.

'Nice try. Eunice up front. Other ladies in the boot.'

Eunice climbed in, set Clarence on her lap, and began recounting the story of the time she'd been "kidnapped" by a drunken performer in a reindeer suit at a Christmas market. Lloyd only heard snippets as he wrestled the trees onto the roof rack and yanked the straps tight. Hopefully the story wasn't completely inappropriate.

The journey back was a blur of darkening skies, Christmas songs, and Clarence's spectacular farts. Lloyd dropped Eunice and the pug at her bungalow, carried the smaller tree into her living room and got it into the stand for her. Eunice gave him a big hug, then whispered, 'You've got a good one there. Don't muck it up.'

His face heated, unsure if she meant Scarlett, or the tree.

Next stop: Scarlett's house. He turned off the main road and parked by the kerb.

Lewis got out and pulled his seat forward so Scarlett could climb out.

'Thanks for coming with us,' he said. 'Next time, save the mud wrestling for when I've got a camera.'

'Thanks, cheeky.'

'Get back in before you get too cold.' Lloyd chivvied Lewis back into the car. 'You ok?' He took Scarlett's hands in his and rubbed them.

'Yeah,' she said, but her voice was a little wobbly. 'I actually had a really good day. Not sure if I'm allowed to say that, but I did.'

'Of course you're allowed to say it. That's my new wish – that my family and you can be happy in each other's company.' He kept his voice low. 'Eve seemed... happy. Happier. Whatever happened down there by the water... I haven't seen her like that in ages. So thank you.'

Scarlett grinned, knocking her boots together to shake off more mud. 'Who knew all it took was a wild pug and some icy mud to heal a teenager.'

He chuckled. 'Maybe you should write a book about it.'

'No one would believe it.' She glanced at the car. 'But let's call it a win for today.'

He wanted to kiss her – god, he wanted to – but the audience was brutal, so instead he squeezed her hand. Her fingers were cold, but she squeezed back hard, like she was pumping hope straight into his veins.

'I'll see you soon,' he whispered.

She nodded. 'You will.'

He walked back to the car, smiling so wide it almost cracked his face in two. As he buckled in and started the engine, he caught Eve's eye in the rearview mirror. She looked at him and didn't roll her eyes this time.

Back at the house, the moment the front door shut, everyone started talking about what to do with the tree. Eve went upstairs to shower, and Lloyd heaved the main tree into the living room, wrestled it upright, and tried to jam the trunk into the stand. It wobbled, then toppled, narrowly missing a shelf of framed photos. He muttered a few choice words, and on attempt number four, managed to screw it in straight.

Stepping back, hands on hips, he surveyed the result. The tree fit nicely into the space at the bay window, and the room smelt like fresh resin and cold air. He breathed deep, already picturing it with lights and all the weird homemade ornaments from Christmases past.

He was still in the trance when Eve shuffled in, now in pink pyjama bottoms and a grey cat Oodie, hair still damp from the shower. She flopped onto the sofa and curled her legs underneath her.

'Tree looks good,' she said.

'You look clean, which is an improvement.'

She gave him a narrow-eyed smile.

Harry and Lewis brought in boxes of rattling baubles and a bag of rustling tinsel, and Lloyd sat down next to Eve, dusting his hands together, as the boys started wrapping up the tree.

'Why doesn't Gran like Scarlett?' Eve asked.

He froze. 'Did Scarlett tell you that?'

'Yeah. She said Gran thinks she's not right for you.'

He let out a groan.

'Is it because she's so young?'

'Partly.'

'How does she even know her? I didn't think she'd met her.'

He raked his fingers through his hair. 'I met her first on the coach trip in the summer when I went to Skye with Gran and the three of you were with Nana and Papa. Scarlett was there with her brother and his wife. We got talking. Both of us were pretty lonely, and... we made friends. But then she went her own way, and I didn't see her again until she started at the bookshop. The connection was still there. Stronger even. I realised I'd missed her and wished I'd kept in touch with her after the summer.'

Eve picked at a loose thread on her pyjamas. 'But isn't it a bit weird? I mean, the age thing.'

'Yeah, it is a bit weird. I'm not going to lie. Sometimes I think it's ridiculous. But we get along so well it doesn't seem to matter. She gets me and I get her.'

'And Gran disagrees?'

'Yeah. But Scarlett's been through a lot. She's only twenty-five, but she hasn't had an easy life.'

'Why?'

'It's not my place to tell you everything about her life, but her parents split up when she was younger. And she's had some nasty relationships.'

'Ok. Like mean boyfriends, yeah?'

'That kind of thing.'

Eve thought for a bit, lips pursed. 'You know Granny and Grandpa on Mum's side? There's a big age gap between them. Eighteen years. No one ever made a fuss. Grandpa acts younger because of it.'

Lloyd blinked. 'I'd forgotten that.'

'He's eighty-two, and she's sixty-four, but everyone says she keeps him young.'

'Yeah, that's a nice way to look at it.'

Eve looked at him, and something in her eyes softened. 'Scarlett's actually ok. She doesn't pretend everything is fine. She's not fake.'

'She really isn't. It's one of the things I like most about her.'

'So, are you going to keep seeing her?'

He exhaled. 'I'd like to, but... well, everyone has to be ok about it.'

Eve leaned over and hugged him. He hugged her back, and she sniffed. 'I'll try to be ok about it.'

'Thanks, snookleberry,' he whispered.

Come Monday morning, Lloyd stepped out of the cold and was instantly grabbed from behind. A cold hand slapped across his eyes dragging him down a little as it was obviously someone smaller than him. He knew from the sweet perfume it was Scarlett, but—

'What are you doing?' he asked.

'Remember I told you Icelanders spend all of Christmas Eve just reading books and eating chocolate?' she murmured in his ear.

'I do.'

'Well, what do you think of this?' She pulled her hand away and spun him around.

The front table of the bookshop was covered in books and bright signs – Jolabokaflod, Christmas Book Flood, with little snowflake doodles all over.

'This looks amazing,' Lloyd said. 'How early did you come in?'

'An hour ago. I wanted to get this sorted before the Monday train rush. May as well start getting people in the spirit for the main event.' She wore her hair down and looked truly beautiful as she straightened a book on the table.

'It all looks fantastic. I'm so impressed with everything you've done here.' He set down his bag and sighed.

'Are you ok?'

'Never better.' He came over, took her in his arms and hugged her. 'I feel like we've turned a corner with the kids. They all seem much more onboard about you and me now.'

Scarlett wrapped her arms around his back. 'That's so good to hear.'

'Thank god for that pug.'

'Who'd have thought it?'

'Eve's still a bit stressed about the play she's doing, but I think she's secretly loving it.' Lloyd stroked a circle on her back with his palm; the physical contact always buoyed him up. 'I wish you could come too.' Though with Rita there, it probably wasn't sensible. How the hell could he convince his mother any of this was a good idea?

'It's ok. You need to keep some things just for your family.' She pressed her face into his chest. 'I missed this.'

'Me too.' He rubbed his cheek on her hair, then ducked his head, and kissed her on the mouth. She let out a small, delighted sound and kissed him back, arms tightening around his neck.

The jangle of the bell brought them up short. An older man with a battered old case stood in the doorway, taking in the scene with a bemused smile.

Scarlett let go and turned bright red. Lloyd coughed, then disappeared quickly up the stairs to the office.

The week passed quickly, and before Lloyd had time to catch his tail, it was the night of the show. He and the kids piled into the car and headed off to get his mum. Eve was already at the school and hopefully not too nervous that her big moment had arrived, though she'd seemed buzzed up about it when he'd dropped her off earlier.

Rita opened the door, braced against the cold, wearing a maroon cardigan and the kind of lipstick that looked like she'd eaten a punnet of blackberries. 'Are you all excited?' she asked.

'You betcha!' Lewis did a ninja move from the back.

At the school, kids with programs roamed the foyer, parents queued for raffle tickets and non-alcoholic mulled wine, and the place was rich with the smell of mince pies and shortbread. The hallways glittered with tinsel, and the sound of chatter echoed through the wide corridor.

At the entrance to the lecture theatre, Miss Morgan – Eve's guidance teacher – stood by the door with a tall man.

'Oh no,' Harry muttered. 'He's my English teacher. Mr Addison.'

'And is he not a good teacher?' Rita asked.

'Na, he's cool. But I just know he'll talk to me.'

Rita frowned. 'I don't see why that's bad.'

Harry was right. The man spoke to him straight away, and Harry's face went plum.

'Hi, nice to see you all,' Miss Morgan said to Lloyd, then smiled at Rita and Lewis. 'Let me see your tickets and I'll tell you how best to get to your seats.'

Lloyd held out the tickets.

'You're going to love the show; I just know it. The dress rehearsal was stunning, and Eve is wonderful.'

'Thank you.' Lloyd smiled, then leaned closer. 'For everything. You've made a real difference to her.'

Miss Morgan patted his arm. 'Not at all. She just needed a little bit of nudging in the right direction.'

'Well, thank you for doing the nudging.'

'No problem. Now, if you want to take the faraway steps to the seats, my lovelies. That'll save you squeezing past people.'

As they made their way up the far-side steps in the auditorium, Lewis grabbed Lloyd's arm and nearly pulled it out of its socket.

'What's wrong?'

'That's Robbie and his dad. Can you ask him if he can come and play one day?'

Lloyd saw the rockstar guy with the long hair, standing with his hands in his back pockets, talking to a man a little further up. His arms were tattooed, and he looked kind of intimidating.

'Oh no, and he's with Mr Halley, my I.T. teacher,' Harry muttered.

Before Lloyd could chicken out of talking to Robbie's dad, a boy at his side jumped down the stairs and greeted Lewis. Robbie's dad said goodbye to the teacher – who gave Harry a brief smile – and followed the boy down the steps.

'Hi,' Lloyd said. 'I'm Lewis's dad, Lloyd. I gather these two are best buddies.'

'Yeah, so I hear.' Robbie's dad ran his hands through his long hair, flicking it back. 'I hear nothing but Lewis this, Lewis that.'

'Sounds familiar, only I get Robbie, Robbie, Robbie. Lewis is hoping for a playdate. Maybe in the new year.'

'Yeah, sure. You can have Robbie any day. I'm always trying to get rid of him.' He glanced at Rita and gave her a lop-sided grin. 'I'm kidding. 'Lewis is welcome at ours any time too. I'll give you my number. Just message me.' He pulled out a pair of glasses that looked like he'd sat on them at some point, then took out his phone and squinted at it. 'My name's Adam. I should have said that before.'

'Aren't you in a band?' Rita asked.

'Yeah, Tavrach.' He gave her a little smile, then held out his phone to Lloyd to show him the number.

Lloyd put it into his phone. 'Do you have other kids in the show tonight?'

'Yeah. Greig, my eldest, is playing Scrooge. His make-up is brilliant. It's weird seeing him looking old enough to be my father.'

They all laughed, then went to find their seats.

Lewis bounced in his. 'I wish Scarlett was here. She loves *A Christmas Carol*. She said it's her favourite.'

Rita's head snapped around. 'Why would she have any interest in a school show?'

'Because Dad likes her. They're kind of a thing.'

Rita stared at Lloyd, then at the boys. 'Don't be ridiculous.'

'She's his girlfriend,' Lewis said. 'And she's really cool.'

'That's enough,' Lloyd said, his ears burning. 'Quieten down, ok?'

'Just own it, Dad.' Harry clapped him on the back.

Lloyd gave him a slight side eye, then they both smirked.

'I don't think anyone's sitting there.' Lewis pointed to the empty seat next to Lloyd. 'Can you message her?'

'She's busy tonight.' Lloyd put his hand on Lewis's knee, hoping to slow the onslaught, but the damage was done. Rita sat ramrod straight, lips pursed and wouldn't look at him.

Mercifully, the lights dimmed a few minutes later. The head-teacher got up and welcomed everyone, reminding people if they took films or photographs, then not to broadcast them on social media. Then he clapped his hands and said, 'Enjoy the show.'

The opening chords of the overture played, and the theatre settled. Lloyd sank into the darkness, letting the drama of Dickens wash over him.

Adam's son, Greig, was brilliant from the start – his make-up was indeed believable – and his acting was great. Lloyd smiled and nodded along.

When Eve walked onto the stage as the Ghost of Christmas Past, an ache of pride and love filled his chest. His mind flew to Amy and how she would never get to see the ups and downs with her kids.

The first act closed to a round of applause, and as the house lights came up, Lewis whispered, 'Can't you ask Scarlett to come for the second bit?'

'Not this time, son.' Lloyd stared at the empty seat beside him and wanted nothing more than to see her there. He couldn't have Amy anymore, but what about Scarlett?

'Can we get some drinks?' Harry asked.

Lloyd pulled out his wallet, handed him some money and watched as he led Lewis off to the drinks queue, pointing out people to his little brother.

'So...' Rita folded her arms, her shoulders tight. 'Is it true what the boys said?'

Lloyd swallowed. 'I wouldn't say we're... seeing each other, exactly. But yes. We've spent time together.'

'How much time?'

He considered brushing it off, but sighed instead. 'A fair bit, lately. She's trying really hard with the kids. And she's good for me.'

'Good for you?' Rita's voice carried a bite, though she shifted uncomfortably in her chair, as though the effort of sitting so long cost her. 'How?'

'Because I feel more alive,' Lloyd said. 'More like myself.'

'This is the kind of mistake people make when they've been through trauma. You cling to the first person who makes you smile, and before you know it, you've let someone unstable into the children's lives. And I—' She stopped, her hand pressing briefly to her forehead. 'I can't stand by and watch that happen.'

'It's not like that. Maybe in the beginning, but not now.' Lloyd held her gaze, his voice calm but steady. 'I know what I'm doing. I wouldn't risk the kids, and you know that.'

'She's half your age.'

'She's not,' Lloyd said firmly. 'She's twenty-five. I'm forty. Yes, it's a gap, but it's not the end of the world.'

'She may be twenty-five, but she acts like a child. Her behaviour on that trip was ridiculous. She's not equipped to be a parent to three grieving kids.'

He set his jaw. 'No one is equipped for that. Not me, not you. We're all just doing the best we can.'

Rita's mouth pinched. 'You used to have common sense.'

Lloyd gave a short laugh, without humour. 'Please don't talk down to me, Mum. I need you to hear this: I won't let you bully Scarlett out of my life.'

She blinked, taken aback.

'She was humiliated on that trip, by a man who treated her appallingly in public. And instead of compassion, she got judgment. From strangers, and from you. That's not fair, and it's not what I expect from my family.'

Rita shifted in her seat, arms folding tighter, but her eyes flickered with something that looked like guilt.

'I love you,' Lloyd went on. 'I know you want to protect me and the kids. But putting Scarlett down isn't protecting anyone – it's hurting all of us. If you can't speak respectfully about her, I'll take the kids and walk away from the conversation. I won't have them hearing you tear down someone I care about.'

For a long moment, Rita didn't reply. Her lips trembled as though she might lash back again, but instead she exhaled slowly, the fight leaving her shoulders.

'I just... I don't want you hurt again,' she muttered. Her voice had lost its bite. 'You've had enough of that.'

'I know,' he said gently. 'And I don't want to hurt the kids, or you. But I need you to trust me. Scarlett's a person I care about. If she turns out to be a mistake, then I'll deal with it. But I'm not throwing away a chance on something that might never happen. I can't live my life on regret.'

Rita's eyes glistened, though she masked it quickly. She gave a small, reluctant nod. 'Well... I suppose time will tell.'

'It always does,' Lloyd said quietly.

This time, when he met her gaze, she didn't look away first.

Time would indeed tell, but he knew one thing for certain – he wasn't going to waste it chasing perfection. Life was never perfect. But something real, something beautiful and a little messy? That was waiting for him, and he was ready to reach for it.

CHAPTER TWENTY-SEVEN

A forest of Christmas lights snaked the length of the Cross Keys' old-beamed ceiling, turning every shadow gold. Holly, baubles and a reindeer made of willow greeted Scarlett at the entrance, and she scanned the crowd for Elise.

She spotted her tucked in a window seat, scrolling her phone and wearing a green cashmere turtleneck and dark red lipstick.

'Hi, sorry I'm late.'

Elise smiled, putting her phone aside, and flicking her long dark hair over her shoulder. 'No worries at all. How are you?'

Scarlett sat down with a sigh. 'Not bad.'

'Tell me everything,' Elise demanded. 'I want all the bookshop gossip.'

Scarlett propped her chin on her fist. 'Bookshop is...' She grinned, shaking her head. 'Amazing. Actually, genuinely amazing. It's the first real job I've had, and I love it. I was never a bookworm and not even that great a reader before, but I'm learning so much. I read sometimes at quieter times, and I love meeting the customers. We're getting more every day.'

Elise took Scarlett's hand and tilted her head. 'This is the best news. I'm so proud of you. It was scary seeing you in such a bad place this summer, but you've done so well.'

'Thank you for helping me out back then. I was a hideous mess. You were so kind to me.'

'Not at all. I was happy to do it.'

'It's ridiculous to think that six months with Leon was the longest I ever managed for a relationship.'

'It was six months too long because he was horrible.'

A server came over, and they ordered drinks.

Elise tapped the table for a second. 'And what's happening with Lloyd? Am I allowed to ask?'

Scarlett sucked her lip; her hands were shaky. 'I love him. Like, properly.'

'What?'

'Yeah, I mean it. Like it's hard to breathe when I think about not seeing him.'

Elise's eyes widened. 'But... how does he feel?'

Scarlett knew what she was thinking – and fearing – that Scarlett had jumped into a pitiful place where she worshipped Lloyd with no hope of him returning the feelings and was wallowing in it until she was in a state.

It wouldn't be the first time.

That was how it had been in the summer when she thought she'd never see him again.

'He likes me too... I know he does.' Neither of them had ever openly said they loved each other, but she almost felt like it wasn't necessary. She felt it in every interaction. 'He's so nice. He takes care of me.'

Elise raised her eyebrows.

'Yeah, that way too. But we're taking it easy. I've met his kids. I've even been to his house, and it's good.'

'Well, I'm glad things are working out for you.' She sat back as the server placed drinks in front of them. 'What does his mother say about it? I remember her not being thrilled about the idea in the summer.'

Scarlett groaned and pressed her palms over her eyes. 'I'm not sure she even knows yet. I think we're both in denial about it. And I don't think my mum is overly thrilled either.'

Elise reached across the table and squeezed Scarlett's hand. 'It's your life. If you want to love someone, then love them. Don't let anyone else's misery stop you.'

Scarlett smiled. 'Is that what you did with Gabe?'

'Pretty much. You know how fucked up our situation was before we got together. It would have been the easiest thing in the world to have run from.'

Scarlett grinned. 'And now you're living with him at his mum's house with peacocks and donkeys.'

'Exactly, and you don't get much crazier than that.'

They raised their glasses, toasting the future, whatever it turned out to be. And Scarlett made another wish – *please let that future be with Lloyd and have his mother's blessing.*

Since the start of December, business had picked up at the Station Bookshop. Scarlett was wrapping a stack of novels in glossy red paper for the jolabokaflod when her phone vibrated on the counter.

Lloyd: Hey. I'm not going to come into the shop today or tomorrow. I have so many online meetings, it'll be easier to do them from home. You're welcome to drop by later if you want. Miss you. x

She smiled at the phone, then set it down to help a customer. Then she found a battered copy of a classic for a lady who wanted "the one where they're all sisters". Just a few weeks ago, she wouldn't have known where to start with that request but working here had made her so interested in stories of all kinds, and she'd now read enough to guess the lady meant either *Pride and Prejudice* or *Little Women* – it turned out to be the latter.

The room buzzed. People queued at the till. With the Christmas music playing and the trains coming in and out, the festive spirit was so real. And Scarlett was lapping it up. She couldn't even remember why she hadn't liked Christmas before.

Between customers, she checked her phone again.

Lloyd: I'm sorry we didn't get you a ticket for A Christmas Carol. I wish you could have been there. Eve will tell you about it if you ask. I think Harry filmed some of it. See you on Wednesday at the shop, if not before. x

Scarlett grinned, her chest going light. She flicked back a message: *Can't wait to hear all about it. I miss you too, but these Christmas crowds are keeping me busy. Will message later with a time to visit. x*

She sat her phone back on the desk and returned to the action. For the next hour, she was a human octopus – making recommendations, refilling the trolley outside, and serving several people before they got on trains and more who got off them.

Lunchtime was just a brief half hour, so she could grab some food and go to the loo. It was no fun upstairs without Lloyd for company.

The afternoon passed in a blur. People queued at the till. An elderly couple bickered over which Sudoku books were "the right level of challenge." A man with a bushy moustache wanted a hardback about the history of whisky, and Scarlett managed to sell him two other books. She hummed to the Christmas playlist, and when she heard the familiar strains of "White Christmas," she closed her eyes and let it fill her up.

At half-past three, she refilled the wishing tree tags and straightened the baubles on the branches. The shop traditionally closed at four, after the last afternoon train rattled through. No more passengers would come until later, when the freight traffic had passed. She was just about to start winding down when the crazy bell clattered.

Scarlett looked up. Rita Miller stood in the doorway, her coat a blaze of warning red against the dim afternoon. She closed the door firmly, flipped the sign from OPEN to CLOSED, and set her bag on the counter with a deliberate movement.

Scarlett froze. Her heart thumped so hard she thought it might shake the decorations from the tree.

Rita pulled off her gloves, smoothing them into her palm. Her gaze landed on Scarlett, and for once there wasn't a cruel bite in it. Just a kind of steady, assessing watchfulness.

'Hello,' she said.

Scarlett's voice came out embarrassingly high. 'Hi. How are you?'

Rita gave a small, noncommittal nod. 'I've been better. But I wanted to have a word with you.'

Scarlett nodded, uncertain if she was supposed to come out from behind the till or just stand there. She opted to stay put. It felt safer. Should she call Lloyd?

'I don't think we need to pretend you don't know why I'm here,' Rita said at last. Her voice wasn't sharp, though – it carried a weary note, almost reluctant.

Scarlett braced for impact. Memories of the coach trip flashed – the moment Rita had called her *Scarlett by name, Scarlett by nature* for half the bus to hear. Lloyd had told her that Rita had been fuelled by cocktails that night, but looking at her now, she looked more than stone sober.

Rita sighed and rubbed her wrist as though it ached. 'I owe you an apology for that day. The truth is, I was in agony. All that sitting on the coach, then trying to walk so much when my back was flaring... With hindsight, a coach trip wasn't a sensible choice for me. And I let the pain make me harsher than I should have been. That wasn't fair on you.'

Scarlett blinked, caught off guard, remembering what Eve had said about her having ankylosing spondylitis. 'Oh. Right.'

'That doesn't mean I don't worry,' Rita continued. 'Lloyd has been through hell. The children too. They don't need another person breezing in and out of their lives. They need stability, not more heartache.'

Scarlett's throat tightened. 'I'm not trying to cause drama.'

'Nor am I, though apparently I have done without meaning to.' Rita leaned forward slightly. 'I know you just want to be happy. I don't begrudge you that or blame you. But happiness with my son... that's not a light thing. This is a family, and it's fragile. And I have to ask – are you ready for that? For the long nights, the grief that sneaks back, the birthdays marked by what's missing, not just what's here? Because that's what you're stepping into. Not candlelit dinners and cute messages, but the grind of real life with three wounded children and a man who still carries scars.'

Scarlett's heart thudded. 'I care about him,' she whispered. 'And the kids.'

Rita held her gaze for a long moment. 'Then I hope you mean it. Because if you run when it gets hard, it won't just break Lloyd – it will break all of them. And that's something I don't know if they can come back from.'

Scarlett shook her head, but words were lodged in her throat.

Rita's expression softened. 'I'm not saying this to hurt you. I can see you care about him. And he cares about you, and he wouldn't say that unless he really meant it. But this isn't a simple love story. Lloyd has been through so much, and the children too. Living inside that grief day after day can wear anyone down – even someone with the best intentions. I just don't want to watch him be left behind again.'

'I'm not going anywhere,' Scarlett said quickly. 'Lloyd means the world to me.'

'I believe you,' Rita said. 'But meaning well and being able to shoulder the weight are two different things. I know you're not a child, but you're young, and this is a lot to take on.'

Scarlett's chest tightened. 'I want to be there for him. For them.'

'I hope you can be.' Rita slipped on her gloves. 'For your sake as much as his.' She picked up her bag, then looked around. 'You really have done a wonderful job here – adding the accessibility ramp was quite genius.'

'Thanks.'

'Has Lloyd spoken to you about renewing the contract after Christmas?'

'Um... not yet.'

'I'll mention it to him.' She gave Scarlett a faint smile. 'I'll leave you to close up.'

The bell shrieked as the door closed, then the quiet settled like snow.

Scarlett stood rooted to the spot for a long minute, her breath snagging in her chest. Rita hadn't attacked her, not like in the summer. If anything, she'd been reasonable. Kind, even. But the words still struck deep. Could Scarlett really live up to what this family needed? She loved Lloyd – God, she loved him – but was love enough?

Her hands trembled as she pressed them to the counter. What if Rita was right? What if a year from now she was drained and desperate, clawing for an escape route, leaving Lloyd to pick up the pieces once again? She'd never managed to make a relationship last longer than six months... Why would this be any different?

She dropped her head into her hands. Her heart swore she could never leave him, but her brain replayed Rita's warning on a loop, each phrase like a poisoned dart.

What if she wasn't cut out for this after all?

CHAPTER TWENTY-EIGHT

Lloyd

Lloyd paced the length of the kitchen, phone in hand, back and forth from the kettle to the window, to the fridge and back. He'd finished work, picked up Lewis, and there was still no reply from Scarlett. Not a word since she'd signed off with, "*Will message later with a time to visit. X*"

That little *X* still glowed at him from the chat screen. A single, tantalising kiss.

She'd probably just had a crazy shift at the shop or was out with friends. Or maybe she'd decided that he was too much, or too old, or too baggage-laden for her and was quietly ghosting him into the digital ether.

Don't spiral, you idiot. She'd told him she cared. She'd shown up for his family, even after the mortifying night with Eve. It was probably just her, being Scarlett, getting caught up in the moment and losing track of time. He tried to convince himself, but it didn't stick.

A thump at the front door snapped him out of it. Footsteps charged through the porch, then Harry's voice rang out. 'Holiday mode activated!'

Lloyd forced his phone into his pocket and met Harry and Eve in the hallway. 'Shoes off, please. I don't want to be cleaning floors tonight.'

Eve scowled at him, but only a little. She'd been on a high since the play, and it showed. Her hair was still wet at the ends from the sleet, and her cheeks were blotchy with cold.

Harry ducked past them and bee-lined for the kitchen. 'What's for tea?'

'Pizza,' Lloyd said. 'Start of holiday treat.'

'Yaas.' Harry peeled his jacket off and launched it onto the peg.

Lewis wandered through from the living room. 'Is the projector still here? Can we do another movie night?'

'I filmed the whole of Eve's play on my phone,' Harry said. 'We could watch that if you want.'

Eve rolled her eyes. 'I said I'd die of embarrassment if you showed it to anyone.'

'No, you wouldn't,' Lloyd said. 'You were brilliant. Your spooky voice was perfect.'

'I was totally upstaged by Greig – you know, the guy who was Scrooge.'

'He was very good.' Lloyd nodded. 'But you definitely held your own. The whole thing was great.'

'So, can we watch it again?' Lewis asked.

Lloyd grinned. 'If that's what you all want, then sure.'

Harry shrugged. 'Can we do popcorn?'

'Popcorn and pizza.' Lloyd raised an eyebrow. 'We might manage it.'

Lewis did a small victory dance. 'And can we invite Scarlett over to watch it? She didn't get to see it and she'll want to because *A Christmas Carol* is her favourite Christmas thing.'

'Well, maybe.' Lloyd glanced at Harry and Eve.

'Ok,' Eve said. 'Fine.'

'She also likes *Love Actually*,' Lewis piped up. 'But is "actually liking love" got anything to do with Christmas?'

Eve snorted. 'It's a movie, you muppet. Not just someone saying they "actually like love".'

'That's a silly name for a movie.' Lewis pulled a face. 'Can we watch it?'

'No,' Lloyd said. 'I'm pretty sure it's at least a fifteen.'

Eve looked at Lloyd. 'So, are you going to invite her?'

This was such a change from last week, Lloyd wasn't entirely sure what to make of it.

'If she wants to come over, she can,' he said. 'But she might be busy.'

'Shall I message her for you?' Harry deadpanned.

'No. I can do that myself, you cheeky thing.'

He pulled out his phone and opened the messages. She still hadn't said anything about times for coming around. Hopefully this wouldn't look like he was being pushy.

Lloyd: Would you like to come round tonight? Harry filmed the school play on his phone, and the kids want to watch it on the projector. We'd all love you to come and watch it too. No pressure though, I know you might be busy. x

He hit send, placed the phone on the worktop, and shooed the boys out of the fridge.

'Maybe you could all get out of your school clothes, then I can put them in the wash and get that done.'

'Let's wear the Christmas jammies,' Lewis said.

'You wear them all year,' Eve muttered as they all traipsed out the door.

They'd barely got to the top when a loud knock came at the door followed by Rita's voice. 'It's only me.'

Lloyd poked his head out of the kitchen. 'Hey. Are you ok? I wasn't expecting you.'

She came into the kitchen and pushed the door. It didn't fully click shut, but it blocked the sound of the kids from up the stairs. Her eyes were narrowed, and she had a deep frown etched into her brow.

'What's the matter?' Lloyd said.

She looked around to check the coast was clear. 'I was at the shop earlier. I spoke to Scarlett. We've... sorted everything out.'

Lloyd kept his expression blank, though every fibre of him itched to shout. 'What does that mean?'

'I apologised to her,' Rita said. 'She didn't say much, but I think she was ok about it.'

'Ok about what? I mean... what exactly did you talk about?'

'Just about where she saw the relationship going. That kind of thing,' Rita said.

He pinched the bridge of his nose. 'I don't know what that means exactly, but I think you've scared her off.'

'How? I didn't say anything bad. I told her I was sorry for what I said in the summer, that the shop looked good, and that I hoped she'd stick with you even if things got tough.'

Lloyd put his hands on his hips and frowned. 'Well, she's not answering my messages now... so, if it wasn't what you said to her then what is it?'

Rita pressed her lips together, then braced herself on the back of one of the wooden chairs at the kitchen table. 'Maybe she just needs time to think. I mean, this isn't an easy situation for anyone to step into.'

'Did you say that to her?' A hot bubble of rage pushed its way up Lloyd's throat. 'I hope you didn't go saying that she was too young for me again. You remember how old I was when I met Amy? I was twenty. So was she. We were students. You didn't like that either. You said it would never work, that she was too young and flighty and I'd regret it.' Lloyd leaned forward, staring right at her. 'I didn't regret a single minute with her. And she was younger than Scarlett is now when I married her. We made it work until she took her last breath. But we were a team. Always. I've made this call before, and I got it right.'

Rita held up her hands. 'I maybe mentioned that taking on you and your family wouldn't be easy, but I didn't try to push her out, I swear.'

'You don't know her. She's had a shit set of experiences with guys. I bet she's completely freaking out now.'

'I only said it would be hard dating a man with three children, who's still grieving.'

He breathed slowly. 'You don't get to decide who makes me happy, or who makes her happy. Or who helps me grieve. That's not your job.'

'Lloyd, that isn't how it happened.'

'The children like her. Even Eve has come around, and you know how hard that can be.'

'I know that... and well, I'm coming around too... What she's done at the shop is really very good. And no one can see the future.'

'Exactly, and I'd rather have a few good months with Scarlett than twenty years being safe and miserable.'

Lewis's voice came from behind the door. 'Dad, can we come in now?'

'We do actually like Scarlett,' Harry added, following Lewis in.

'Yeah, Gran.' Eve shrugged. 'I totally didn't at first, but after we fell in the mud... Well, she was good for a laugh.'

'How did you fall in the mud?'

'It was Eunice's pug's fault.'

'Listen.' Lloyd held up his hands. 'While you're all here, I need to say this out loud. For me. For all of you.'

Rita's eyes widened.

He took a shaky breath. 'I'm in love with Scarlett. I don't know if it will last, or even if she'll want to try, but I want her in my life. I want her in your lives.' He looked at the kids one by one. 'Not as a replacement for Mum, just as herself, as a friend. Someone who can enrich our lives.'

Eve looked momentarily horrified. Maybe the 'L' word was too much, but she recovered herself and glanced at her gran. Rita exhaled, not quite a sigh.

'Maybe it's not what you hoped for me,' Lloyd said to her, 'but she makes me happy. If you can't support that, at least let it be.'

Rita met his eyes. 'Of course I'll support you if that's what you want.'

'I'm cool with it,' Harry said.

Eve didn't even roll her eyes. 'I guess I am too.'

'I definitely am,' Lewis said. 'And if she starts living with us, that means I can keep the black Christmas tree and you can have the projector, Harry.'

Lloyd tried not to laugh. If anyone could cheer him up, Lewis could.

Rita looked at the three of them. 'I promise the only reason I went to see her was to clear the air. Maybe she doesn't accept my apology. I really don't know.'

'I don't know either.'

Rita wiped the corner of her eye with a knuckle. 'I didn't mean to ruin it all.'

He let out a sigh.

'Why have you ruined it?' Eve frowned between Rita and Lloyd. 'What happened?'

'I think I've put my foot in it.'

Lloyd rubbed his forehead, and despondency settled over the kitchen. Nobody seemed to know what to say.

'Come on, everyone. Don't let the Scrooge faces in,' Eve said, then put on her spooky voice. 'I am the Ghost of Christmas Past, and I order you to ditch the gloomy mood.'

Rita chuckled and ruffled Lewis's hair. Harry nudged Lloyd as his phone buzzed on the counter, and he grabbed it.

Scarlett: Sorry I didn't reply sooner. I think you're an amazing guy, but I don't think this can work. I can't guarantee things will work out. My track record in relationships is so bad. And I don't want to cause you any more pain. I hope you understand. xx

He read it again, then once more, heart sinking with each pass.

'What's up?' Harry said.

'She's not coming to watch the film,' Lloyd said.

Lewis flopped onto a seat. 'But why? Didn't you tell her we wanted her?'

'I did. And... well, I'm not sure she wants to see me again.'

Rita eyed him. 'Did I scare her away?'

'I'm not sure.'

'Seriously, Gran?' Eve raised an eyebrow. 'Leave the scaring to me. Can I see the message?'

Lloyd handed her the phone, and she read it. Eve nodded, then a wicked grin spread across her face. 'I have an idea.'

'What is it?' He looked up, met her eyes, and saw the old Eve – the real one with the cheeky streak who took no shit from anyone – so like her mum.

'It's brilliant, that's what it is. But you all have to help. All of you.' She eyed Rita. 'Including you, Gran. And you can't get out of it.'

Lloyd looked at his mum and then at Eve, with a weird bubbly sensation in his gut.

'Oh, and we might need Eunice,' Eve added.

Lloyd's bafflement increased. What the hell was she planning?

CHAPTER TWENTY-NINE

Scarlett

Scarlett knew she had to get up. No matter how warm and safe the duvet felt, she couldn't hide beneath it forever. But the thought of facing the day made her stomach twist.

She'd never made a relationship last more than six months. Not once. Somehow, she always ruined it, or picked someone who was wrong for her, or found herself running when it got too serious. What made her think it would be any different this time – with Lloyd of all people? He deserved someone steady, dependable, not a walking disaster who didn't know how to stay the course.

Yesterday's meeting with Rita had gone far better than Scarlett could have expected, but instead of relief, all Scarlett felt was pressure. If even Rita – fierce, protective Rita – was willing to give her a chance, then she couldn't bear to let her down. Or Lloyd. Or the kids. The mountain of expectation loomed too high, too steep, and she wasn't sure her heart was strong enough to climb it.

Eventually, she rolled over and blinked at her phone through crusty eyes.

Lloyd: I'm sorry. I wish things were different. I want you to be happy, even if it's not with me, or even if it's only as friends. I'll see you at the shop today, and we can talk. I care more than you know. xx

She wiped her nose, rolled up in the duvet tighter, and tried to dissolve. But even the cocoon wasn't enough; her brain was a boot stamping on her chest. How could she face him? End this before it got too far. Not showing up for work was exactly what the old Scarlett would have done. When the going got tough, she bailed and blamed everyone else.

But that wasn't who she was anymore. Not now. This job mattered. Today and the jolabokaflod tomorrow. She'd put so much work into it she wanted to be there – even if it had completely lost its shine.

'Scarlett? You're going to be late for work. Are you ok?' Her mum knocked on the door.

She tried to say yes, but it came out as a sort of choked groan.

Patricia came in, then sat on the end of the bed, fussing with the edge of the duvet. 'Are you ill?'

'I've messed up. Again.'

'What are you talking about?'

Scarlett buried her head in the pillow. 'Lloyd.'

'Oh, sweetheart. What happened?'

'How can I be right for him? It's not like I'm going to be any good for him or his kids in the long run, is it?'

Patricia said nothing for a moment, just stroked the end of Scarlett's hair with two fingers. 'I don't like you talking like that, but it's your choice. I mean, if you don't think he's worth it—'

'He's worth everything to me.' Scarlett sat up, the tears hot and sudden. 'I know I'm mad and probably delusional, but I love him. I care about him more than anyone else ever. And it just… never works out, does it? I didn't choose for all these exes to be horrible to me. I didn't choose to have a dad who screwed us over. But I've done some stupid things in the past and how can I be sure I won't mess up again?'

'You can never be sure of that.' Patricia reached out and hugged Scarlett. 'You've just got to keep trying your best. If he means this much to you, then you should fight for it. Or at least talk to him properly before you give up.'

Scarlett huffed into her mum's shoulder. 'What if I never fit?'

'Try. Remember Lilah? You and I were both heavily against her when she and Aidan got together. But it worked out. They never gave up.'

'What if I'm not what he needs right now – or ever?'

'Look, if you want him, then go to him. If you're meant to be together, you'll figure it out.'

Scarlett nodded, but her chest still ached.

'Get dressed, and I'll drive you to work. I have the box of crafts for the Jolabokaflod. Maybe I could set it up today?'

'Yeah, sure.' Having her mum there might dilute her interactions with Lloyd. 'But if Lloyd's there, don't say anything to him about any of this, ok? Let me speak to him.'

'Of course.'

Patricia lifted a cardboard box labelled 'Crafts for Jola-xxx' in purple Sharpie – clearly, she couldn't spell the whole word – and they made their way to the car.

At the bookshop door, Patricia stood back as Scarlett unlocked it. The wall behind the till was covered in Jolabokaflod posters – she'd made them herself and should have felt proud. Instead, her mood slumped again, heavy as wet paper. And when she opened up at nine o'clock, Lloyd hadn't turned up.

Where was he?

Avoiding her? Or just busy with more meetings?

Thankfully the bookshop was busy and kept her mind off things. The schools had wound up for the Christmas break, so quite a few kids came in with parents, and even some older kids on their own. Scarlett served them all, her mind straying to thoughts of Harry and Eve. Were any of these kids their new friends?

Patricia hung around, setting up the crafts display in the side room. 'You should see the likes on the social media page,' she said, coming through and waving her phone. 'People are really excited about this book flood thing.'

Scarlett smiled or tried to. 'Yeah. I'm pleased people are taking it on board. It's a good idea.'

A young couple came in, and Patricia whispered, 'That's Georgie Porter, the tennis player. She lives here now. I remember watching her on TV.'

'I know. I've met her. She's Elise's friend.'

'Oh my god. Wow.'

Scarlett hushed her mum as Georgie and her boyfriend wandered around looking at the books. When she approached the till with a pile of romances, she grinned at Scarlett, and recognition dawned on her.

'Hey, nice to see you. Do you work here now?'

'Yeah.' Scarlett started scanning the books.

'That's great. The last time I saw you, you weren't working. I'm glad you found somewhere. This place is the cutest.'

Scarlett agreed. Though maybe the next time Georgie came in here, Scarlett wouldn't be working here anymore. She'd managed a whole month – not much better than her usual efforts.

After Georgie and her boyfriend left, Patricia looked up at the clock. 'It's nearly lunchtime.'

'Yeah.' Scarlett flipped the sign to CLOSED. 'Let's go upstairs and have a break.'

Patricia had brought soup in a thermos, and she raked about in the cupboards for bowls, while Scarlett put the kettle on. Her phone still had nothing new from Lloyd.

Why hadn't he come in?

Maybe he'd had an emergency with one of the kids. Should she message him and find out? Or was it really not her business?

They ate in silence for a minute, then a sudden, violent hammering on the shop door made them both jump.

'What the hell?' Patricia said.

Scarlett bolted down the stairs, heart hammering. Through the glass, she saw Eunice, bundled in a rainbow of scarves and hats.

'Let me in,' Eunice called. 'It's urgent.'

Scarlett opened the door, her heart hammering louder than the crazy bell. 'What's happened?'

Eunice swept in with Clarence trailing after her, and Scarlett waited for a response.

Patricia came down, her face etched with worry. 'Is everything alright?'

'Oh, hello.' Eunice flicked her gaze to her. 'Who are you?'

'Scarlett's mum. Why? What's going on?'

Eunice bustled over to the CD player and stabbed at the buttons until the Christmas music returned.

Scarlett looked from her mum to Eunice, then at the door, which Eunice had left wide open, letting in a rush of cold air.

'Are you going to tell us what's happening?' Scarlett moved to close it.

'Look for yourself.' Eunice sidled over beside Patricia – who was looking completely baffled – then gave Scarlett a conspiratorial wink and pointed at the entrance.

A slow-moving shape loomed there. At first, Scarlett thought it was another customer, but as the person got closer, she realised it was Rita Miller. Scarlett froze. Rita was holding something – a board, maybe, or a placard.

Scarlett's internal organs flipped, then somersaulted. She took a step back, mouth gaping.

Rita adjusted her bobble hat, squared her shoulders, and held up the board to Scarlett. In huge black marker, the first side read:

SORRY FOR BEING A MEDDLING OLD BAT

Scarlett gawked. Next to her, Patricia snorted in disbelief, and Eunice let out a bark of laughter.

Rita flipped to the next side.

YOU WILL NOW BE VISITED BY THREE GHOSTS

Scarlett turned to Eunice, who just winked, then to her mum, who mouthed, 'Is she drunk?'

But Rita was stone-cold serious, standing with her feet apart, holding the sign with both hands. She pulled her lips into a tight line and lowered her head like she was humbled, then she stepped aside in a stagey little sweep, and another figure materialised. Eve.

She had a string of fairy lights tangled around her neck, and her face was pale with a faint dusting of glitter on her cheeks.

With a smirk, she put on an eerie voice. 'I am the Ghost of Christmas Past. I'm here to remind you of everything that came before, and to say that memories, bad or good, are here to shape us and help us face new challenges. Remembering my mum and others we've lost will always be ok. Moving on isn't a betrayal, just an adaption... adaptation...' She flapped her hand in front of her face. 'That word is hard to say.' Then she regained her ghostly voice. 'Even when things change, we should always take the best bits with us and keep them in our hearts.'

A lump built in Scarlett's throat. Patricia put an arm around her shoulders and squeezed.

Eve took a big, dramatic bow, then stepped aside.

Out stepped Harry, clutching a wrapped box and wearing a Christmas jumper with a giant Santa on it. He looked like a reluctant elf.

'This is too much,' Scarlett whispered, but she couldn't stop smiling.

Harry shuffled forward, eyes on the ground, then straightened and looked Scarlett dead in the eye. 'I'm the Ghost of Christmas Presents. Like, literally presents. So I brought this.' He held up the box and shrugged. 'But also, I mean, we just want everyone to be happy. If being happy means you and my dad are a thing, then we're cool with it. You made him smile for the first time in ages. And you brought the projector. So... Merry Christmas.'

He deposited the box on the floor in the doorframe, then backed away, blushing furiously. Scarlett bit her knuckle, fighting the urge to cry.

'This is so weirdly beautiful,' Patricia said under her breath.

Lewis shot out, wearing a ninja cat hoodie, and tinsel wrapped around his head. He skidded to a halt, then struck a superhero pose.

'Ghost of Christmas Yet to Come, reporting for duty!' he said.

Scarlett laughed so hard she nearly doubled over. Her mum was wiping tears.

'Future is scary, but you gotta live it anyway!' He glanced to the side, and Scarlett heard Eve whispering something. 'I want everyone to stay together, even if it's weird at first, and even if people say it's not allowed. Cos I think it should be allowed! And I'm the youngest, so I know best.'

Scarlett was full-on crying now. Through the tears, she saw Lewis marching forward. He took her hand.

'As the Ghost of Christmas Yet to Come, I'm going to show you what we all want in our future.' He dragged Scarlett out of the shop, into the cold air on the platform. She briefly noticed that several people had stopped to watch before Lewis dragged her around the corner to where Rita was holding her sign, Eve and Harry were grinning. And beside them, looking half fearful, half bemused, was Lloyd.

Scarlett's knees went a bit wobbly. He looked at her with a shy, hopeful smile – like he couldn't quite believe any of this was real.

She couldn't either.

Letting go of Lewis, she wiped her face and tried to find words, her eyes never leaving Lloyd.

Rita stepped forward. 'I hope I didn't scare you off yesterday. I honestly didn't mean to. You really have done a wonderful job in the shop, and if Lloyd is happy, then so am I.'

Scarlett blinked, tears threatening again. 'I wasn't scared off... I guess I just don't trust myself.'

'Well, you should. You made some wild decisions, I must say, but you did them because you followed your heart.' Rita smiled and dabbed her eyes. 'It took courage, especially with meddlers like me on the loose.'

Lloyd walked over, and everything else faded out. He stopped just in front of Scarlett, close enough for her to see the nerves and joy fighting it out in his eyes. 'Hi,' he said.

'Hi.'

'Are you ok?'

She nodded, though she definitely wasn't.

He smiled, and that was it – she launched herself at him, arms tight around his neck. He hugged her back, strong and warm, then lifted her off her feet and spun her around.

Squealing and laughing, Scarlett was weightless and spinning. When her boots landed back on the ground, Lloyd kissed her, right there in front of everyone. Scarlett leaned into it, her hands on his cheeks, melting into a pool of warm chocolate.

When they broke apart, the whole group was watching them, along with several random passengers, half-smiling, half-sniffling.

Scarlett felt like she'd fallen out of time. Lloyd's arms were solid around her, his breath warm in her hair, and for a second, she thought maybe she'd passed out on the shop floor and was dreaming the whole thing. But the kids were there; Eve smiled, though rolled her eyes at the same time; Harry beamed, and Lewis clapped like mad.

Scarlett and Lloyd just kept laughing, hugging, then pulling back to look at each other, and hugging again, as if checking it was all still true.

'I love you,' Lloyd whispered. 'I can't see the future, but I know how I feel in the present. And I really, really love you.'

Scarlett blinked, tears spilling down her face. 'I love you, too. This might sound crazy, but I loved you when I met you in the summer. There's always been something about you.'

'I know. I felt it too, though I didn't understand it. Even now I don't completely comprehend it, but maybe that's what makes it so real.'

'And so good.'

'Yes.' He ran a thumb down her cheek, still smiling, like Christmas had arrived two days early.

Rita approached, wringing her hands. 'I truly hope we can put what happened in the summer aside. I can't promise I'll ever be less of an old bat, but if I make mistakes, just call me out on them.'

'Yeah,' Lewis said. 'We do it all the time.'

Rita ruffled his hair, and Scarlett grinned. 'I'll remember that.'

Patricia hung back, watching, but Lloyd caught her eye and stepped forward. 'Hi. I'm Lloyd. I guess you're Scarlett's mum.'

'Yeah, Patricia.' She stuck out a hand, then, on impulse, gave him a hug. 'Thank you for making my daughter happy.'

'She does more for me than I can say.'

The kids joined them in a group hug, and tears flowed as Scarlett felt the warmth and happiness.

'You can't tell me you didn't see this coming,' Eunice declared. 'This is all because of the wishing tree.'

Scarlett laughed. 'You're a genius.'

Lloyd smiled at her, eyes soft, and she squeezed his hand.

He smiled, blue eyes shining. 'It was all Eve's idea.'

'This is the best Christmas ever.'

He gently placed a kiss on her cheek. 'And here's to many more. The past will always be in our hearts. The present is a time to live and love in. And the future is an ongoing adventure.'

Scarlett nodded. 'One hundred per cent. And I'm ready.'

She'd never felt so ready or so happily festive in her life. As they went back inside, Scarlett brushed her hand over the wishing tree and thanked it and the universe for making all her Christmas wishes come true.

CHAPTER THIRTY

Lloyd

Christmas Eve and the Jolabokaflod were in full swing. The shop was only open until twelve, but the first of the three hours of opening was the busiest Lloyd had ever seen. So many people had turned up and were shoehorned between the shelves, buying books – both pre-wrapped ones and others from the shelves.

Lewis was manning the hot chocolate station with Rita, and Harry was running up and down the stairs fetching the water. Eve was on the till with Scarlett, and Lloyd almost felt jealous at the sight of his daughter leaning in and whispering something to her. If they could be friends, it would be the most incredible outcome – beyond anything he'd wished for.

The wishing tree was out for its last day – until next year. It might have seemed like one of Eunice's cuckoo ideas at the beginning, but now it was going to be a shop tradition for as long as Lloyd owned the place.

He caught Scarlett's eye, and he grinned. She beamed back at him. They still had lots to think about – plans and decisions to make. But none of it was pressing. There was no rush. Just being together and growing what they had was all that mattered.

A burst of giggles came from the hot chocolate stand, followed by Lewis's voice: 'It's Jolabokaflod, not Jolly Bacon Flood.'

Scarlett snorted, and Lloyd turned to her. They both burst out laughing.

The bell on the door shrieked, and in came Aidan and Lilah.

'That's Scarlett's half-brother,' Lewis said to Rita. 'Though I can't work out which half.'

Rita frowned at him, then said, 'Yes, I know.'

Lloyd's insides squirmed a bit. Rita and Aidan had last seen each other on the coach tour. So much had happened in between.

Lilah had made it to the counter and was chatting with Scarlett, who seemed to be introducing Eve. Aidan hung back like he was half listening, then his eyes fell on Lloyd.

Aidan gave him a half smile, then turned to Scarlett. 'You two, uh—' He paused. 'Are you official now?'

Lloyd exchanged a look with Scarlett. 'Yeah.' She nodded, and Lloyd moved closer.

'We're going to make a go of things,' he said.

Aidan's face did something complicated. 'That's cool.' He shrugged, then slapped Lloyd on the arm. 'I hope it works out for you both.'

'Thanks.' Lloyd caught Scarlett's eye again. Neither of them knew if it would 'work out' or even what that meant. But they were definitely going to be happy for as long as possible.

The door shrieked again, and Elise, in a grey wool coat, came in with Gabe trailing her, hands stuffed in his pockets.

Aidan put his arm around Lilah as Elise made straight for the counter. Gabe went to Aidan and nudged him with a wink.

'This is incredible,' Elise said to Scarlett. 'Look at all the people.'

Scarlett blushed. 'I didn't do anything.'

'Yes, you did,' Eve said. 'It was all your idea.'

'She's a genius,' Lloyd said.

Elise smiled at Scarlett and then Lloyd. 'Am I to assume all is well here?'

'It's the best,' Scarlett said.

'You're official?' Elise's eyes widened.

'Yeah. Didn't you see the announcement on the national news?'

Gabe snorted. 'The Glenbriar gossips are usually a lot quicker.'

'I think it's so sweet,' Lilah said. 'The way you met was fate.'

'I'm not sure I believe in fate.' Lloyd locked eyes with Scarlett. 'But I am very glad you spoke to me on that coach trip. If you hadn't...' He held out his hands. 'None of this would have happened.'

When twelve o'clock arrived, they served the last few customers and locked up. Rita had already cleared away the hot chocolate stall, and Eve, Harry and Lewis were packing away the wishing tree, ready for it to be stowed somewhere safe for next year.

Rita sidled over to Lloyd and tapped him on the elbow. 'Can I have a word?'

He followed her through to the side room where Scarlett was boxing up the few wrapped books that hadn't been sold. Rita glanced around, then squared up with a brisk, business-like air.

'Just so there's no doubt,' she said, her voice quiet. 'I want to fully apologise for the summer. For the things I said and the way I said them. I let my pain and my fears get the better of me, and I took it out on you.' She flicked her gaze to Scarlett. 'That wasn't fair, and it wasn't kind.'

'You're right,' Lloyd said. 'It wasn't. You nearly pushed Scarlett away, and I can't let that happen again. I need you to respect my choices from now on, Mum.'

Rita's mouth tightened, and she nodded. 'I know. I was wrong to meddle. I just... I only ever wanted to protect you. And the children.'

'I get that,' he said. 'But protection doesn't mean control. Scarlett isn't the enemy here.'

'I can see that now,' Rita said. 'She's brought laughter back into this family, and I'd be blind not to notice. I may still worry – it's my nature – but I'll try to keep my worries to myself.' Her eyes softened. 'And I hope you'll forgive me for being slow on the uptake.'

Scarlett hesitated, then gave a small smile. 'Well, I guess it was a bit of a surprise. But thank you.'

Rita let out a long breath, her shoulders dipping. 'I'll give you space. Tomorrow, I'll be with Eunice for lunch, so you can enjoy your Christmas without me fussing around.'

'Are you sure?' Lloyd said.

'Of course. Eunice needs the company, and you'll doubtless see enough of me at other times. Just look after each other, will you?'

'We will,' Lloyd said, and he put his arm firmly around Scarlett's waist.

Rita smiled and went into the other room, calling to the kids.

Lloyd glanced at Scarlett. 'You know that Christmas Day is messy for me now anyway.' He increased the pressure on her waist. 'I'm taking the kids to Perth in the morning to see Amy's parents. Our Christmas lunch won't be until later. If you want to spend time with your family, that's fine. Or you're welcome to spend the day with us. I'm happy either way.'

Scarlett blinked, sucking on her lip. 'I could come over in the afternoon and join the games. I like the sound of that.'

Lloyd kissed her cheek.

'Why don't you invite your mum and Eunice around to play too?'

'Are you sure?'

'It's Christmas. My mum might want to come too... but run it by the kids first. They might want a quiet day.'

'I doubt it.' Lloyd chuckled. 'It sounds like too much fun. Besides, they can have a quiet day on Boxing Day. But I'll ask them just in case.'

When Lloyd put it to them, everyone seemed pleased with the idea. Eve and Harry had some ideas for games that sounded very complicated, but Lewis wasn't bothered what they did as long as they could play the cereal packet game.

'I'm nowhere near bendy enough for that,' Rita said.

'I'll take you on,' Scarlett winked at Lewis.

'Bet you can't beat me,' Eve said.

'How much?'

'Er... I'm not sure we should be encouraging gambling.' Lloyd put his hands on his hips, but both Scarlett and Eve laughed.

It was almost one o'clock by the time Lloyd locked the shop. Scarlett was holding his hand, but it felt like a full-body hug having her so close – so openly. The kids had wandered up the platform and were chatting with Rita.

The Christmas lights strung along the shop window blinked down on them.

'Do you want to come home with us? I'd love it for you to stay over tonight and wake up together on Christmas morning.'

Her eyes widened. 'Would that be ok?'

'Of course.' He squeezed her hand. 'If you want to.'

She let out a little laugh. 'Yeah. I want to. I just...' She chewed her lip. 'Are you sure it won't weird out the kids?'

'I think they'll be fine about it now.' He tugged on his gloves. 'Like I said earlier, my Christmas day schedule is messy, but I could drop you at your mum's in the morning before I take the kids to Perth. Then I could get you later for the games.'

'Ok, let's do it.'

'I love you.' He leaned in, took hold of her shoulders and gently pressed a kiss to her lips.

They caught up with the kids at the car. Lewis did a little jig on the icy pavement, then bounded ahead to open the doors.

By the time they reached the house – after briefly stopping for Scarlett to grab an overnight bag – the windows glowed with fairy lights. The black tree stood sentinel in the hallway, festooned with ninja cats and one lone batman action figure.

Scarlett peeled off her jacket and boots, and Lloyd headed into the living room to put on the fire.

Eve drifted in behind him. 'You did good, Dad,' she whispered.

He got up and pulled her in for a hug. 'Thank you so much.' He kissed the top of her head. 'For bringing this about. Your idea yesterday was brilliant.'

'It was fun.' She pulled away, and her hand drifted to the family photo on the mantelpiece. Tears welled in her eyes. 'I miss Mum.'

'I know.' He hugged her tight. 'We all do. But letting in more love will always help. It doesn't erase the love we felt in the past, just strengthens us in the present and the future.'

'Yeah.'

For a moment, they stood just hugging until Lewis and Harry bundled in and both made a dive for the remote control.

'Why don't we watch my school show now?' Eve said. 'We didn't get to it the other night and Scarlett's here now, so she can see it.'

'Sounds like the perfect plan.'

Lloyd made some popcorn as everyone got into their jammies. When Scarlett appeared in her elf PJs, he grinned. 'I knew you were an elf in disguise.'

She sidled up to him and kissed him. 'I love you.'

'Likewise.' He returned her kiss, then passed her the bowl of popcorn. 'Can you take this into the kids while I get into my jammies?'

When he got back, the five of them curled together on the big sofa, and Lloyd sat with his arms around Scarlett and Lewis.

Harry pressed play. The little phone projector cast the video on the far wall – Eve's performance as the Ghost of Christmas Past, all glitter and eerie voice, making the perfect scene with Greig's brilliant Scrooge.

This was the life. Maybe not the one he'd planned, but he'd take it.

When the film was done, they read books, played Uno, ate chocolate and chatted until it was bedtime. Everyone hung their stockings on the banister, and Lloyd read *The Night Before Christmas* aloud.

Then he kissed each kid goodnight, and they all hugged Scarlett.

Once all their bedroom doors were closed, Lloyd went into his bedroom after Scarlett and put his arms around her from behind. 'This is such a Christmas treat to have you here.'

She twisted in his arms, smiling up at him. 'Don't you have to fill up the stockings now, Santa?'

He kissed her slowly. 'Not until later, when they're all asleep.'

She melted against him, and her whole body relaxed. 'How will you stay awake?'

'Hmm... good question. You got any ideas?'

'One or two.' She grinned. 'You know what I wished for on the wishing tree?' she whispered.

He stroked her cheek. 'What?'

'I wished I could see you again. And then you turned up. Then I wished on my birthday candles that we could be together. They both came true.'

'And what do you wish for now?'

'Just for this love to last.' She tucked her face into his neck. 'And I feel sure it will.'

He pulled her closer. 'I do too. I never thought I'd feel like this again. Having you here is the most precious gift.'

'Let's cuddle.' She got into the bed, and he followed her, propping himself on one elbow, and watching her pull her hair out of its messy updo.

'You're so beautiful,' he said.

She curled against his chest, tracing slow circles on his tee with her finger. 'Are you sure you're ok? I'd hate it if this was too much.'

He shook his head, kissed her hair. 'It's never too much. It's exactly what I want. What I need.'

Scarlett shifted, straddling him, eyes bright and wild. 'Should I say Merry Christmas now or wait till midnight?'

'Both,' Lloyd said. 'Say it now, at midnight, tomorrow morning, whenever you like.'

She grinned and ducked down to kiss him. It was hot and deep and full of promise.

'Happy Christmas,' she whispered. 'I love you.'

He smiled, heart too big for his chest. 'Happy Christmas to you too.'

Maybe he would never fully believe in fate, but how could he deny that sometimes wishes came true? The magic of Christmas shimmered in the air as he kissed his new love, amazed by how much could change in a single season, and already full of hope and dreams for every Christmas yet to come.

The End

MORE BOOKS BY MARGARET AMATT

Scottish Island Escapes

1. A Winter Haven

2. A Spring Retreat

3. A Summer Sanctuary

4. An Autumn Hideaway

5. A Christmas Bluff

6. A Flight of Fancy

7. A Hidden Gem

8. A Striking Result

9. A Perfect Discovery

10. A Festive Surprise

The Glenbriar Series

1. Stolen Kisses at the Loch View Hotel

2. Just Friends at Thistle Lodge

3. Pitching up at Heather Glen

4. Two's Company at the Forest Light Show

5. Highland Fling on the Whisky Trail

6. Snowdown at the Old Schoolhouse

7. Starting Over at the Crafty Bee Barn

8. A Surprise Proposal in the Rose Garden

9. Cutting it Neat for the Wedding

10. A Classy Affair in the Country

11. Mix Up under the Mistletoe

12. A Fresh Start on the Bridle Path

13. Last First Kiss at the Village Church

14. Fight or Flirt on the Scenic Route

15. Love Match on the Road Home

Love on the Edge – Barra Series

ACKNOWLEDGMENTS

Huge thanks go to my wonderful husband for always supporting my dreams (and for patiently enduring all the writing chat that never stops!). And to my son, whose curiosity and enthusiasm for storytelling always makes me smile – watching him create his own worlds is one of my greatest joys.

I'm also incredibly grateful to the editors who helped shape this book, and to the fellow authors and friends who continue to cheer me on behind the scenes – your support means the world.

But most of all, thank you to the readers. Whether you've just picked up one of my books or have been with me from the start, I appreciate you more than words can say. Your messages, reviews, and recommendations keep me going and remind me why I love doing this so much. I hope these stories bring you as much joy as I had writing them.

Big love.

Margaret XX

About the Author
Margaret Amatt

Margaret has told and written stories for as long as she can remember. During her formative years, she spent time on long walks inventing characters and stories to pass the time.

Writing books is Margaret's passion and when she's not doing that, she's often found eating chocolate, walking and taking photographs in the hills around Highland Perthshire. Those long walks still frequently bring inspiration!

It's Margaret's pleasure to bring you the **Scottish Island Escapes** series, **The Glenbriar Series** and the **Love on the Edge – Barra** series. Each series features interconnected stories for those who enjoy inhabiting Margaret's world but each and every book can be read as a standalone if you'd rather dip in and out.

You can find more information about Margaret on her website or by signing up for her newsletter

www.margaretamatt.com